FOSTER ME

ARIANA OMAN

ISBN 978-1-68526-817-6 (Paperback)
ISBN 978-1-68526-819-0 (Hardcover)
ISBN 978-1-68526-818-3 (Digital)

Covenant Books
11661 Hwy 707
Murrells Inlet, SC 29576
www.covenantbooks.com

PROLOGUE

January 24, 1998

Dear Suzette,

My hand is shaky. I had a feeling this would be difficult to do. This note and releasing you, perhaps they are one in the same. After all these years, I should be done writing to you, yet I have this one last note.

The comforting aroma of homemade soup is permeating the house, filling me with memories and thoughts of you. It's amazing that soup would remind me of you, strange that anything would. A lifetime has passed since I touched your hands, since I kissed your cold, thin hands lying in mine.

It slips. Like a shadow when light disappears, time slips out of sight, yet it's there always moving on, dragging life with it. I have held on too long. I'm no longer a child, but, my dear mother, you will always be Mom.

Vegetable soup doesn't smell anything like a hospital, although that's where my mind drifts, into your hospital room. For weeks, you waited to pass through the veils of reality. I wished for time to stop and begged God to let you stay. I prayed. I offered to trade places with you, hoping that it would be me instead of you. I knew it was a hollow prayer. I prayed anyway. You had five daughters who needed you. Why didn't the world stop revolving when your last breath escaped? I held my breath hoping to keep you alive. I waited for time to halt and bring you back.

I used to say breast cancer stole your life, but nothing has been stolen. Your life ended and mine went on. Tears would not call you back into a body that could no longer sustain your life. I knew you were gone. I laughed, Mom. I couldn't cry, yet I could laugh. Samantha and Nadine were angry that I giggled while we dressed for your funeral. Granddad, he understood. It was not laughter that seeped through my young lips. Your father heard my ache. Though it did not erase the shame, Granddad defended my giggling.

We were told over and over while your body lay in a coffin that time would heal the pain. Time does not know how to heal. Time is the space that severs five daughters from their mother. For three years, you struggled with the angel of death hanging over your shoulders. For three years, we were tossed from this aunt, that uncle; I was a foster child long before I became one. While you were gone for months at a time, your phone calls and postcards connected us to you, yet all the medical treatments out of the country only distanced you; they didn't save your life. With no father to rescue us, fate demanded that we five girls live in different homes. I now know that you were supposed to pass on. Your daughters were destined to walk separate paths. We were to find our own way in the world, without you to love and guide us. You died, yet your secrets remained with us and in us; we each dealt with them alone.

This past May I attended Tasha's wedding then helped her pack for her new life in California. I discovered slides of you and tucked one in my pocket. I had an idea, the perfect gift for my younger sister. For her thirtieth birthday, I sent Tasha a picture. She tells me she hasn't decided where to put it. Initially, it was in the bedroom then found its way to the living room. Tasha will eventually find a place for you. It's just her heart; twenty years ago it was broken, and she's still gluing the pieces back together. Your family told us not to cry. As with the rest of us, Tasha needed to mourn but was not allowed. I think she sealed off your memory instead.

I've never visited your grave. Indiana seems so cold to me and so far away. I know you left us sometime in June. My sisters know the date you were born and the date you died; I refuse to remember. The fact that you died is all I need to know. Cammy named her first daughter after you. Samantha calls me on your birthday. Nadine has your wedding ring. Tasha has our family slides and pictures, all but one is stored away. I didn't want anything to remind me of you, yet I have a letter I've clung to. Thirteen. I was thirteen when I began the letter. Like tall buildings without a thirteenth floor, I wish I could have leapt from twelve to fourteen eliminating my thirteenth year.

Enclosed inside this note is that letter which contains my unspoken words. It reveals my path, that of a foster child. I have refused to read it, until now. Before I end this note, I will read my letter to you. It took me years to write it, years to live the words I wrote to you.

A whisper in my mind, your last breath took me with you. It's time, Mom. Time for me to move on and allow the space between you and I to remain. I must reclaim my breath, my life. You've been my power, my voice, and you've been my emptiness.

CHAPTER 1

September 18, 1976

Dear Mom,

Nadine succeeded in making an impression on Aunt Erika, although the outcome was not exactly as she intended. I know your brother told us to wait at the gate, but Nadine was in charge. As soon as we walked off the plane, she lit up a cigarette and dragged me to the baggage claim area. She has a way of encouraging me to do the things she wants; Nadine threatened me with violence. Being two years older than me has earned her the right to boss me around, yet it doesn't make her any smarter. I think something happens to females just before they turn sixteen. She's been really dumb lately. I remember the same thing happened to Samantha.

On the plane, Nadine revealed her plan. She said we had to establish ourselves with Aunt Erika. I don't think Aunt Erika was impressed with Nadine's lit cigarette hanging out of her mouth nor did my older sister look very established either. There was a lady on the plane sitting next to Nadine who said we were brave to be flying by ourselves. Nadine said we didn't have a choice and told her about our situation. I looked out the window and wondered if you were among the clouds, I didn't feel alone.

What is it like to die? I know we have a soul, and I know we have three places to go: heaven, purgatory, or in Satan's lair. You already suffered when you were sick, so I think you're in heaven. I wonder where heaven is. I mean is it similar to the clouds the plane flew into, or is it a different world from this one? I hope you're not that far from us. It may be harder for you to be with all five of your daughters now that we don't live together or in the same state.

According to Tasha's letter, Samantha has her own apartment. She didn't go to anyone; she's eighteen. Apparently, she supports herself with a waitress job. Samantha likes Indiana. Besides, I think she wants to be near Tasha and Cammy. I'm relieved to be back in Florida. Indiana is not home to me; the smell of dust and cornfields is so unnatural. I could never live where saltwater mist is absent in the air.

One suitcase. That's all we were allowed to bring. My whole life fits in a suitcase. I left behind the furniture piece I selected. After you died, Aunt Beth let each us keep an item then sold what remained of our home. The antique lectern was my choice. Obviously, I couldn't take it with me. Aunt Beth cleared out its belly. Instead of guarding our family pictures and slides, my lectern has a new function. It's positioned in front of the VanHusen living room window with a Boston fern sitting on it. I suppose it's to guard their house from intruders, although the fern doesn't appear intimidating. Aunt Beth told me I am welcome to adopt the fern whenever I'm ready to claim my lectern. I have a feeling that may be a while. I doubt Aunt Erika wants another piece of furniture in her house. I'm questioning if she wants us.

By the time she found us at the baggage claim area, Aunt Erika was red in the face, and her veins popped out near the temples. It was weird staring at someone who looks like you did, before you got sick. She doesn't have your eyes. Hers are gray like mine. Aunt Erika knows how to use them too. She threw a look at Nadine that would have killed me if I were on the receiving end. At that moment, I was glad it was Nadine who was in charge because she absorbed most of Aunt Erika's wrath. She deserved it. Nadine has a way of making things a mess.

Your sister ordered us to wait at the arrivals area by the curb while she fetched the car. I sat on my suitcase and cried. I don't know if it was because of Miami's heat, Nadine's smelly cigarette, or Aunt Erika's cold reception. And my attempt to hide my face was feeble. Aunt Erika noticed the tears as she grabbed the suitcase from under me. After loading it in the trunk, she asked me why I was crying. I thought about telling her that I left behind three of my sisters and that my mom just died, but this she already knew. Besides, I was unable to say those words, so I said nothing. Aunt Erika clenched her teeth then told me to stop crying. I understood. It was not a request. It's hard to stop crying when you're already trying not to cry. The compulsion grew stronger. I tightened my neck muscles inside until they stiffened into rods of pain then opened my eyes wide to prevent the tears from pouring out. A few escaped. No one noticed.

Nadine made a strong impression, Mom. I don't think my crying helped either. Aunt Erika spewed venom all the way to Miami Shores; she lives thirty minutes from the airport. It gave her plenty of time to explain the house rules and define our chores. I was afraid I wouldn't remember everything. Aunt Erika anticipated our stupidity. She substitutes speaking to us with written communiqués. It seems I come from a family of prolific writers. Your sister leaves at least three notes a day on the bathroom mirror or on the refrigerator. The half-hour ride from the airport is the most oral communication she has granted us since we've arrived.

I thought Nadine was going to open the car door and jump into the traffic when she heard we were enrolled in a Catholic high school and would be expected to do well. After eight years of Catholic school, I was hoping things would change. I'm tired of living the role of a gifted child. So what that I'm insightful and have a thesaurus for a brain. So what that I like to write and know how to formulate a proper sentence. I wish the IQ test was never invented. I want to be normal and attend public school like the rest of the world. Tasha and Cammy will be going to public school. My complaints are in vain. It looks like I'm stuck in the parochial system until I flunk out or become a nun. We both know how remote the chances are that either of those destinies will manifest.

Aunt Erika dropped another bomb in Nadine's lap at the end of our long journey from Indiana. Even though Nadine protested, we are to go to church every Sunday. I don't like going to church either, but I was not about to say so, especially the first day we arrived. Then Aunt Erika pulled up to her house and welcomed us to Miami. I didn't feel welcomed. I still don't. We're staying in Cousin Marcy's bedroom while she's away at college.

Nadine emptied the contents of her suitcase into our allotted three dresser drawers, leaving no room for my clothes. I found a cardboard box to protect my belongings. I tuck it under the bed. It's not a proper dresser, I know. It's not my room either. The closet is filled with Marcy's stuffed animals and hanging clothes. We never open the closet; Aunt Erika forbade us. We share a queen size bed, and Nadine thinks she's the queen. She hogs the covers every night after she smokes her cigarette and puts it out in my plant. She says the ashes fertilize the soil. I had rescued a fern from the thorny rose bushes by the garage.

I wait until Nadine goes to sleep. That's when I write Cammy and Tasha. Their letters are sad. All they write about is you, and the weather. I don't know if they miss you more because they're younger or if they miss you more because they didn't have as much time with you. Your two youngest daughters are having to acclimate to a colder climate. They miss Florida. They miss you. So do I.

When I sleep, I forget that you're gone. Then I wake in the morning and it all comes back to me when I look around the room. This is not our bedroom, this is not our house, and even though she looks like you, Aunt Erika is not our mom.

Your sister has one offspring still living in the nest: Tony. Marcy is a freshman at Florida State University, someplace in North Florida near Georgia. Anyway, Aunt Erika is already planning for Christmas break. It's not even Halloween and she's preparing the family room so that Marcy can sleep in there when she comes home. I feel like we invaded the Davidsons' house.

Tony attends Archbishop Curly, but I rarely see him at school or home. He's a junior, and I'm a low-life freshman. At first, I believed Tony was shy and preoccupied with his tennis team status. I've since reconsidered my assumptions. No doubt he has learned to speak. Maybe he believes Nadine and I are unworthy of his words. Or maybe he's afraid we will usurp his room if he gives us eye contact. At least the cleaning lady is friendly. I practice my Spanish lessons with her. Maria helps me with my accent, smiling to me when my pronunciation sounds remotely Spanish.

The sun is rising. I can see it peeking through the trees. It took me weeks to become accustomed to tree branches tickling the windows at night. Actually, Nadine's snoring is more disturbing than palm frowns brushing against the house. Soon, I'll go downstairs. My morning chores include making citrus fruit cups and setting the breakfast table. I'm bored with peeling grapefruits every morning, but that's my assigned duty. Aunt Erika has everything perfectly timed so we don't interrupt her family routine. She makes Tony's lunch while I ready the breakfast table. When the Davidsons eat breakfast, Nadine and I make our lunches. It never occurred to me that we were weird because of our vegetarian diet. I thought we were normal until I came to live here. Nadine tells me you smoked pot and were a hippie. Perhaps you were more apt to experiment because you were the youngest in your family. Experimental or not, our diet excludes us from your sister's family breakfast dining table.

Nadine and I are taking a class together: typing. Aunt Erika insisted. She says that knowing how to type will help us when we're in college. To insure against our excuses, she brought home an electric typewriter from Uncle Will's office. I obediently practice my typing, but higher education is the last thing on my mind. I'm a straight-A student mainly because I don't have anything else to do except study. The Davidsons leave early in the morning and come home just before dinner. Even after they're home, the house remains quiet. While Nadine and I wash dinner dishes, Uncle Will wanders into the Florida room to read the evening newspaper, and Aunt Erika flits off to one of her classes. She's taking sewing, gourmet cooking, and Spanish. Nadine says under her breath when Aunt Erika leaves that she should take a "How to Be Nice" class.

It's Nadine's job to set the dinner table. She's an incurable slob. The table cloth is always crooked. I straighten it for her so she doesn't get yelled at. Aunt Erika is strict. She doesn't have your penchant for hitting, although her tongue is equally as sharp.

I'm going to hide this letter before Nadine gets up. I love you, Mom. I hope heaven is where you've gone. I don't enjoy praying, so it may be a while before you get out of purgatory if you ended up there. Granddad says in his letters that he prays for you every day. It must

5

be hard to live long enough to lose your wife and most of your children to cancer. All he has left is James, Erika, and Ruth. Well, you'll never have to experience that. One day we will join you. Nadine might be there before the rest of us. She smokes three cigarettes a day.

*****

Much has transpired since I last wrote you. This morning I woke before the sun and stared out into the night, looking for the words to tell you. I think I used them all for my honors English class. The sun's rays are beginning to crack through the darkness, and I'm forced to write instead of contemplate. So here it goes.

My English teacher, Mrs. Conroy, is encouraging me to write short stories. I have been giving them my mornings; that's why I've not written you. Mrs. Conroy believes my writing is years beyond my age and is doing her best to convince me to join the Writers Club. I'm hesitant to commit. It means once a week I won't be riding home on the bus with Nadine. The city bus is our pseudo-school bus, and I'm afraid to ride by myself. On the city bus, sometimes the Cuban men say things in Spanish to Nadine and me. I know enough Spanish to ask where the bathroom is. Besides a few popular cuss words, I'm not exactly at the level of conversational Spanish, but I know what the men are saying without understanding the words they use. I wish Tony would sit near us. Invariably, he finds his way to the back of the bus and studies. His classes must be extremely demanding. Nadine's form of defense is a harsh scowl which usually keeps the more flirtatious men at bay. I can't join the Writers Club because of my social curse: I'm burdened with cuteness. Even the bus driver winks at me.

I hope I grow as tall as you were, although I'm currently experiencing a slight slowdown in the growing department. At four feet, eleven inches, I'm the shortest kid in school, and I'm cute, not sophisticated or lovely. I'm the one Father Worley pats on the head when he comes into class. Halloween reinforced my unwanted *cute* notoriety when I unwittingly wore Marcy's costume.

Last weekend Nadine and I went to the school Halloween dance. I felt ridiculous wearing Marcy's fifth-grade pumpkin costume; Aunt

6

Erika said she didn't have any other costumes small enough to fit me. Nadine dressed up like a whore, and Uncle Will seemed embarrassed when he dropped us off. The two of us were hilarious now that I think about it, a whore and a bright orange pumpkin at her side. As soon as we walked inside the gym, Nadine merged with her junior friends leaving me to fend for myself. I hate being a freshman.

My costume earned me dubious recognition. The president of the Pep Club, Jose, nicknamed me. Munchkin. Unfortunately, I think the name is going to stick. Jose was one of ten Draculas. At times, I was unsure if it were Jose I was dancing with or if another Dracula had snuck in while I was practicing my disco turns. It's strange that only seniors were the ones who would ask me to dance; perhaps it is due to their seniority. At our school there are four boys to every girl. Since the first day it opened, Archbishop Curly was the exclusive domain of the male gender. Due to a drop in enrollment however, the doors have been open to girls for the past two years. A brother attending Archbishop Curly is the sole requirement for a female student to attend. Special allowance was made for Nadine and I. I guess a cousin is technically close enough to being a brother. Tony didn't go to the dance. It was probably a good thing because Nadine made another impression on the Davidson family.

While I was shaking my pumpkin buns on the dance floor, Nadine was drinking by the railroad tracks. I engaged in a search and rescue when she was not by the curb at the time Uncle Will instructed us to meet him. I found her with her friends and naively thought she had a bad case of the giggles. That was only the beginning. The whiskey she drank was to take hold of her mind and body, revealing a side of Nadine I was unprepared to witness.

After some persuasion, Nadine got into the car. Okay, it was more like she stumbled into Uncle Will's car. He didn't say anything, yet I could see him studying her in the rearview mirror. During our ride home, the alcohol kicked in, and Nadine's giggles erupted into malicious words. I need to practice writing dialogue so I'll do so here. Pretend you were there, Mom, although I'm glad you weren't.

Nadine said to me, "Close your ears, Ariana." My older sister then looked at the back of his head and said, "Your wife is a witch.

She's an evil witch, Uncle Will." He stared at her reflection in the mirror. I did my best to hush her, yet the more I nudged, the more the words flowed from her over relaxed mouth. "She treats us like we're worthless. I hate her. Why do you let her treat us like this? Why don't you stand up to her and tell her it's wrong? You're her husband. Why is she doing this to us? Don't just look at me. Say something," she demanded.

"She's your aunt," he said clearly. I noticed his eyes were serious, but his lips twitched. Nadine probably couldn't see his lips because she sat directly behind him. I think all she could see was his strong stare.

"Yes. She's my aunt. My dead mother's sister. And she's a witch. I hate Catholic school. I hate having to be picked up by my uncle. I want my own car. I want my own car." Nadine turned her head toward the window, and her body weight followed her eyes. The car slowed down as Uncle Will pulled into the driveway. Nadine must have realized where we were because she began protesting. "I'm not going in that house. I'm not going in that house where that witch lives. Nope."

Uncle Will's eyes questioned mine. I must have had a more bewildered look on my face than he did because he drew in a deep breath of air.

We opened Nadine's door, and she poured out of the car as if she was an octopus. She had no skeletal system. Uncle Will and I stared at her, no doubt wondering what we were to do. I was afraid she might have been hurt when I heard the beginning of a scream.

"IIIIIII'm not going in that house. She's a witch. She's a rotten witch."

I leaned over the body lying on the ground and said, "Nadine, get up. We have to go. You can't stay out here all night. C'mon. I'll walk you upstairs."

Uncle Will shook his head and said to me, "We're gonna have to carry her." I looked at him as if he were crazy. Nadine is nearly double my size. He was already tugging at one arm when I reluctantly grabbed her other arm. I did more talking than pulling knowing my words would be more effective than my strength.

"Naddy, please. I can't lift you. Please walk." I must have reached some part of her consciousness which stirred her body enough to move toward the front door. When Aunt Erika opened it, I knew Pandora's box had been opened as well.

Nadine looked up and attempted to focus her eyes. Aunt Erika asked me what was going on. I was surprised by her inability to grasp the obvious.

Uncle Will said, "She's been tipping the bottle."

Nadine stirred to life probably because she recognized Aunt Erika's voice. "You're a witch," she slurred.

Aunt Erika threw a look at me and said, "Get her upstairs and into bed." I knew it was not a request.

With all my might, I struggled up the narrow staircase with Nadine propped on my shoulder and leaning into my pumpkin hips. Uncle Will was behind us, pushing Nadine up the stairs. She landed on the bed sideways, and I didn't care. Her breath was putrid. Her body lay limp. I turned around to find Aunt Erika standing behind me.

"Where did she get it?"

"I don't know. She said it was whiskey when I found her by the railroad tracks. Some of her friends were there. I assume they gave it to her."

"How much?"

"She said it was a little bottle, but she drank the whole thing."

"Take her clothes off."

Even unconscious, Nadine detests Aunt Erika's voice. She lifted her head in our direction and muttered, "Witch." She then leaned over the side of the bed and threw up. I rolled my eyes and sunk my sore shoulders knowing I was the one who would clean the mess. The smell was grotesque. I started for the door to fetch a bucket and mop. Aunt Erika was gone, so I dutifully remained in the room with Nadine.

I changed out of my costume. An old T-shirt and jean shorts replaced my pumpkin, cute image. I didn't bother with pajamas knowing it was going to be a long night.

"Get her to aim for the bucket." Aunt Erika handed me a bucket and some rags. But it was too late. Nadine, I was suddenly reminded, had a second helping for dinner. I swallowed hard. On my hands and knees, I soaked up a horrid mixture of alcohol and undigested food. Nadine turned onto her back, rolling in her disgrace. My sister delivered the last of her stomach contents on herself. She mumbled then let out a hushed wail. Finally, Nadine collapsed on my side of the bed and passed out.

"Keep the bathroom door open and this door open. She may get up looking for the bathroom. I'll stay at the top of the stairs in case she's confused and goes in that direction." Aunt Erika was emotionless. Her hands were clutching a pillow and a blanket.

"It smells in there. I have to clean—"

"Do it in the morning. I don't want to wake Tony with more commotion."

"Where am I supposed to sleep?" I asked, staring at the liquid covering the wood floor.

"The bed," answered Aunt Erika. I looked over at the lifeless body that lay in its own disgust. Your daughter, my sister, soiled more than herself.

I fell asleep with the repugnant odor of alcohol gripping my nostrils, seeping into my lungs. Before dawn, I woke to the same smell. The fluid on the floor had formed into a cloud, hovering over Nadine as she snored. I wandered through the dark on my way to the bathroom and saw Aunt Erika sleeping at the top of the stairs. When I came out, she was gone. I looked for a note just in case she left one there. But there was no note. Your sister slept at the top of the stairs after all the insults Nadine discharged. She sacrificed for your daughter. I don't know if I would have.

Using the faucet by the garage, I rinsed out vomit-soaked rags. Nadine met me outside and asked where Aunt Erika had gone. I was unsure if my sister was looking for a battle or if she was hoping to apologize.

"There's a note on the refrigerator. They're at the country club. She said for us to have the room cleaned by dinner time."

Aunt Erika had left us to the mess and our shame. Though it was a week ago, it seems like a lifetime has passed. The course has changed at the depth of our lives.

I can hear Aunt Erika in the kitchen. It's time to peel grapefruits. My hand refuses to end this letter or say goodbye. Until the next time that I add to these pages...

I love you, Mom. And I'm sorry.

CHAPTER 2

Nadine tells everyone that she has been sentenced to the Davidson family for two years. Reaching eighteen is a coveted prize for a sixteen-year-old, especially one who feels jailed. She's not stupid. We both know that because of her drunken display, Aunt Erika will make Nadine's life miserable, and by virtue of being her sibling, I'm not exempt from the torture. I have four years to endure Aunt Erika's wrath, and worse, I'm the youngest in this household. It will be me and Aunt Erika and Uncle Will. I can't picture it. I don't think it will happen that way.

How odd it feels to be the youngest. I had accepted my role as the neglected middle child, even liked it. Tasha and Cammy are middle children in Uncle James's family. It's as if we traded places. They're lucky to be in a large family, sandwiched between cousins.

The Davidson house is often empty. The demand for dentistry must increase as the holidays approach; Aunt Erika has been spending Saturdays at Uncle Will's office. Nadine has a waitress job after school and on the weekends. She's saving her tip money for a car. When Tony isn't playing tennis, he locks himself in his bedroom. I feel isolated from the world while studying alone in Aunt Erika's house.

The solitude was reflecting on my grades. Even Nadine showed concern. I was bringing home perfect scores on every test. Then I became a member of the Pep Club. Jose talked me into it. I think it was just in time, before I transformed into a walking blob of brain matter. My English teacher is disappointed that I joined another club before hers. I explained to Mrs. Conroy that I would have to wait for my left hand to heal before beginning the Writers Club. Typing is actually difficult now.

I was playing volleyball during PE and had my hands in the wrong position. I don't know what I was thinking when I prepared for a setup instead of a serve. The ball caught my fingertips and bent my left hand backward; my fingernails cut into my wrist. Coach said my hand was hyperextended. The day after it happened, I was pulling dishes out of the cabinet and almost dropped them. My hand was more traumatized than I realized. Standing next to me, watching the plates quickly land on the counter with a crash, Aunt Erika called me a hypochondriac.

Coach suggested that I go to the doctor for an x-ray; she thinks I broke my hand. Aunt Erika won't take me. She says I'm faking it. I'm not. Coach doesn't think so either and spoke to Father Worley. He said to wait another week to see how it's healing. Coach wanted to call Aunt Erika and convince her to take me to the doctor. I begged Coach not to because I didn't want this to become a family issue. I mean, Coach helps Tony with his tennis even though a pro teaches him lessons at the country club. A call from Coach would cause there to be another note on the bathroom mirror or snide remark from Aunt Erika during dinner if she thought I was trying to make trouble. She's protective of Tony. If Coach were to say something, Aunt Erika would see it as an attack on Tony's reputation.

The Davidsons belong to a country club somewhere in Miami Shores and use it as their escape from Nadine and me. On our first Sunday in the Davidson household, Aunt Erika drove us to church. Unannounced to us, the sole purpose of her courtesy was to show the way. It was the first and last time she would endure our presence on a Sunday morning. She and Tony leave for the early mass on Sundays then drive directly to the country club. Evidently, Uncle Will meets them on the tennis courts after his morning walk.

Nadine and I have no other choice. We accept our subordinate status and walk to church every Sunday. It's bad enough that we're required to attend mass. Having to walk three miles changes the churchgoing experience into an insult. The way your sister's family eludes us gives cause for me to wonder. They must know your cancer was not contagious. Maybe they're taking precautions. They wouldn't want to become vegetarians or be struck with a tragic fate like ours.

Occasionally, Mrs. Mac gives us a lift to church and insists that we sit with her and her son, Jimmy. They live across the street from the Davidsons. Jimmy is three years younger than me, yet he's more of a gentleman than Tony. I think he has a crush on me, or perhaps Mrs. Mac instructed her son to be cordial. She seems to know what's going on in the Davidson house. Not that there is anything going on to speak of, it's what's missing that gives her the moral permission to care.

Mrs. Mac has not outright offered to drive us to church. She nonchalantly pulls over and offers her transportation services. I appreciate Mrs. Mac's delicate maneuvers to avert butting in family matters, and I'm thankful for the ride. It helps me to avoid thinking about the cracks on the sidewalks.

I feel anxious when we walk near the old ficus trees; their roots have dug under the sidewalk causing the concrete to split. I'm careful not to step on the cracks. In my mind, I compulsively repeat the same words over and over, "Step on a crack, break your mother's back." Nadine noticed my preoccupation with the sidewalk, and I confessed my obsession. My less than compassionate sister suggested I pray instead.

Mom, I think I'm trying to keep you alive. That or I'm at the doorstep of madness. I know you're dead, yet my unconscious mind is slow to accept. You're in my dreams, talking to me as if you never died. Then I wake in the morning and relive your death all over again.

I wonder what is a dream and what is real. Father Worley says that reality is a perspective. In religion class, we've been studying the phenomenon of paradoxes. I know you are a soul and you live beyond your body's life, yet I know you are dead. Death makes life complicated. Or is it that life makes death complicated?

I had a dream that seemed real. Actually, I'm uncertain if it was a dream. One night I crawled into bed feeling sad and asked God for comfort. A hand appeared with its palm facing me. It paused in the air, and I heard a voice in my head, although I don't remember what it said. The hand moved toward me. It was large enough for me to curl into, so I slept in God's hand while he held me. That was the best night's sleep I've had in months. I woke feeling loved and protected.

If it weren't for a uniform, I'd be forced to wear my birthday suit to school. I don't dare ask Aunt Erika for anything, especially something personal like clothes. Nadine has offered to dip into her savings and take me shopping. I told her it would be a waste of money. I'm anticipating a growth spurt to erupt any time now. What a thrill it will be to walk into the Pep Club meeting one day and be as tall as Jose. He would probably continue calling me Munchkin, but my nickname would have a new meaning.

The Pep Club is planning a senior class trip to Walt Disney World in the spring. Jose has secured permission for me to be included. Being cute has its advantages. Besides, most of my classes are senior courses. I'm practically a senior, just younger and shorter.

Mrs. Conroy has asked me to submit a short story in the school writing contest. I'm apprehensive, and I'm afraid. When I put words to paper, I'm doing more than creating a story. I reveal my inner self, and I bear my soul. Though a partial college scholarship is enticing, it's not worth exposing myself to six critical judges. Mom, writing is more than a form of expression. It's a mirror, a microscope, and it is a voice for my soul. I don't even let Nadine read my stories. I doubt she would comprehend how deeply they run to my core.

On the weekend days that she's not working, Nadine escorts me on the city buses destined for the mall. I don't particularly like the mall, but it's a change of scenery. I prefer the library. The books inspire my imagination. Nadine says the mall is more entertaining than the library. She has a point, although she forgets the library is at least within walking distance. Without city buses and Nadine's mean stare to protect me, the mall might as well be in China.

During our mall adventures, Nadine usually treats me to lunch. She works hard for her spending money and generously shares it with me. We aren't paid an allowance; however, on school days, Aunt Erika leaves on the credenza fifteen cents for milk. You know how I hate milk, so I save the money. I've enough to buy Nadine a gift for Christmas. I know she'll be surprised.

Your father faithfully writes me once a month. We are devoted pen pals, and through our words, we've become friends. Using handsome penmanship, he writes long letters on faded baseball stationery from the forties. I wonder if he knows it's 1976. It doesn't matter; this year I'd rather forget. I have a feeling Granddad feels the same. He writes, "Life is a journey, and some years are like some roads you wish you hadn't taken."

A month ago, I received a letter from someone I thought was left behind in the past. Mary Pat Brennan found me, and I'm glad. "We've been friends since we were two years old, and losing your mom and moving away isn't going to keep us apart." I've reread those words a thousand times. I hide her letters next to yours. We have resumed our friendship via the mail. Mary Pat sent her school picture. Her hair is darker, but I don't know if she's taller than me. Soon, it will no longer be a mystery. The Brennans invited us to spend Thanksgiving with them. I think Aunt Erika is relieved to know we will not be ruining her precious family holiday. Mr. Brennan made arrangements with Aunt Erika. He'll be picking up Nadine and me on Wednesday morning. I'm excited about going to Satellite Beach. Mary Pat promised to invite my classmates from Holy Name of Jesus for an afternoon reunion.

There is more to share, but the time has come. I am obliged to peel grapefruits. I loathe this chore. I've developed an aversion to the smell of citrus. It reminds me of a stinging, burning sensation. You would think after all this time that I would find a way to avoid eye contact with grapefruit acid. Aunt Erika shakes her head out of disgust when she sees me reach for the kitchen towel to wipe my eyes. Working in a dental office has reinforced her abnormal leeriness about germs. One morning Aunt Erika rushed into the kitchen screaming about my not having washed my hands. I asked her how she knew, especially since at the moment I was unsure. Your sister admitted to listening for the faucet to run prior to the sound of the knife drawer being opened. Since the incident, I've become more aware. It's not quite the same feeling as having a guardian angel, more like a wicked witch hovering over my shoulder.

I have half a mind to spit in the fruit cups this morning, yet I'm afraid of what would happen if Aunt Erika heard me spitting in the kitchen. It could kill her. She's too mean. She'd probably kill me.

*****

It felt strange to be back in Satellite Beach. Deep down I expected you to be there. I needed the Thanksgiving dinner with the Brennans more than I realized. Mrs. Brennan talked about you, telling us what a friend you were to her. I had forgotten that you were more than our mom. She seems to miss you as much as me. Before Sunday mass, Mrs. Brennan and I lit a candle in your honor. I hope you felt our prayers. I hadn't prayed in a long time. I could say the Hail Mary in my sleep. Fifty years from now if I never say the Hail Mary and wanted to then, I'd remember the words. It's imprinted on me, like my name. Mary Pat asked about Aunt Erika. I eluded the question, but Nadine wouldn't shut up. I was concerned the Brennans would feel sorry for us.

The reunion with my friends wasn't what I expected it to be. I'm no longer in their class. It wasn't a reunion with my classmates from Holy Name of Jesus. Instead, it was a reminder that I don't belong to them anymore.

Midterm exams are here. I've studied until my brain has melted into mush. To relieve the monotony, I've adopted the habit of reading Uncle Will's newspaper in the evenings. News is a diversion, not exactly light reading though.

Typing class requires no studying; however, I've been practicing for the speed test. My left hand has been reluctantly cooperating. It's excruciating to open and extend my fingers fully. Quite unexpectedly, my easiest class has become my most difficult. One poor decision during a PE class weaves its way to my report card. What heavy fate I must bear to have a simple typing class threaten my grade point average. Coach has shown me exercises for my hand and encourages me to repeat them throughout the day. I'm learning that my will may not be enough to overcome my destiny. I'm wary of where this journey is leading me. I look behind and see pain; I look ahead, and it's dark.

After all these years of going to church, I have no answers to my questions about life. I don't think the Catholic faith has insights into living. Mom, it's not that Nadine and I hate church, although it is boring. We don't comprehend the purpose of going to mass. Am I holier because I've listened to a priest? Am I a better person because I've confessed my sins or received Communion? Am I closer to God because I've entered a church? I believed it would be a mortal sin to stop going to church. Now I don't think so. Nadine says she's an atheist. Two years ago, she vowed to become a nun. She doesn't know who she is or what she wants. I don't like Sunday mass, but I also know I'm not an atheist. Well, going to church has brought me closer to an angel: Mrs. Mac.

Mrs. Mac and I have a Sunday routine. Nadine works, the Davidsons race to the country club, and Mrs. Mac drives her family and me to the bath club. The Macs gave me a standing invitation. Mrs. Mac has taught me how to play backgammon and orders me a beer with lunch. No one breathes a word about the Davidson family. The Macs are wise not to make enemies of their neighbors.

I've grown fond of the Macs' beachside cabana and the smell of sea mist in my hair every Sunday. I have a feeling the bath club is more exclusive than the country club. It gives me a tinge of satisfaction to know I go to the bath club and the Davidson family doesn't.

By the way Aunt Erika was acting, one would believe the Queen of England had arrived. Close. Marcy is home from college. I get the feeling that she resents us for taking over her room. Upon her entrance, she said hello to Nadine and me. She hasn't granted us another audience.

Nadine is at work, and the Davidson family is putting up a Christmas tree as I write you. I was invited to join the manufactured happy family gathering, but I don't like eggnog.

Granddad sent a check for ten dollars and a handwritten Christmas card. He said he was hoping this would be his last Christmas. Eighty years isn't that old. He goes to his card games every week and complains about how the winters in Indiana make it difficult to get around. Granddad was forced to join another group of card players; his card playing buddies are dying off. I never thought about it until I read his Christmas letter. He is one of few from his era. I think he feels lonely, Mom. Aunt Ruth wrote me a letter telling me how Granddad slipped on the ice and bumped his head. Granddad has a hard head. I think that's where Nadine gets hers. I've lost too many people this year. I asked God to let Granddad stay a while longer. I depend on his letters written on his yellowed baseball stationery.

CHAPTER 3

I know I haven't written in a couple of months. Things have taken a sharp turn around the corner, and I'm doing my best to hang on.

It's not exactly a growth spurt, but I have grown an inch since we arrived in August. Actually, it was Mrs. Mac who noticed. Anyway, Aunt Erika gave me money for a new swimsuit, and Nadine dragged me to the mall. After much debate and numerous trips to the dressing room, I decided on a one-piece. It's hot pink. Nadine says I look like a neon rabbit. I'm hoping my head will grow into my ears. I don't remember if you had big ears or not. Nadine has normal size ears. There's nothing normal about me.

Remember the milk money I told you I was saving? Well, on my way out the door to an afternoon movie with my friend, Julie, Aunt Erika handed me a five-dollar bill. I gave it back telling her I had money of my own. Her veins popped out of her forehead around the temples. At this point in our affiliation, few words are necessary for communication. I answered her penetrating stare and admitted to saving my milk money. She hasn't given me any since. Nadine said I was retarded for not shutting my mouth and taking the five. She's right. I didn't think I would get punished for saving my milk money. Even Mrs. Mac thought I was being industrious.

As it turns out, Aunt Erika had been doing her own saving up. She had been busy after the holidays, I've learned. And Nadine got her Christmas wish after all. A woman, Jessica Lareau, came to the house the other day to speak with Nadine and me. She explained that she's from the Catholic Services Bureau and she has been assigned to us. Mrs. Lareau is a counselor for foster children. Aunt Erika is giving us up. "Rescinding her guardianship" were the delicate words Mrs. Lareau used.

Next month we're going to court to officially change our status from the Davidson domestic problem to the Catholic Services Bureau's foster children. Mrs. Lareau explained that foster children are wards of the state. I had to look up the word *ward* to understand what she meant. From the sound of it, I thought it was an insult. In a way, I guess it is.

Nadine seems relieved to know we will be leaving at the end of the school year. I don't know how I feel. We are to appear before a judge and answer questions. What's there to ask? I mean, we don't have a choice. No one else wants us. Aunt Ruth is old and already has Granddad to care for. Uncle James has too many kids as it is; the VanHusen house bulges with their five children plus Tasha and Cammy. Besides, I prefer to be in Florida. Indiana is too far from the ocean.

Mrs. Lareau said she is searching for a Catholic family who is willing to accept two sisters instead of separating us. She let us know we are considered hard to place because of our age. Aunt Erika was not in the same room when Mrs. Lareau spoke with us, yet we felt her presence. I had the feeling Mrs. Lareau wanted to say more but didn't.

Uncle Will said to me while we were alone in the kitchen yesterday, "You must think we are pathetic." His eyes revealed his shame.

I answered, "No." I thought the opposite. I figured that was what the Davidsons thought of Nadine and me. Pathetic. Aunt Erika has conveyed it thousands of times and in a thousand ways.

So the State of Florida is going to be our legal guardian. I hope it will be kinder than Aunt Erika. I wish Mrs. Mac wanted two more kids. She told me that Aunt Erika was doing her best and that I was probably better off as a foster child. I'll miss the bath club.

I'm thankful we are allowed to finish out the school year. I'll be able to go with the seniors to Disney World. Jose gave me a T-shirt. In bright orange letters, "Munchkin" is written across it. I'll wear it on our trip, although it doesn't apply. I'm five feet tall. Tasha is almost three years younger than me, and she's already five feet tall. I wonder what is stunting my growth.

Mrs. Conroy gave me a writing journal after the Christmas break. She explained how she had a strong compulsion to buy it when she was shopping with her husband. I told her I would use the journal, but I have no intentions of doing that. I have this letter, your letter. I need to write you instead of rambling in a journal. Mrs. Conroy knows that we are leaving in three months. Her eyes filled with tears when I told her. She bravely restrained the sorrow from running down her cheeks. She's the kind of person who becomes emotional while reading a cartoon. I used to cry. I used to feel. Now, I'm just numb. I hope Mrs. Lareau can find a home for us. Another Catholic home, oh joy. I think I'm going to convert to Judaism. I don't think they do this stuff to their kids. Maybe Mrs. Lareau can give us to the Jewish Services Bureau.

My fern died. I found cigarette butts just below the surface of the soil when I pulled it out of the pot. Nadine killed my plant. If cigarettes can do that to a plant, think what they're doing to her lungs. She defends my complaints about her smoking saying that you smoked for years. I remind her that you died and how you died.

*****

The judge was a woman. I didn't expect to see a woman. She wore a black robe as I had imagined, but I had no idea it would be a woman. Mrs. Lareau told us the judge had a stroke and this was her first week back on the bench. If Mrs. Lareau had not informed me, I would have thought the judge was as drunk as Nadine on the night of the Halloween dance. My judge slurred her words.

She asked me a question, yet I don't remember what it was because she then told me to spit out the gum I was chewing. I didn't. Not because I was being obstinate, I was straining to comprehend her words. Then the judge yelled at me louder and more forcefully. I understood then and removed the gum, sticking it in my uniform's pocket. My hesitation agitated the judge and confirmed her assumptions. She asked if I realized that my aunt could no longer tolerate my insolent behavior. I glanced at Aunt Erika and figured it was true, but not for the reasons the judge was probably told before we were

allowed to enter the courtroom. Aunt Erika's eyes remained fixed on the judge. Your sister had to have felt my momentary stare into her soul. I told the judge that I understood.

And I do. I do understand. You were her dying sister with one last request, to take your near-grown daughters and see them to adulthood. How could she tell you no? How could she be honest with you? Your sister has a life of her own, a family of her own, a world in which we are intruders. She became our guardian because you asked her to. And she resented every second of her obligation.

It was necessary that Aunt Erika portray us as uncontrollable. Now the State of Florida has assumed her burden. Your sister was relieved of her guardianship because we are pathetic. I wished that Mrs. Mac could have been in the courtroom. I think she would have spoken up for us. Mrs. Lareau was there holding our hands and representing us instead.

Jessica Lareau is from Canada and has a slight French accent. I like her accent; it reminds me of you. You were so French, so elegant. I remember you as a tall, thin woman with full lips. Granddad must have known when you were born that you acquired most of his French genes. Naming you Suzette was being true to you. I think you would have been embarrassed to see two of your daughters in a courtroom admitting they were pathetic. Mrs. Lareau told us it was for the best. For who is it best? Aunt Erika? For us? The state of Florida?

During the drive back to Aunt Erika's house, Mrs. Lareau was quiet, keeping her accent to herself. I stared out the window, and Nadine—well, she smoked a cigarette and announced that she was no longer Catholic. Our former legal guardian drove in a separate car because she has a separate life.

Aunt Erika is at her cooking class. Tony and Uncle Will are gone. They didn't leave a note on the refrigerator. I guess the note writing is done. We skipped dinner. Nadine said she was too tired to eat. The idea of food is unappealing after having been given to the state. I'm sitting on the edge of the bed continuing my letter to you, and Nadine is smoking a cigarette and walking around the block. I don't want to be here either.

Nadine was right all along. I should have established myself when we first arrived. Why did I grovel for Aunt Erika's mercy? We had been judged and sentenced long before our plane from Indiana landed.

*****

Walt Disney World was a blast. Jose escorted me on all the rides and held my hand when we stood in lines. He's going to Harvard in the fall. He's intelligent, good-looking, and unfortunately, he doesn't find me sexy or sophisticated. Jose tells me I'm cute. His parents were chaperons for the evening. They think I'm cute too. Jose's dad told me that his company made my Munchkin T-shirt; he seemed tickled to see me wearing it. The school bus pulled into Archbishop Curly's parking lot at one in the morning. I felt disappointed that the trip had ended before Jose had mustered up enough confidence to kiss me. He drove me and his parents to Aunt Erika's house and gave me a peck on the cheek after he walked me to the front door. I think the kiss was more because he's Cuban than anything. I will miss him the most. Mrs. Conroy says Jose will be a famous writer one day. I think if he can find a way to convert his accent into words, he'll be famous. His accent is what entices people to listen closely to what he has to say. He's too reserved to be a writer.

I was amazed to find Aunt Erika reading in the living room when I walked in the house. She doesn't want me in her home, but she'll wait up for me late at night. I suppose she wouldn't want to explain to Granddad why one of us were killed while under her care. I wonder how she explained our new status as foster children. I take that thought back. I don't want to know what she told Granddad.

While en route to their home, Mrs. Lareau told us about Shari and Tim. In tainted English, she described them as Catholic, thirty-seven years old, and young at heart. The Andrews had asked for a daughter and were twice as happy to learn there are two of us. I feel like a horse being auctioned off.

For a few hours we were to converse with Shari and Tim, so they could determine if we were suitable. Mrs. Lareau drove to the other end of Miami, to Kendall. I think it borders the Everglades. I could have sworn I saw an alligator on the side of the road as Mrs. Lareau turned into Winston Park.

Nadine tucked cigarettes into her purse, and I pulled them out when she wasn't looking. I left her smelly tobacco in the car. Aunt Erika had taught me when to grovel and when to establish. This was not the time to establish ourselves.

A dog greeted us at the door. Shari gave us a warm hug and Tim smiled, a lot. Before we left, the Andrews proudly showed us to their backyard where they have a camper that sleeps four. Nadine was more interested in their Jeep.

That evening the Andrews spoke to us more than Aunt Erika has in seven months. The only problem is that they are childless. We will be their first attempt at being parents. I miss a big family with screaming kids and chaos. I never felt alone in a big family, neglected maybe but never alone. I don't like loneliness; it's a hopeless feeling.

Nadine was angry at me for taking her cigarettes; she wanted the evening to be more focused on her than it was. The Andrews thought I was cute. They made the mistake of saying so. Mrs. Lareau seemed pleased. I guess we have a new home as soon as the school year ends, and there we will remain until we reach the age of eighteen, if Nadine doesn't muck this one up.

Kendall is in the boondocks. It's too far from the ocean. Beggars can't be choosy. At least, it's a home.

CHAPTER 4

Finals required every ounce of concentration I could summon. Distractions weren't the problem. I lost my drive. I studied mainly because Jose encouraged me. Sitting next to him in study hall was my sole motivation for studying. I simply wanted to be around him. I like his company. Jose was impressed with what he thought was my determination; I don't think he gets it. Going to college is light-years from now, if it exists at all. Furthermore, high school isn't a preparation for college like it is for him. It doesn't matter. The last day of school was our last day in Aunt Erika's home. She doesn't care if I failed the ninth grade or not. If I had to repeat it all over again, I wouldn't be doing it under her roof.

Our report cards were sent in the mail, and it's official. I was an A student for my ninth year of schooling. That was my last year in Catholic school, thank God. No pun intended. Nadine and I will go to the same high school again, but we will be on split sessions.

At least for her final year of high school, Nadine will be in public school: no more uniforms, no more nuns, and no more religion classes. A public high school is to be built a few blocks from here; it won't be open for another year. I will attend that school when I'm a junior. Right now it's a bean field.

We've moved to the edge of the United States, Mom. Julie told me that alligators run faster than humans. Jose said there is nothing to worry about since they're almost extinct. Compared to Miami Shores, Kendall is on another planet. With all this practice, I'm learning how to leave without looking back. Jose will soon be at Harvard, and Julie has other friends. Mrs. Mac gave me her address, like I didn't know it; she only lived across the street. Jimmy gave me a miniature backgammon game and that was that. Oh, Mrs. Conroy gave me a book by Mark Twain. She said it was all his essays and told me he was rejected many times before he was published. I think she was hinting for me to persist despite the setbacks. She had imparted to me her knack for reading between the lines.

There were no tears nor hugs when Aunt Erika appeared to say goodbye. Mrs. Lareau waited in the foyer while your sister reinforced her strategy that dispossessed us, the invaders of her home. Aunt Erika told Nadine she was extremely immature. No news flash there. Then Aunt Erika turned to me and said she wouldn't touch my maturity with a ten-foot pole. I pictured her standing across the room with a bamboo pole in her hand. I had half a mind to yank it from her hands and whack her with it. I don't know what is mature and what isn't, but I know a loving soul, and I know when someone isn't.

While adding items that refused to fit into her overstuffed suitcase, Nadine carelessly rummaged through mine. I didn't want her to find your letter, so I tucked it under my shirt. Knowing Nadine, she'd use your letter as if it were an ash tray not unlike she did with my fern.

After we plopped our suitcases in the trunk, Mrs. Lareau pulled up to Mrs. Mac, who was standing at the end of her driveway. She gave me a kiss and a hug and waved us goodbye. I watched Mrs. Mac from the back-seat window. I thought she was brave doing that in front of Aunt Erika, who was probably peering out from her living room window.

Mrs. Lareau was quiet during most of the drive to Kendall. I think she was deciding on what to say. When we were a few minutes from the Andrews's house, our counselor spoke up. It astonished me to learn that Aunt Erika was on her mind. Mrs. Lareau needed to explain, or perhaps she wanted us to know she wasn't deaf or blind. She said Aunt Erika is rigid. I know what that word means; it just sounded weird being applied to a person. And it fits. Your sister is rigid. Nadine describes Aunt Erika the best saying with a guttural sound to her voice, "She's a witch."

Albeit we share a bedroom, Nadine and I each have a bed and a dresser. Shari spent our first afternoon together discussing how to decorate our room. She said we can paint the dressers whatever color we want and showed us how to make macramé hangers. I asked for a replacement fern once I learned that Nadine is not allowed to smoke in our bedroom. The American Lung Association will be happy to know that my exposure to second-hand smoke has tripled. Shari and Tim are ardent smokers. It baffles me, the preoccupation with sucking on a lit wad of dried leaves.

There are immediate benefits to living with the Andrews that I did not expect to gain from a Catholic home: Nadine and I aren't required to go to church. After an entire month of being here, we have yet to ask to attend a Sunday mass. Though the Andrews don't go to church, they definitely have the Catholic predilection for drinking. My Italian foster parent says she was raised on wine instead of milk. Every night Shari pours me a half glass of California Chablis with dinner. I like wine about as much as I like milk. Nadine drinks her full glass then discretely finishes mine.

We live with three cats, but one of them won't come out from under the Andrews's bed except to eat and hiss at me if I'm around. Buffy, their dog, is an adorable mixture of several breeds. Two years ago, Shari gave Buffy to Tim when he came home after a business trip. She described how Buffy was tiny enough to fit in one hand. Buffy has grown into a medium-sized dog complete with one ear that points up while the other droops down.

Shari's New Jersey accent is heavy, making it difficult for me to comprehend her words. Nadine says Shari's accent isn't the problem; it's my hearing. You were sick and out of the country, so we decided not to tell you. I had developed a serious ear infection when I was twelve years old. When my fever reached a hundred and four, Samantha rushed me to the hospital. We waited in the emergency room for over an hour. I preferred my bed to the waiting room, so I insisted that Samantha drive me home before a doctor examined me. It was a mistake because of what happened.

I know now that my eardrum burst. At the time I didn't know what was going on. In the middle of the night I felt a huge, loud sound filling my ear. The ache was so intense that I thought my head would explode. Then my right ear bled. I never want to feel an ache like that again. The doctor had said my ability to hear in the range of the human voice was damaged, but from that ear I can hear high and low pitches that most people can't. Nadine says it makes me more dog than human. There's a delay of a couple of seconds before I can differentiate sounds I hear. To compensate, I tend to watch people's lips. As I grow accustomed to hearing someone, I'm able to comprehend without seeing the words formed. It's no big deal. Most people don't realize there's anything different about me except that I talk loudly.

I would have to be completely deaf not hear my sister's screams at night. Nadine scares the wits out of me; it sounds like she's being murdered. Her nightmares began two weeks after we arrived. A few times Tim has come into our room to wake her. He asks her about the dream she was having, and invariably Nadine doesn't remember. Nor does she believe us when we tell her she's been screaming. She rolls her eyes and drops her head on the pillow, and the next morning my sister acts as if nothing happened.

The Andrews apparently told Mrs. Lareau about Nadine's disturbing nightmares. Last Saturday our counselor brought someone with her for our first home visit. Patrick Muldune is an ex-priest and now a counselor. His Irish accent sends chills down my spine; it reminds me of Catholic school. Our family visit was quickly diverted to a private meeting with Nadine. I was asked to go outside with Buffy. I had no complaints until three hours had passed with no ending in sight. Buffy was accommodating; she showed me her favorite digging spots. We sat under the palms and drew in the sand. I don't know which one of us was more excited when Mrs. Lareau came outside to fetch us. Buffy prefers air-conditioning over hot, steamy summer days in the backyard.

Mom, I don't know what the Andrews and Nadine talked about with Mrs. Lareau and Patrick Muldune. Nadine won't tell me. She has emotional flare-ups, and the next thing I know, the Andrews ask me to go outside while a family discussion ensues. My sister is making up for that impression I stole from her when I snatched the cigarettes out of her purse.

The summer is boring here in the Everglades. Well, it's not that remote. We actually live in a neighborhood, but the kids are much younger than us. School doesn't start for another month and a half. I didn't realize I depended on school to meet friends. Nadine and I babysit once in a while for the neighbors. I'm saving my money for a trip to see Tasha and Cammy next summer. They're slack in their letter writing. I worry that they'll eventually forget me.

Granddad is loyal to the pen and paper. I wonder if Aunt Ruth knows he writes about her. He has few topics of interest, and she is among them: card games, friends, weather, Aunt Ruth, and prayers. It's fascinating how father and daughter have become companions in their waning years of life. In the course of almost a year, I've discovered that Granddad is a spiritual man. I used to think he was religious, but after rereading some of his letters, I've decided he's more spiritual than Catholic. Your father wants to leave this life; he feels he has completed it. I wonder if all old people play this same wait game.

God must be testing Granddad and me for endurance. Eventually this long, boring summer will end. Shari and Tim work all day while Nadine and I do chores and sunbathe in the backyard. We're camping out this weekend to mark the end of our honeymoon. Mrs. Lareau describes the first month in a foster home as a honeymoon. She says things in the Andrews household will settle into a routine. I believe a routine will be difficult to accomplish without school as my guide.

We have a campsite reserved at America Outdoors in Key Largo. And Buffy has special permission to accompany us. Shari asked me to make sandwiches for the trek. The Andrews eat meat. Making sandwiches for them is going to be a challenge. I attempted to trade chores with Nadine; she's responsible for the laundry. My sister refused to budge knowing she has a cake chore. I didn't expect her to, but it was worth a try. Shari plans to come home early from work today to pack the rest of the camping equipment and supplies. When Tim gets home, he'll load us in the Jeep and drive us down to the Keys.

I rarely see Tim. He usually has a beer in his hand and laughs a lot. He works for Eastern Airlines, in the sales department. I had assumed he was a pilot, but Shari set me straight. She used to work for Eastern; that's where they met ten years ago. Anyway, Tim's from Miami, and as fate would have it, he graduated from Archbishop Curly. He said he never imagined he'd have two daughters that attended the same school as he especially since it excluded girls in his era.

Shari and Tim skip breakfast. That means I don't have to peel grapefruits ever again. It's my job to feed the "kids" instead. Initially, Buffy was stubborn when it came to swallowing her heartworm pill. After several experiments, I've found a way to win her cooperation. I employ the Pavlov method. When she swallows the unmasked pill, I give her a lick of liverwurst. I used to hide the heartworm pill inside the liverwurst, but she found a way of separating and spitting it out from the side of her mouth. She's a smart dog with a rather nimble tongue.

When Nadine goes into Shari's room and talks to Luis on the phone, that's my time to write you. Nadine and Luis met at Curly and started dating about a month before we left Miami Shores. She likes him more for his car than anything else. From the sound of her voice, I think their conversation is ending. I'll continue your letter at another time.

*****

I have found my goal in life: camping. I live for it. America Outdoors is situated on the edge of the Atlantic Ocean, in the heart of Key Largo. It's only an hour away but feels like a separate country. Quaint, sandy campsites are tucked in between huge sea grape trees and tall gumbo limbos. For most of the weekend, I laid under the water next to the sea wall and breathed fresh air piped in from a snorkel. The sun's light and heat penetrated my watery world and tanned my skin. It's an awesome feeling to be under the ocean, skimming my butt on the sand as waves ripple over me. My eyes adjusted to the saltwater. I opened them to stare past the surface of the water, watching white puffs of clouds float by. A baby stingray passed near me, its gliding fins reflected the slow motion of the Florida Keys.

I lived under the water only running back to the campsite long enough to eat and have a wine cooler. Coolers were Tim's suggestion. I find them more agreeable than a glass of wine. Shari makes mine with mostly water and a touch of Chablis to give it color.

By virtue of being a dog, Buffy isn't allowed on America Outdoors' beach. Friday evening, I snuck her to the boat launch and proudly introduced her to the Atlantic Ocean. It was love at first sniff. Excepting her doggie bathtub, this was her first experience with a body of water. Buffy's instincts to swim lured her in the water. Twenty minutes later, she barely noticed I was waiting for her on shore.

In Key Largo, the stars are brighter and seem closer. They were teasing me into believing that if I reached, I could touch them. On Saturday night, the four of us lay on beach chairs and stared at the night sky for hours. In between shooting stars and the rising moon was Nadine's complaints. She was bored. Nothing satisfied her, not the beach's serenity, not the stars' promises, not even wine coolers. Nadine loathes camping. She was as miserable as I was happy.

I was reluctant to leave Sunday evening. During the drive back, Shari and Tim decided to camp out once a month. Nadine rolled her eyes, and I beamed.

With the intent to create a personal reading program, I selected some books from the Andrews's den. Shari retrieved one of the books she saw I had stacked in the corner near my bed. She acted peculiar when she explained that it was inappropriate for young eyes. I was intrigued and wanted to read it even more. She must have tucked it in her room some place because it wasn't on the bookshelves when I searched for it the following day. The name of the book escapes me. I remember the title had the word *chain* in it. I've decided to begin with *Jonathan Livingston Seagull*. The title seems fitting for a summertime read.

For entertainment, I read. Nadine commandeers the Andrews's bathroom. She borrows Shari's makeup and curling iron. My sister looks like a clown by the time she's done wielding the makeover wand. I don't say anything though. Lately, she's been hypersensitive.

A week ago, we saw a psychiatrist. Shari insisted on it. Mrs. Lareau objected but arranged for the appointments anyway. Our counselor was concerned about the message it would send to Nadine and me.

Evidently, the psychiatrist volunteers for the Catholic Services Bureau; he didn't have an office of his own. He looked out of place sitting behind Mrs. Lareau's tiny desk. I lost the coin flip and was first to lie on the proverbial couch. Nadine followed.

We waited in the lobby while the psychiatrist spoke with Shari and Tim. Mrs. Lareau must have seen this as her opportunity to play counselor because she asked us what it felt like to be foster children. Opposite of Nadine's compulsive need to communicate, I had nothing to share. What's there to feel? We're foster children.

Mrs. Lareau called today for our weekly conversation. After much persuasion on my part, she admitted that the psychiatrist recognized my acumen and said that I use it as a survival tool. I had to look up *acumen*, although I had an idea what it meant by the pride Mrs. Lareau conveyed. Nadine didn't fare as well in his professional opinion. According to Mrs. Lareau, the psychiatrist said my sister has a chip on her shoulder and believes the world owes her. I asked Mrs. Lareau if we had to go back for more evaluations or if one session was enough to determine that we were nuts. After recovering from an unexpected laugh, she confided in me. The psychiatrist asked that Shari come back for counseling, but she has refused. Our foster mother was insulted by the psychiatrist's suggestion. Mrs. Lareau didn't say, yet I had the feeling that Shari thinks Nadine and I are the ones who are screwed up. I wouldn't mind psychiatric counseling because it hurts when I think about you. Maybe counseling would help. I never talk about you. Nadine does. I'm waiting for the Andrews to figure out Nadine has wrapped them around her pinky. That will be one big eye-opener for them.

For each foster child under their care, the Catholic Services Bureau will be mailing out checks in the amount of one hundred and eighty dollars. Mrs. Lareau said it's for clothes. As foster children, we are entitled to a clothing allowance before school begins. I plan to accept more babysitting jobs. A hundred and eighty dollars will only cover the basics. I won't have a parochial school uniform to hide in. Shari is planning to take me clothes shopping at Miracle Mile in Coral Gables. She said it would be a mother-daughter thing. I thought it was obvious that I already have a mother.

Nadine is spared the shopping ordeal I must endure. Before leaving Miami Shores, she bought clothes with the money she was saving for a car. After meeting Luis, Nadine figured she could have both, a car and clothes for the price of one.

Nadine had no excuses to exempt her from the introduction circuit; she was stuck with me as we were paraded. The Andrews have displayed us to all their friends who live in the Miami area. Most of their friends are married with grown children. With no kids as a distraction, conversations with the Andrews's friends are actually agonizing. The Polanskis are the exception. They have one son five years younger than me. He has a neighborhood full of friends who play in their pool and wrestle. I feel at home in their house and wish the Polanskis were foster parents.

I'm the youngest in this household, again. I find myself missing Tasha and Cammy when I'm alone. They're lucky they ended up with the VanHusens. At least they're not foster children.

Shari dragged me to the dentist; he's a neighborhood friend. The Andrews are baffled why Uncle Will never brought us to his office for a checkup. I shrug my shoulders instead of attempting to explain the Davidsons' need to disregard me.

I am forced to quit a habit. It's time. Besides the obvious dangers it poses to my teeth, bubble gum is not exactly flattering. I have cavities that need to be filled. The dentist wants me to wear braces as well. He has an orthodontist friend who needs a tax write-off. After January, I'll look like a metal mouth geek. I better make friends before I turn into a tax write-off; otherwise, there will be little chance once I smile.

Nadine is with Luis this evening. He drove all the way here to escort her to a party in Miami Shores. I hope she doesn't get drunk and barf in his new car. Shari and Tim are sitting outside. Their evening routine is simple: They move from the dining room table to the patio table; cigarettes and after-dinner drinks are essential elements to their unwinding. I prefer my books. Since no one is around, tonight I'm continuing this letter.

I'm supposed to clean the dishes, yet I am delaying the inevitable. I hate the dishes. Shari uses every pan in the kitchen when she makes dinner. It takes me nearly an hour to clean up after her.

Remember when all six of us would pile into the kitchen after dinner? That's when you taught us folk songs. And Tasha and I discovered we lack an ability to sing. Neither making dinner nor cleaning the dishes was a chore back then. I loved being in the kitchen listening to your voice as you sang and harmonized with Samantha and Nadine. Cammy was the perfect percussionist when we handed her a spatula and a pan. Those songs, they float in and out of my mind as I do the dishes by myself.

The Andrews just called for Daughter Number Two. Tim nicknamed us. Nadine is Daughter Number One, and I am Daughter Number Two. I prefer Ariana, but he thinks it's cute to number us. Why does he have to number us? There's only two of us. It can't be that difficult to remember who is who.

It's time to do the dishes. Nadine has the easy chores, laundry and vacuuming. I have the dubious honor of cleaning the bathrooms and the kitchen. I don't like being the youngest. I now have more compassion for Cammy than I did.

*****

Showing off their new daughters, the Andrews display us for their friends. Only we're not that new, just to Shari and Tim. Our foster parents proudly describe our personalities to anyone who will listen. I'm cute and bright, only they say "gifted." Nadine's trouble, but they haven't figured it out yet.

Our household has grown since I've pulled out your letter from under the mattress. While we were visiting Shari and Tim's friends in Ft. Lauderdale, we discovered two female puppies down the street. Shari insisted we adopt them. She says they're just like Nadine and me, two sisters who needed a home.

Nikki and Elki are a German shepherd and husky mix and look like fur balls with four black enormous paws. They are adorable, to say the least, and run circles around Buffy. She and I hide in the bedroom to avoid being consumed alive. Puppy teeth easily penetrate exposed flesh. Tim pulled out a thirty-five-millimeter camera to record their puppiness. I have not relinquished his camera since. From a wilting leaf to Nadine's makeover sessions, I've taken pictures of everything. I hope I remember to remove her pictures before Nadine sees the developed film. She threatened me with violence if I photograph her. Unlike my sister, Tim enjoys hamming it up in front of the camera lens. During one such photo session, I didn't have the heart to tell him I had not put a roll of film in.

School begins next week, at the end of hot August. Shari told me to enjoy the fleeting moments I have of freedom because I'm enrolled in the accelerated program. Her idea of freedom is boredom to me. Attending Killian will be a relief. Against all odds, Nadine and I have survived the summer, in another home. The further time takes me away from you, the more I realize that our family is really only a memory. We are in the past, not a hope or a promise of what could be but simply what was. There is no going back, but I can't seem to let go.

"What does it feel like to be a foster child?" Mrs. Lareau's question haunts me. I now know why I don't have an answer. While photographing Nikki and Elki, it dawned on me that I've been a foster child since I was ten. I don't remember what it feels like not to be a fosterling. The day you told us you had cancer was the day I became a foster child. Although he was not our father, Ben was your husband. In your absence, he cared for us while you battled a disease that seemed more like a relentless monster. I thought cancer was the worst thing that could happen to us, until Ben sexually molested Samantha. I wonder if you knew when you filed divorce papers that he was a drunk in addition to all the other names you called him. Samantha replaced Ben; she was our temporary guardian. She wasn't much better than him, although she never placed us in danger of sexual perversions. Uncle James and Aunt Beth opened their home for a summer while you lay dying in a hospital room. Aunt Erika endured us for nine months, long enough for us to fully develop and be born as legal foster children. And in between were your friends like Mrs. Brennan who made cheese casseroles and smiled to help us feel less abandoned.

I just thought of something. I never once wondered where Dad was during all this separation. I somehow knew and accepted that when he divorced you, he divorced his five daughters as well. In grade school, I was embarrassed that I had no father. Everyone except our family had one. After a while I barely noticed he was missing. Now, I have no mother. Being a foster child is different than being motherless. Why doesn't Mrs. Lareau ask me what it feels like to be alone, to be motherless?

Years of wearing a uniform has left me naked in more ways than one. Shari selected a peach cotton shirt for my public school debut. She says it brings out my tan. For the first day of school, my foster mother told me that the right outfit is critical. She's right about initial impressions. Within the first week, students assign themselves to their proper social group. In my case, it's difficult to determine which group I belong to. I'm one of the brains yet typically socialize with the regulars. I find the geeks interesting and end up sharing projects with them if we're in the same class. I've always avoided the druggies. Nadine, she hangs with that group. It may take me a while, but I find one or two good friends and stick with them. I somehow become popular, although that's due more to my cuteness than any intentional politicking.

I predict three weeks will pass before we are fully adjusted to split sessions. Nadine will catch the bus at seven in the morning. She should be the one to go to school at noon since she likes to sleep in. We may both be attending Killian, but my sister might as well be in a separate school system. Nadine will be a senior. Seniors have developed a refined attitude during their previous three years of high school. She'll snub me at every opportunity. Anyway, I think she'll be on the prowl for another boyfriend. Luis wrecked his car.

We're going camping this weekend. Nadine volunteered to remain home and watch the puppies. I'm glad Shari saw through that one; Nadine has to come. Nikki and Elki will stay over the dentist's house while we're gone. I'll miss them, but I agree with the Andrews—the fur balls are too young for camping.

I'm hoping we'll see dolphins. Some of the camping regulars we met during our last camping trek said dolphins swim near the shoreline this time of the year. I long to swim with the dolphins. If that were to happen, I would go out to sea and never come back.

I wonder if dolphins have their version of foster children.

CHAPTER 5

Patrick Muldune and Mrs. Lareau teamed up again. It's a kick in the pants to hear them talk—he with an Irish accent, she with a French. More family discussions means more walks with Nikki and Elki to Hidden Lake. Buffy stays home in the air-conditioning.

My last three Saturdays were spent with the fur balls while Nadine had an audience of four adults. I stare out to the lake for hours, so do the girls. Nikki is perfecting her instinct to chase birds. The older and less mobile ducks swim in the middle of the lake, away from her puppy barks. Elki is a digger with a nose for frogs. The girls keep a fuzzy ear out for Tim's pager. When a high pitch beep blares, they know it's time for us to head back. We have a routine: baths then doggie biscuits before we enter the house.

I'd rather go camping than walk to the lake. There's something magical about lying under the water instead of standing out over it. Submerged, I can see the world from the other side of the water's surface. With all her sea urchins, barracuda, and sharks, I choose the Atlantic Ocean's realm over the Andrews's house. I don't have a name when I'm under water. I am no one's daughter and no one's sister. I'm immersed, surrounded, and one with the underworld. I am not alone or invisible because the Atlantic Ocean knows all who exist within her.

Complete attention has been focused on my seventeen-year-old sister. Nadine's screaming nightmares grew more frequent. Then she graduated to threats. Tim understood my concerns that Nadine might become violent and that I would be a likely target. She had already ripped a set of sheets to shreds. Shari gave up her project room, converting it into a bedroom for their Daughter Number One. Since she has had her own room, we haven't been woken by any screams or vicious words in the middle of the night. Tim teases saying it was me who was causing Nadine's upset. He's not very bright.

I don't know what's going on with Nadine. I doubt that during their family discussions she reveals she's been smoking more than cigarettes. I've seen her friends at school. They have a reputation for selling pills to the druggies in my class. Nadine's angry all the time; we barely talk. Shari thinks it's because of our schedules. Nadine's after-school job isn't an interference. It gives us the distance we need. I know you wanted us to remain close, but I choose to avoid my sister.

Nadine has a new boyfriend, Bill. When he comes over, Bill hands me the keys to his car and tells me to find my way around the block. I recognize the ploy for what it is. Bill's generous gesture is to dismiss me from the house while the Andrews are at work. I wish his car were a stick shift; I want to know how to drive the Jeep. In a year, I'll be old enough to drive. In three years, I'll be eighteen and legal. I doubt I'll drink. The smell of alcohol reminds me of Nadine.

I asked Mrs. Lareau during this week's telephone conversation if there were any foster families available. I was hinting at my ache for more siblings; I want a family, not a home. She told me to concentrate on the foster home I'm in. My counselor didn't say, but I have a feeling the answer to my question is, "No."

Before he leaves, Patrick Muldune makes it a point of asking me how I'm doing. He looks me in the eyes and waits for a reply. I've learned to smile sweetly and tell him that I'm happy. Patrick Muldune doesn't care how I am doing; he wants to be sure I won't go ballistic like Nadine. She has less than a year before she reaches her eighteenth birthday, so it doesn't matter to her that there are few if any alternate foster homes. I have three years remaining on my foster child sentence. I hope she doesn't mess things up again.

Adjusting to public school has been stressful; I have anxiety dreams about it. There's one dream in particular that is recurring. In it, I sit down to take a test and find the material is completely foreign to me. As the dream progresses, I realize that I've been absent from the class all semester. I usually wake up with a racing heart and dripping forehead. Panic used to erupt, but I have countered my natural response to the dream. I taped a copy of my class schedule next to the bed.

For PE I chose modern dance over soccer. My decision was based solely on access to air-conditioning. I don't like to sweat. I admit it's inharmonious to live in the subtropics and have an aversion to sweat. "Life is full of inconsistencies," as Mrs. Conroy would say.

I've discovered, to my amazement, that modern dance is a natural medium for self-expression. Air-conditioning was my lure, and this creative vehicle has me hooked. Every day before I walk to the bus stop, I practice my dance routines. When he was home from work one day, Tim asked me where I learned yoga. He was either delirious from fever or my assumptions about him are accurate: he's not very bright.

Our modern dance instructor demonstrates exercises that are guaranteed to maintain tone, shapely figures. My figure is not exactly shapely. At this point I'm shooting for tone.

My foster mother suspects that I'm a late bloomer. What else would she expect from Daughter Number Two? To confirm her diagnosis, Shari insisted on a medical checkup. The doctor announced that I'm healthy. I noticed he didn't use the word normal when he was describing me. It's as if I stopped developing at the age of thirteen. Nadine is considering breast reduction, and I'm secretly hoping I will sprout boobs before my high school graduation ceremony.

The idea of riding on a school bus was appealing until I learned it was more desirable to have an older friend who has a car. For nine years of schooling, I envied my public school counterparts who rode a school bus. Now that I'm in the public school system, riding the bus is uncool. I don't know why I pursue normalcy. I should give up and accept that I'm not.

Most of the Winston Park circle of friends believe that honor students are socially inept creatures destined for a life in the university system. Melissa and Carrie know differently. Although they avoid me once we're on the bus, we chat incessantly at the bus stop. I harbor no ill feelings; I understand they have to maintain their distance. Social groups have their rules. I abide by mine, parking my nose in my text books while on the bus.

Thanksgiving is around the corner, which reminds me, I haven't written Mary Pat Brennan this month. The Polanskis are having a turkey bash at their house. I'm looking forward to it. We were told to bring a swimsuit, but I'm too embarrassed to wear mine. I'm not interested in looking like a neon rabbit on turkey day. Besides, the last time I was floating in the Polanski's pool, Shari asked her friends if they thought I have a physical defect since I have yet to bloom. She must have thought my hearing is worse than it is. That day, I wanted to permanently sink to the bottom of the pool.

Mrs. Lareau and Patrick Muldune are creating a series of group counseling sessions for the teenage foster children in their care. Nadine warns me that she has no intentions of going. I rebut saying that participating in group counseling once a month wouldn't kill her. Nadine disagrees.

It's time for me to tuck your letter back in its hiding place. Nadine and Bill are saying goodbye in his car. The dogs need to be walked before Shari and Tim come home; they went out for a late dinner. The Andrews invited me to join them; they regularly forget I'm vegetarian. What is there for me to select from a steakhouse menu?

*****

Studying for midterm exams was more challenging this year, not because my classes are unusually demanding. The Andrews's home was transformed from the perfect study environment into a carnival atmosphere. Shari was given an early Christmas gift: a piano. As I studied in my room, the sound of her less than fluid fingers on the piano keys motivated a Christmas wish. I hoped Tim anticipated piano lessons in his Christmas budget.

Adding to the excitement, two more unexpected gifts arrived before Christmas: snow-white kittens. We think they're boys. Shari found them in a shoebox near her office building, and Tim named them Nickle and Pickle. I think hidden deep within his psyche is a desire for twins because Tim apparently has a long list of matching names.

The kids ferociously unwrapped treats and toys on Christmas morning. Wrapping paper was everywhere. I found green and red reindeer paper soaking in Buffy's water bowl during my morning routine. My few minutes originally spent feeding the kids in the morning has expanded into an hour-long chore. This household is bursting at the seams. Last week we had to move litter boxes into the garage and install a kitty door. Three canines and five felines require every second of my spare time.

Shari loves Christmas. She must have dipped deep in the savings book to give us so much jewelry and clothes. I gave the Andrews a popcorn air popper. They acted excited. It's shoved under the cabinet next to the pizza warmer we never use.

It was a bountiful Christmas for me. Santa slipped a camera in my stocking. It's a one-ten, but it's a camera. I wonder if Tim will allow me to use his thirty-five millimeter for special occasions.

The pictures from our Christmas dinner are in the family photo album. Two daughters miraculously appear among the Andrews's family and friends. Instant Kodak moments and a more complete family, that's what foster children bring childless homes.

Granddad sent his annual Christmas check and a short letter. Aunt Ruth added a few lines at the end of his letter informing me that your father had a stroke. The right side of his body is affected. Not only is his handwriting slipping, but so is his hearing. I think I'll write Granddad to let him know partial deafness is sometimes a blessing.

Tasha and Cammy called to wish us a merry Christmas. I had thought Nadine forgot how to cry, but apparently she hasn't. Tears ran to her quivering lips after we hung up the phone. I gave her a hug and whispered, "Don't think about it, Naddy. Don't think about it."

Shari and Tim went on a four-day camping trip during the Christmas break. It was a turning point for Nadine and me. My sister was given permission to have a few friends over Saturday night. Shari trusted Nadine's promise that no boys would be allowed in the house. Nadine grinned ear to ear when our foster parents drove off in their Jeep with the camper in tow. Their Daughter Number One had plans, and Bill was at the top of her guest list. I warned Nadine that the neighbors would tattle. She did it anyway.

By eleven thirty, Nadine's Saturday night party was in full force. Underage inebriates poured out from the house and into the street. Things were out of control as they usually are when Nadine is involved. Music was blasting, and people were stripping. Nadine was not immediately available to monitor the chaos because she was preoccupied with Bill. I was told my sister and her boyfriend were in the master bedroom, but I dared not verify. I don't have the stomach for that.

One of Nadine's classmates gave me a drunken hug then slumbered onto the floor, taking me with him. His dead weight pinned me to the tile. We remained in this position until someone heard my muffled requests for assistance and pulled him off me seconds before I turned blue from asphyxiation.

At around one in the morning, Nadine's coworkers walked through the front door. They asked me for a mirror or a piece of glass, and I pointed to the kitchen table. Nadine's mysterious guests emptied powder from a zip-lock bag and divided it into thin lines using a razor blade. Motivated by curiosity, I naively observed each step of the process. Then I was offered the first snort. Curiosity melted into disgust when I realized what they were doing. I walked away, not bothering to reply.

Anticipating trouble, I had locked the kids in the garage. But Nikki and Elki were discovered despite my efforts. I wonder how anyone was able to maneuver past Buffy. Her protectiveness quickly changes into ruthlessness when she feels threatened. My little fur balls were lapping up beer from a makeshift bowl when I found them in the front yard. It's amazing how fast life can turn upside down.

For the enjoyment of the front yard loafers, overzealous party participants propped the stereo speakers on the living room window sill. I knew that was the last straw for the neighbors. I sat down next to Nikki and Elki; we patiently waited for the police. Sam pulled up in his sheriff's car instead. He lives two blocks over.

Sam and his partner, a black German shepherd, were defiantly ignored. Then he turned on his siren. Watching intoxicated youths scatter was actually entertaining. I rolled my eyes at the sight of Nadine stumbling out the front door, shamelessly tucking in her unbuttoned blouse.

The kitchen table crowd must have bolted through the garage and out the back, leaving the door wide open. Thankfully the kittens and cats remained hidden in the garage rafters. That is where I found them while Sam had a discussion with my sister and her boyfriend. If given a choice, I again would elect rescuing two sharp-clawed, white fur puffs from the rafters rather than standing outside facing Sam. He didn't pull any punches when he lectured Bill and Nadine.

Sam met me in the garage. I think he was in the "adult lectures the kid" mode when he opened his mouth, but nothing came out. I was brushing Buffy, doing my best to settle her down. Sam must have recognized the look in my eyes when he stared into them. He put his hands on his hips and shook his head.

I replied to his gesture, "I know. She has a way of making a mess of things. Does beer hurt them?" I asked looking over at my Nikki and Elki.

"They may get gas. Shepherd mix?"

"Yeah," I said, turning back to Sam. "As usual I'm the one who has to clean up since she's drunk."

"Your sister isn't drunk. She's high." His words entered into my good ear and clung to my brain. "Clean up tomorrow. I'll help you lock up for the night," he said as he turned the dead bolt on the garage door. "Some kids don't give up. They may come back."

"Are you gonna arrest Nadine?"

"I'll do worse. I'm gonna speak with Shari and Tim when they get back."

I crossed my arms and let out a sigh. "I'll have to do dishes until I'm forty."

"I'll put a good word in for you," said Sam.

Beer cans were everywhere; I know because it was me who plucked them from the yard Sunday morning. I left the inside of the house for my sister. She was dragging the last garbage bag into the garage when the Andrews pulled in.

Nadine is on a month restriction, and I received a stern reprimand for not overthrowing Daughter Number One from her throne and usurping control. The Andrews went relatively easy on me. I have yet to thank Sam. I'll walk to his house after dinner.

It surprised me that Shari and Tim were not anymore upset about the cocaine than the party itself. Actually, I was more shocked than surprised. My foster parents readily admitted they take pleasure in a snort from time to time. Am I the only straight person left on the planet?

Mom, I'm sorry we're screwing things up again.

Last night I had another anxiety dream. I was at school and walking down the crowded main hallway. Somehow, I forgot which class I was heading for. The second bell rang, and then all the classroom doors closed; I was left standing in the empty hall. The silence was deafening.

Throughout the day, this residual sensation of dead silence has resonated inside me. I'm afraid it has become part of me.

*****

Shari says it happens in threes. One loss is all I can bear. That should be the absolute limit for anyone. One death per year.

Tim came into my room this morning delivering frantic words. He walked out before my eyes had a chance to focus. Though I didn't understand what he had said, I knew it was serious. I thought it was Nadine, but it was my precious Elki. She dug up a toad. It was no ordinary toad. This one is from South America, the kind that seeps poison from its glands just under the skin.

Little Elki was limp, lying in his arms as he pulled open the Jeep door. Tim and I exchanged looks, not words. I jumped in the passenger seat, and he lay her in my lap. Elki didn't stir. I held her tight and talked to her, yet I could feel her life slipping from my hands. Elki didn't take a last breath like you, but I knew.

I was in my pajamas yet didn't realize it until we were at the pet hospital. The vet told us that she was gone by the time we brought her in. Oh, my sweet Elki. My constricted throat muscles refuse to release their grip. I want to scream at the world, and I want to cry, but I've forgotten how. The tears fall without a peep from my mouth.

Mom, please find Elki and let her know we miss her terribly, especially Nikki. She's been looking for her sister. Tell Elki I love her and that I'm sorry I let her dig for frogs by the lake.

CHAPTER 6

The dentist greedily extracted four teeth from my mouth, and the orthodontist generously shoved braces in it. I'm sporting clear plastic brackets on my front teeth. Beets, carrots, and tea are absolute no-no's because they'll likely stain the glue and plastic. The list of foods to avoid is longer than a roll of toilet paper. Two years of sharp braces, a restricted diet, and tiny rubber bands, I hope I'm gorgeous after all this socially sanctioned torment. During our group counseling session, Mrs. Lareau noticed the plastic and metal additions to my mouth and commented on my cuteness. Normally I would resent the label, but her French accent makes cute sound exotic.

Foster group counseling has changed the dynamics in the Andrews's home. Mostly, it is Shari and Tim who've changed. They swap stories in the adult group sessions and are learning what it takes to be parents. The Catholic Services Bureau prefers people who have experience in the parental role, a logical prerequisite. But when there is a shortage of homes and a plethora of homeless foster children to be placed, beggars aren't choosy.

Patrick Muldune conducts the foster parents' group sessions while Mrs. Lareau monitors ours. The six of us sometimes forget she's there. No one talks about college or graduating from high school. Instead, we talk about surviving as foster children.

I was familiar with Victoria's background before she spoke a word. While living in Aunt Erika's house, I had no idea that the tragic newspaper article I had read would be sitting in front of me, rubbing her sweaty hands in a cold classroom. Victoria and her older sister were the only survivors when their van was hit from behind. She lost them all in a matter of seconds—her grandparents, parents, and brother died in a crumpled van. One more operation will straighten

Victoria's mangled arm, yet it won't take away the memories of the accident.

I listen to Victoria, really listen to her. She's lost her family; there's no one left except her sister. Victoria is small like me. She has braces like me. She's alone like me. Her foster mother is rigid like Aunt Erika. Her sister works and doesn't come to group counseling, just like mine. Victoria has my same fate. Nadine says we have bad karma.

Shari and Tim apologized for excluding me during their discussions with Nadine. Evidently, their group counseling members have ganged up on them. On our way home from last month's meeting, Tim said with tears in his eyes that he was sorry he named me Daughter Number Two. He explained that it was never intended to indicate rank or who was more loved.

Words are not an eraser that can wipe everything clean.

Yesterday we had a family meeting before Nadine ran off to work. Shari and Tim dropped a load on us to consider. They asked us to call them Mom and Dad. Apparently, they regret having us call them by their first name.

"Forget it," was Nadine's answer. My sister has a way of saying what she means. I feel obliged to have some tact attached to my communications. Mrs. Lareau warns me about tact saying that mixed messages are more hurtful than directness. Tim and Shari are foster parents, not Mom and Dad. How am I going to give them this answer when their hearts are so eager to hear the name they've longed to be called?

I plan to tell them tomorrow on our way to group counseling. I pray Shari can accept it and not take it as a rejection, but I know better.

*****

The Easter Bunny was charitable this year. In addition to a basket of treats, he delivered an earache. It was a humbling reminder of my childhood. Though I have outgrown the ear infections phase of my life, fate demanded one more episode. Earaches don't occur during the day when I can care for myself. They sneak up in the middle of the night and render me immobile. The throb was relentless. I must have moaned without realizing because Tim turned on the hall light and looked in on me. Within minutes, Shari handed me cup of hot herbal tea; I could taste the swig of whiskey she added to it. Buffy made herself comfy in my bed while I sipped on the brew.

Shari and Tim propped a heating pad under my head and told Buffy to stay with me for the remainder of the night. The throbbing persisted despite their remedies. But I felt better anyway. It was my bad ear. A constant dull buzzing sound has plagued me ever since the infection. I know I should say something, but the Andrews will ban me from underwater tanning if I do.

I anticipate a four-point-o final grade report this year, which is amazing considering I'm in Mrs. Sholenowski's class. My English teacher has a passion for red ink. The rumor among the honor students is that Mrs. Sholenowski has heavy investments in companies that manufacture red pens. She handed back my most recent short story; it was dripping red ink. On the bottom she wrote a note: "There are college scholarships for writers. I suggest you apply." I appreciate Mrs. Sholenowski's trite gesture to make up for the red ink marks all year, but she doesn't get it. I'll be lucky to graduate from high school drug-free and with one personality. I've counted four distinct personalities in Nadine.

The bean field is nearly transformed; Miami Sunset looks like a castle. There are no windows, and a pair of circular towers stand on either end. Half of Killian's tenth graders will be transferring in the fall to this new high school. We voted on the name of our team and the school colors. Ours will be the first graduating class, in 1980. Two years from now I will graduate high school. I can't image it.

Carrie and Melissa have switched their alliances in the course of the school year. They sit with me on the bus. And they smoke, not on the bus but at the bus stop. Melissa is better at it than Carrie. I don't think Carrie inhales. They haven't experimented with drugs, but my friends are considering expanding their horizons. They're saving their money in anticipation of purchasing a bag of marijuana. Nadine looks stupid when she's stoned; I think Carrie and Melissa would look even sillier. Smoking pot or smoking cigarettes is the same, bad habits that smell.

Speaking of silly, Nikki has yet to fill out her lanky, tall body. She towers over Buffy. When she stands on her rear legs, Nikki reaches over my head. Her rambunctious puppiness has become a problem in the house. Nikki's tail invariably finds Tim's beer can and whacks it off the cocktail table. It's a nightly routine soaking up beer from the living room carpet. The Andrews have resorted to putting her outside when no one is home. Nikki is the designated outside dog. I'm waiting for Tim to name her Dog Number Two.

Group counseling will adjourn for the summer when school ends. No doubt Tim and Shari will be relieved. They seem irritated with the parental coaching they've been receiving. We haven't been over the Polanskis' in a while. I suspect the Andrews don't want parenting advice from them either.

Between Nadine and camping, life in the Andrews home has been hectic. I've been avoiding writing this, but I might as well put it on paper, thus purge it from my mind. Nadine has moved out. She didn't wait for the school year to end. I can't believe she left me behind. She's staying at Nina's house. Nina's mom obviously bought my sister's poor me speech; Nadine diligently practiced the finer points of manipulation on Shari and Tim and perfected it.

You are probably owed an explanation. I don't have all the facts, yet it isn't that difficult to complete the picture I have of things. The neighbors from across the street spoke with the Andrews about a serious matter. Okay, I'll end the tactfulness. Nadine was caught with her pants down.

The Palinis' children discovered Nadine and Bill in the bushes, engaging in more than kissing. The lovebirds were too engrossed to notice they had an audience. Apparently, Mrs. Palini personally investigated her children's claims and learned firsthand that Nadine is not a virgin.

I would like to make it clear how embarrassed I am and inform you that your second daughter is not. You must have skipped her when it came time to impart inhibitions and made up for the mistake, giving me an extra dose.

A resulting family eruption continued for about a week. Mrs. Lareau and Patrick Muldune came to the rescue on Saturday; I was happy to leave the house that day. It had been a while since Nikki and I walked around Hidden Lake. The Catholic Services Bureau's attempt was in vain. Nadine was determined to shatter the Andrews's dream. Now they're down to one last hope. It's up to me to carry the burden of being a daughter to my foster parents.

Bill drove Nadine to the Andrews's house yesterday. She apologized for leaving me to deal with Shari and Tim. My sister had done that months ago, left me to the Andrews. Emotionally, Nadine left when school started. Moving out made things official.

As soon as they graduate, Nina and Nadine are moving to the University of Florida in Gainesville. My sister is not interested in college; she's looking for a free ride, and Nina's mom bought her a ticket. I don't know the legalities of Nadine's situation. Because she is so close to turning eighteen, I doubt anyone is going to place Nadine in another foster home or turn Nina's mom into a foster parent. I'm done with worrying about Nadine.

Nina's mom just called and invited me over for dinner. After school lets out, I'll ride the bus that goes to her neighborhood. Watch Nadine not be there.

Tim has been battling Eastern Airlines; his employer isn't convinced that a foster child is a family member. The question is financial dependency. Since the state of Florida pays the Andrews a monthly support check in the amount of one hundred and eighty dollars, foster children fall short of the definition of immediate family members. Tim reassured me he will pay for my flight to the Bahamas if it comes to that. My foster father has a sales meeting in the Bahamas two days after school ends; Shari and I will accompany him. This will be my first trip outside the continental United States. Shari says the Bahamas are like the Florida Keys, only better.

I have good news, Mom. I weigh eighty-five pounds and am five feet, one inch. I must have grown while Nadine was having her tantrums. Before she left, my sister commented that I'm developing hips. It wasn't hips I was hoping for, but hips—yeah, I'll take hips.

Shari is taking me shopping for a bathing suit. I want a two-piece. My foster mother says I'm better off with a one-piece. Shari warned, "Ariana, you're not filled out yet. A two-piece may fall off you."

CHAPTER 7

The Bahamas are luscious and untamed. Their pristine, white beaches captured my imagination as we meandered along steep cliffs during the ride from the airport. Turquoise waves delivered fluffy, milky bubbles to the shoreline; I envisioned digging my bare feet in the hot sand. Focusing my mind on the coastline distracted me from our perilous situation. Bahamians drive on the wrong side of the road, and there is barely enough road to drive on as it is.

Our carefree taxi driver cheerfully dumped us off at the hotel curb. With gratitude, I placed my feet on solid ground then looked up to see David Smith standing in front of me. Only two days before, David was in my science class at Killian. His appearance baffled my rational mind, so my creative left brain manufactured an explanation for his presence. I had been teleported into another dimension after the airport taxi fell off a cliff.

Okay, my imagination is slightly distorted and clearly more colorful than the actual explanation for his presence. David's father works with Tim in Eastern's sales department. David was surprised to learn I was the foster child he had heard about. I was intrigued when I realized the man who is having an affair with the sales secretary is David's father. Once Tim discovered the connection between David and me, he begged me not to breathe a word about the affair. With or without Tim's plea for silence, I would not have crushed David's world by divulging office gossip.

Though I was flattered when David and his brother invited me to join their private tennis tournament, I declined. Tennis is too country club for me. I wrestled up my own entertainment: mopeds. For a fifteen-year-old lacking a driver's license, they're the most exhilarating transportation vehicles ever invented. Propelled by a small motor, I weaved between shops and through alleys exploring the heart of Paradise Island. I breathed in the island's essence and fell in love with reggae music and the smell of roasted corn. Shari and Tim camped out at their favorite spots on the island, the casinos. My foster parents must have thought they died and went to heaven. Casinos are the ultimate for those who flourish among cigarettes, drinks, and winning delirium.

For the perfect ending to an unforgettable weekend, the Andrews waited until we were flying home to reveal their summer plans. They and the VanHusens had engaged in secret negotiations. For an entire month, I am invited to stay in your brother's home. In exchange for my airline tickets, I agreed to complete some projects around the Andrews's house.

Mom, I have waited two years for this. Soon, I'm gonna reunite with Tasha and Cammy. I can't wait. I hope I grow another inch before I see them. I leave for Indiana in July, giving me plenty of time to bloom.

Thankfully this summer has not been as boring as the last one. The weekend after our Bahamas excursion, we went camping in Key Largo. The Andrews braved bringing Nikki, and she proved her maturity. She also revealed that she's more dolphin than dog. Once she dips her paw in the Atlantic Ocean, there's no hope to keep Nikki on the shore. The Andrews and I are official members of the regular camping crowd, so no one says anything to me about Nikki being on the beach, probably because she paddles around in the water most of time. Buffy is content to remain at the campsite with Shari and Tim. They bought a hammock and secured it between two gumbo limbo trees. The Andrews's idea of a perfect camping weekend is spending the daylight hours swinging in their hammock. At night, they share drinks and commiserate with the regulars at the beach campfire. Turns out Key Largo is a weekend haven for overworked, middle-aged Miamians. After I walk the kids down US1, I hang out in the hammock and stare at the night sky until the Andrewses return. During the day I make an effort to come out of the water long enough to photograph our memories. Buffy won the

Kodak moment that weekend; she was sporting her new camping visor. That dog has more personality than Nadine.

Before school let out, I learned that next year I'll be attending Miami Sunset, home of the Sunset Knights. Our colors are black and gold, and our graduating theme will be "First in Tradition." It's awkward. Hopefully we'll think of another class slogan before we graduate.

I found the book Shari hid from me last summer. She must have replaced it in the den believing that I lost interest. My foster mother doesn't know me very well. The book borders soft pornography. It is rather boring and poorly written. Out of spite, I've perused through some of its pages during the day while Tim and Shari are at work. I guess that means I may have a rebellious streak in me. That's a relief. I was beginning to believe that perhaps I was destined to become a nun.

I have been diligently upholding my end of the agreement with the Andrewses. Yesterday, I planted hibiscus bushes around the air-conditioning unit. Unfortunately, I will have to redo that project; Nikki has mistaken my landscaping efforts for digging holes. Today, I washed out the garage. Tomorrow I'm taking a break from my household projects; I'm going to the beach with Melissa and her mom. My friend needs the support. Her mother has been reading pop-psychology books, and now she wants to practice bonding.

I suspect Shari has been attempting the same thing. After dinner last night, my foster mother sipped on cognac and told me a story. Initially, I thought it was a lecture about driving, but as her story unfolded, it became obvious that she had a different motivation. I'll tell you the story as Shari told it to me:

A teenager, a girl about seventeen, was driving home from school with a friend. It was in the 1950s. Shari said they were in a big car; I pictured a powder blue '57 Chevy. Anyway, the teenage driver leaned over to her girlfriend's side of the front seat to grab a pack of cigarettes out of her purse. Simultaneously, a little girl was on her bicycle riding home from the library. By the time the teenager lifted her head to see where she was steering, it was too late. Though she swerved, the bicycle's back wheel was clipped.

I expected that to be the end of the story, then the plot thickened. The driver punched the gas pedal instead of the brake. Her girlfriend screamed for her to stop, yet the teenager continued speeding down the street. I asked Shari if the teenager finally stopped. She didn't give me a clear answer. Despite her refusal to confirm, I decided the story was about a hit-and-run. Shari asked for my opinion.

"Why didn't the driver stop?" I asked. I wanted the whole picture before I delivered my reproach.

"She was afraid of getting caught. She thought the kid was probably dead."

"Did the kid die?"

"No. But the little girl was seriously injured. The teenager—"

"Wasn't thinking about the kid at the time," I finished her sentence.

"What do you think should happen to the teenager?" Shari asked.

"A hit-and-run...she left that kid on the road."

"There were people—"

"Not the driver. She kept going, didn't she?" I asked.

"Right. Sh-She kept going."

"She should be punished more because she ran than the fact that she hit the kid. I wouldn't want to be that teenager facing the little girl's parents trying to explain to them why I ran. Accidents happen, but you don't run especially when it's a kid."

Shari finished her cognac, thus creating an excuse to wander into the kitchen for a refill. She didn't say so, but I figured she was the teenager. I regret that I didn't show more compassion; I was identifying with the kid at the time.

My foster mother wandered back to the living room mainly because of social obligation. We talked about my summer projects around the house, her work, Nikki's compulsion to knock over Tim's beer, everything except her story. While we engaged in the art of small talk, part of my attention drifted to the hit-and-run. I deduced that at the age of seventeen, Shari had been arrested and was brought to trial. Three months ago, I was given a clue. But it wasn't until last night that I saw it for what it was.

My civics class had recreated a murder case that was reported in *The Miami Herald*. For the mock trial, each student was assigned a role. I was one of the investigators working for the prosecution and discovered a valuable resource for my preparedness—my foster mother. She had described with uncanny detail the courtroom proceedings during a trial. When I inquired how she knew so much, Shari replied that she had been a juror more than once. At the time, I didn't question her answer. I had no reason to believe otherwise.

While sitting on the sofa and smelling her cognac breath, I solved a mystery I had pondered from time to time. The Andrewses had not adopted their dream daughter probably because a criminal record is a stumbling block in the adoption process.

I realize my foster mother was looking to me for some kind of exoneration. Shari is carrying a load of guilt. She lost her chances of getting pregnant when she was twenty-two. She blames the cancer on herself. Until she reached that pinnacle age, Shari managed to drown herself in parties, alcohol, and cigarettes. Then her body rebelled to the mistreatment. Cancer is a ruthless and unforgiving disease.

Shari is the first person I've met who has survived cancer. She may be living, but she isn't free of its wrath. My foster mother was engaged to be married at the time of her hysterectomy. Her fiancée broke off their nuptial plans weeks after the surgery; he wanted children from his loin. Tim was adopted; he probably never thought twice about Shari's infertility.

Guilt cannot be measured, and it cannot be seen. I thought it was an emotion. I now recognize it as a form of self-punishment. And here I felt guilty about reading a dirty book on my summer break.

*****

Dear Mom,

I didn't bring your letter with me to Indiana. It's not that I forgot. I couldn't risk anyone finding it, especially my cousins. It's safer under my mattress at the Andrews's house than in a suitcase at the VanHusens'. Besides, I convinced myself that by being around my sisters, I would be less compelled to write you. Obviously, that was faulty thinking. I'll staple this to your letter when I return to Florida.

Two years is like two centuries. Tasha is as tall as me, and Cammy is not far behind. I had to adjust to having two younger sisters again. After I relinquished the impulse to impress them, they let go of their distrust. Now we're best friends.

Uncle James's house is smaller than I remembered it. Tasha and Cammy share a bedroom and one bed. They don't seem to mind it though. Life has delivered fewer experiences for them to know the difference. I guess that's one of the advantages of being younger.

My cousins asked what's it like to be a foster child, and Aunt Beth seems curious about Shari and Tim. Instead of the truth, I likened a foster home to living in paradise. Though I'm willing to admit I went overboard on the sugarcoating, it's better than appearing pathetic in their eyes. No one has uttered Aunt Erika's name.

Tasha and Cammy ask about Nadine, and I'm careful to leave out certain details. The drugs and Bill are aspects to Nadine that are better left hidden from admiring young eyes. My dear sisters are curious about you, and I tell them all that I know. I didn't realize being with you when you died gave me a sense of closure they don't have. Cammy is having trouble completely accepting your death.

The VanHusens didn't waste time. On my second day here, I was assigned chores and thus became an official member of the family. Three rows in the garden are mine to weed and hoe, and it's my job to make salad for dinner. Preparing a meal for ten people requires immense planning and coordination. After coming from a home of three, I was in awe of our first dinner together as it lay spread out on the table; I insisted on taking a picture before everyone sat down. Meals are minor in comparison to the laundry. The VanHusens would do well to invest in Whirlpool's stock.

I love being in the middle of the country with cornfields and dirt roads that stretch for miles. I also love being in the middle of a large family. Silence, my ugly and constant companion, has been absent since I've been here.

Why is it that people who don't enjoy writing are the ones who ask for long, frequent letters? Within a week of arriving, the

Andrewses called and complained about my slack letter writing. Aunt Beth introduced me to the perfect solution, postcards. Postcards are like a frozen candy bar. They're brief, sweet, and they're satisfying.

Last weekend, the VanHusens loaded us in the van and drove to the Indiana State Fair. Hoosiers take their fairs seriously, and the VanHusens are no exception. Their excitement was infectious. As soon as we poured out of the van however, disappointment overtook my senses. I don't know what I expected. Perhaps one must be a Hoosier to appreciate their state fair. I found the carnival rides bearable and avoided the animal showcases altogether. "Manure takes some getting used to," as Uncle James had explained.

Aunt Beth added my name to the family swim club membership. The eight of us walk to the pool in the morning and stay until thunderstorms threaten. I love the hike to the swim club almost as much as swimming. We skip across a meadow that blesses the eyes with blooming wild flowers and envelops the nostrils with the scent of wild mint. Tasha says that Indiana is very different in the winter, when the meadow is covered under a blanket of snow. Their lush and alive meadow vanishes in three months. I can't imagine it.

Cammy is fearless. She's taught herself how to jump off the high dive. I made several attempts to follow Cammy's bravery. Each time, I succumbed to my fear of heights while on the ladder and had to scamper down before reaching the diving platform.

The VanHusens's neighbors have a gelding in their backyard, and Tasha has befriended him. I pretended to be a professional photographer while Tasha displayed her equestrian skills in a soybean field. What a sight to see little Tasha, who's not so little, riding a horse bareback. My camera has exposed more rolls than I can count. Aunt Beth ordered double prints so Tasha and Cammy will have mementos of my visit. It bothers me when I'm reminded that this is only a visit.

We spent this afternoon with Aunt Ruth and Granddad. Granddad's body has slowed down during the last two years. However, his mind is keen. He won every card game I played with him. I resorted to cheating, but it didn't pay off. He still won. Aunt Ruth showed me your pictures hanging on the family room wall. I was disheartened to see we barely resemble each other when you were my age. Granddad said I have your penetrating eyes.

Your father has compensated for his hearing loss. I'm forced to shout for him to hear me, yet he hears me like no one else. Granddad listens with his heart.

*****

Samantha just pulled out of the driveway.

It's eleven o'clock at night, and I am sitting at the kitchen table. I have the stove light on; it barely illuminates these words I write. The VanHusens's quiet house consoles me, and the surrounding darkness is comforting.

I had no idea I harbored such anger inside me. The words that flowed from me this evening were coming out of my mouth, yet I was shocked to hear them. Though my anger needed a voice, I'm afraid my words cut into Samantha's soul. She had asked me why I didn't hug her, and she knew my answer was a lie. We were sitting in the diner where she works, at the table she serves. Samantha had picked me up at the VanHusens's then drove downtown.

"What's up with you?" Samantha had asked me.

I answered with spite in my tone, "You think you're our mom, but you're not. You're the oldest sister. That's all. You were born first. You're not any smarter."

"Ariana, where's this coming from?" she demanded.

"You hit Mom. I saw you hit her. She was sick, Samantha. You swung and hit her in the chest. I was in the dining room, and I saw you hit Mom."

"Yes. I hit Mom. I got pissed, and I hit her. And you didn't see me crying afterward. You walked away before you heard Mom and me—"

"How could you? How could you hit her? She was dying."

"Is that why you're being cold to me?"

"No. You think you were such a loving substitute for Mom. You were high, Samantha. You got high all the time. Sam, you took the money Mom gave us for food, and you got high. I was the one up in the morning making breakfast for Cammy and Tasha—"

"That's bull. Yes, I got high. I was seventeen years old holding our family together. I kept us together by being a parent to my four younger sisters. You don't know. Uncle James was going to split us up."

"We are split up. I'm a pathetic foster child, Samantha. I have no one. No one."

"You have me," Samantha said softly.

I was relentless, saying, "When's the last time you wrote me? When's the last time you put money aside for a long-distance call to Florida? You like playing mom when it's convenient to your self-image."

"That's not true."

"No? You're a waitress at a diner. What do you have to feel good about? You're probably still drinking and getting high. You have this warped idea that you somehow rescued us from a fate you'll never know. You'll never know what it's like to live in other people's homes when they don't want you. You won't know what it's like to be a foster child, Samantha. You got high. You barely came home long enough to make dinner. I tucked the girls in at night. I was the one who heard Cammy crying in her sleep. I was the one who made sure they wore clean clothes every day. You were in your own world getting high."

"Okay. I got high. That's a lot of responsibility to be dumped on a seventeen-year-old. I was a senior in high school. My mother was dying. I had the bills, the house, Uncle James breathing down my neck-"

"I'm partially deaf because of you."

"I'm sorry, Ari. I'm sorry you…I'm sorry."

"Not sorry enough. Tell me, when you get high, does it all go away? Does the pain go numb? Does Mom's image leave your mind? Do you ever think what it's like for us when you're getting high?"

"I was doing the best I could."

"You hit Mom. She comes home to die and you hit her. How dare you."

"She hit me first."

"She hit us all, Samantha."

"Why are you so angry with me? What makes you so righteous? You were never friends with Mom. You didn't have the conversations we had. You didn't hear her cry on the phone. She leaned on me. I was her friend and her daughter. She wanted me to watch over you girls. I heard the struggles she went through with Dad. I witnessed how he beat her—"

"It doesn't matter. She's gone. I don't see it the way you do."

"What's gotten into you?" Samantha asked.

"I'm tired of hearing what you did for us. Our lives are broken. Have you looked at us lately? We're separated. Living separate lives in separate homes. You haven't learned anything. Two years and you're living the same disgusting life. There's a world out there, Samantha. You don't visit with Tash—"

"Beth and James think I'm a bad influence. They think I'll get the girls to take drugs or something."

"So that's why they don't like you coming around? You may think you've sacrificed your life for us. I think you were hiding. You still are. Drugs and alcoh—"

"Who are you to judge me?" Samantha squinted her eyes.

"You were the one I looked up to. You were the one who graduated from high school. You were the one, Samantha. We saw your accomplishments and reached for them. You gave up. You just gave up. I don't want to be a waitress. Why can't you do better than this? Is this what I'm destined to do?"

Samantha stared at me. A tear fell from her right eye, but she didn't blink.

Her tear softened me, and I resented it. "Do you cry alone? I do. I feel numb most of the time, but at night I can cry, alone."

Samantha's eyes remained fixed on my face. I bit my lip and glanced down at the table. My sister had unconsciously folded her hands. For a moment, she was the eighth grader I had admired. She was wearing her Catholic school uniform, sitting at her desk with her hands folded.

I sighed and said, "Do you realize you were my hero? You were the one who would tow me on her bicycle so I could go to the library."

Samantha smiled. "You and your library. If I hadn't towed you, you'd walk. It'd take you all day, but I knew you would have walked if I didn't take you."

I nodded my head. The flow of words had ceased. My anger had reminded us of our past and the hollowness it carves into our lives. There was nothing more to say. Samantha reached her hand across the table, and I accepted her gesture to secure a truce. An hour passed before we were able to hug.

Our eyes don't see things the same way. Samantha sees herself as someone who stepped into your shoes while you were gone. What I saw is changing. Samantha is a waitress in a small-town diner. Forgiving her will be hard. But I will forgive her; she's my sister.

When Samantha pulled out of the driveway, I smiled to her. It had been a long time since I gave her a warm smile. I can still feel her warm, tight hug.

*****

I'm in the Atlanta airport waiting for my flight to Miami. This two-hour respite between my family and the Andrewses gives me time to adjust. Leaving is so empty; I almost wish I had not gone to Indiana. The silence and my aloneness are more pronounced.

My last moments in Indiana were full. I absorbed the cornfields, the soft chill in the air, and the sight of Granddad as Aunt Ruth drove up the driveway.

Granddad's eyes held me in place as he struggled to free himself from the car. I could feel his strength through his wobbly hand as he grasped mine. He took me aside and whispered into my ear, "Don't forget, not even for one second, that you are loved." Granddad held my hand tight, and I prayed that he would never let go. I told him that I would see him again. Your father shook his head saying, "I've outlived my family, and I want to join them. It's time." I refused to say goodbye to my grandfather. I kissed him on the cheek instead.

Granddad understood. Though we are prolific pen pals, in person few words pass from our lips.

Tasha and Cammy waved to me as I boarded the plane. I wonder if they know my heart ripped open wider with each step that took me further from them. Soon, I will see the Andrewses and the kids. I'm looking forward to seeing them, yet my thoughts remain at the VanHusen house.

During the last week of my visit, we plowed the vegetable garden under and then a cherry tomato fight erupted. Tomato skins and seeds were flying everywhere even splashing against the side of the barn, fifty yards away. We had to hose ourselves down. Then a water fight ensued. Gardening is an exhilarating hobby. Too bad Nikki is a digger. I'd love to plant a garden in the backyard.

I and the three eldest VanHusen siblings snuck the dilapidated station wagon for a drive. Evidently, driving on dirt roads demands more skill than I had imagined. After pushing the car out of a ditch, I lost my driving privileges among my fellow car thieves. The experience convinced me to sign up for driver education at school this year.

This summer has been an incredible journey from the floor of the Atlantic Ocean to the cornfields of Indiana. I think I'm ready now to be a junior at Miami Sunset, home of the Sunset Knights.

CHAPTER 8

It's overgrown, the Boston fern that Aunt Beth has on top my antique lectern. She had supplied me with a couple of its shoots, wrapping them in a wet paper towel and plastic wrap. I'm amazed that they survived the trip to Florida in my suitcase. Tim helped me plant them in the front yard, near the water faucet. It's not a meadow or vegetable garden, yet the bright green ferns remind me of Indiana.

Mrs. Lareau welcomed me back to our weekly telephone conversations. During my absence, she went home to Canada and inadvertently reinforced her funny pronunciations. I had forgotten my counselor has a French accent. She relayed the news that Victoria's arm surgery was a success. Victoria's struggle with her rigid foster mother, however, was not. She's now living in a group home until another suitable foster family can be found. Victoria, she has bad karma.

If you could see me now, you'd say I was in my glory. Buffy is on my bed, and Nikki is lying next to my feet. Nickle and Pickle intermittently jump onto the window sill, taunting Nikki into a game of chase. I'm kneeling, leaning my elbows into the bed, and I have this page of your letter draped over a school book. Buffy is sprawled on top of the remaining pages. Each time she shifts her position, she disperses your letter between the sheets. Despite over watering it, Shari managed to maintain the life of my ivy plant. Fate has not given me a large foster family, yet I feel at peace being with the kids, my plant, and your letter.

Since leaving Indiana, I've had a month to settle into a routine: school, soccer practice, and studying. Miami Sunset is less intimidating than Killian. Being closer in proximity is the main reason.

Though I had to adjust to the concept of walking two blocks to school, I don't miss riding the school bus.

I joined soccer mainly because I was solicited by the coach. She said that girls soccer was a few players shy of becoming an official team. I asked her why she thought of me, and she replied, "You have long legs." I was at soccer practice that same day, my long legs and all.

Wearing cleats has been a challenge. Mostly it's my feet that are challenged. They want to run out of my cleats at every opportunity. Coach insists on cleats even if they are a handicap. She says insurance and lawsuits take precedence over comfort. Being a natural sprinter has eased my transition into soccer. I'm learning how to maneuver a soccer ball, yet bouncing it off my head has caused some complications. If my angle is slightly skewed, I walk home with a headache.

There's an extra benefit to being on the girls soccer team besides leaving sixth period early for the games. The football team practices on the field next to us. Jordan Russo is captain, and I think I'm in love. Unfortunately, I'm not the only one in love with him. Half the soccer team melts when Jordan looks our way. He has a Toyota truck and is currently unspoken for. As far as potential boyfriends go, the female students of Sunset have designated him as fair game if not the ultimate prize.

I like having normal school hours instead of a split session. Studying in the evening is easier for me. The Andrewses do their unwinding while I nestle in my room with books, papers, and pens. Unlike my other classes, driver education is an easy A. My English teacher, Mrs. Roth, is a heartless illiterate. She's constantly calling on me to read passages during class. She knows I feel embarrassed. That's why she calls my name. Gary, he sits behind me, says Mrs. Roth has a reputation for pushing the quiet ones. I'll have to learn to speak up, maybe become a loud mouth like Gary. Though, he's only disruptive when he's sniffing glue. I'm not interested in sniffing glue just to avert Mrs. Roth's quest to humiliate.

I have good news and bad news: Jordan Russo is in my French class. It's good for the obvious reasons yet bad for my grade point average. For the first time, I'm afraid of failing a class. Instead of conjugating French verbs, I'm constantly thinking about French kissing Jordan.

Before school began, I finished Shari's dirty book and lent it to Melissa. She has yet to return it to me. I wonder if Shari has noticed it's missing from the den's bookshelves. My foster mother, I have learned the hard way, doesn't miss much—including my shoes. I lost them or, more precisely, unintentionally left them. Before school ended last year, I rode the bus to Nina's house. Anticipating a long walk from the bus stop to her house, I donned a pair of sneakers. I jumped off the bus leaving my new school shoes behind. Summer passed without Shari saying a word. I figured she had no clue my closet was deficient one pair of shoes. I was a fool to think my foster mother forgot about the shoes she selected and bought for me.

Shari waited until I returned from Indiana to ask where my shoes had gone. I knew she would take it personally that I lost them, so I lied and said I left them in Indiana. When will I learn that cheating and lying don't get me anywhere except in more trouble?

Shari instructed me to write a letter asking Aunt Beth to return my shoes. I wrote Aunt Beth all right. I confessed my absentmindedness and explained why I lied to Shari. Then I asked Aunt Beth to write back saying she was unable to locate my shoes. The letter never arrived in Indiana. Shari had snatched it from the mailbox and read it. I was on restriction for two weeks. I wonder if Shari realizes she could go to jail for tampering with someone's mail even if it is in her mailbox.

The case of my lost shoes put a damper on their big news. The Andrewses had asked Mrs. Lareau if they could adopt me and sprung the question on my first night back from Indiana, during dinner. Shari and Tim must have felt lonely the month I was gone.

My tactfulness almost landed me another disaster. I told the Andrewses that I loved them like parents. I neglected to add the remainder of my thought until Mrs. Lareau stepped in after a few weeks of confusion. The Andrewses never considered that I would reject their offer. I guess they thought I was absolutely pathetic needing a family when I already have one. At almost sixteen, who wants to be adopted? I explained that I would be the only one in my family with a different last name. Adoption would separate me further from my sisters. The Andrewses found that difficult to comprehend. I wish they had never asked to adopt me. I'm shocked Shari's criminal record allows it.

*****

I'm afraid our camping adventures have ended; the last one was before I left for Indiana. The Andrewses like anything new, as long as it is new. Camping is over a year old. It's not new. I miss the beach. I miss the stars. And I miss my underwater world. Since my visit to Indiana, the simplest of pleasures have slipped from my life. I was hoping things would be better this school year. Silly me.

Melissa finally returned Shari's book. For weeks I had hounded her for it, worried that Shari would find out about my treacherous act. But now it doesn't matter. Nothing I do is right. Being caught reading a dirty book would be chucked on top the enormous pile of horrible misguided deeds I've committed lately.

When I came home from soccer practice today, I threw my cleats in the refrigerator then stood in front of my closet looking for something to drink. Lucky for me, Shari was home early enough to witness my dazed performance. Coach's workouts are too demanding; my foster mother doesn't agree. Shari relentlessly complains that I'm absentminded.

Twice this week I've left the clothes in the dryer, Shari gave half hour lectures for each offense. I earned a weekend of no TV for leaving a bar of soap in the kitchen sink. I know it's appalling to do that to someone who works all day, leaving soap in the sink for them to find. My nails should be ruthlessly yanked from my fingers. I know. I'm a rotten child deserving severe punishments for my crimes.

My foster mother has enlisted Tim's participation in her campaign to prove—actually I don't know what she's attempting to prove. I suppose it's another *pathetic* campaign. Perhaps this is different. Because I declined their adoption offer, this may be a *punishment* campaign for denying Shari her dream. This past weekend the Andrewses played a joke on me. It lacked humor though. None was intended. Tim appeared in my doorway with the telephone receiver in his hand, unattached to the telephone. The cord was dangling on the floor as he shoved the hand receiver into my face saying, "It's for you." I thought he had lost his mind. Instead of saying so, I played along. I hesitantly grasped the hand receiver then said, "Hello?" A cruel and hysterical laugh erupted from Shari. She was around the corner in the hallway.

The Andrewses decided the episode proved once and for all that I was preoccupied and in my own world. Their antics proved more than the obvious. I wonder if they can see themselves behind their accusations, judgments, and punishments.

Things are escalating beyond the scope of our immediate situation. The Polanskis were over for dinner last Friday. Their mission was painfully obvious to me. I'm no fool. I know when I'm on trial and when simple questions are not so simple. I rebuffed the Polanskis' probing questions. I was polite however; the accused are supposed to appear innocent.

That evening the Andrewses and the Polanskis went to the movies, leaving me with a mess in the kitchen. I wandered off to my room instead of tackling the dishes right away. I fell under the spell of studying and forgot about the dishes piled in the sink. Because of the Andrewses' response when they came home, the Polanskis apparently made a decision based on the evidence they collected. Strict parenting was my sentence.

Tim stormed into my room at one o'clock in the morning; I was asleep, buried under my books. He dragged me out of bed while Shari shoved her alcohol breath in my face. Leaving me to the suds and silence, the Andrewses thankfully went to bed. Nikki occasionally whined to me; she was outside by the kitchen window. I wanted to whine as well, yet I stopped myself. It was too late or too early to be yelled at again. At two in the morning, I dried the last pan then crawled back to bed. I didn't bother changing my clothes just in case the Andrewses had more chores to be completed in the middle of the night.

I heard about "the dishes still left in the sink when we got home" again the next day. While Shari lectured, my mind wandered.

I imagined leaving my body and floating into the ethers. To my disappointment, it was a fleeting fantasy, and it didn't help me escape from Shari's dissertation about responsibilities, cooperation, and her disappointment in me. My foster mother says she always wanted a daughter. What Shari really wants is a doll to dress up and bring on shopping excursions. I'm not that type of daughter. Malls give me a headache.

Shari doesn't seem to grasp the concept of being a foster parent, let alone a mom. She plays the role of a parent as if she were playing a piano. My foster mother dislikes lessons and rarely practices the basics. Believe me, Shari lacks a natural talent to compensate for her deficiency in parental experience.

Mrs. Lareau agrees that the Andrewses' disciplinary actions are excessive, yet she defends my foster parents. My counselor diplomatically relays that the Andrewses are concerned that I am withdrawing. Without hesitation, I freely confirm their concerns. Who in their right mind wouldn't withdraw?

I'm beginning to see the function of my foster counselor. She is a mediator and liaison instead of my protector and my voice. When it comes to Mrs. Lareau's role, I had things wrong.

*****

The Andrewses are playing a new game. I wonder if the Polanskis have anything to do with it or if it's an origination from my foster parents. When they walk by, Shari and Tim give a solid tap on my head, enough to startle me and leave a residual sting. I've complained, but they counter, saying it's a "love tap." I've asked why tap at all, and they claim it is to bring me out of my world. They don't get it. I mentally check out to escape from them. And the more I withdraw, the more they tap me on the head. I don't know how to stop the cycle, so I stay in my room when I'm not at school, soccer practice, or in one of the five clubs I've joined.

Though the love tap is bothersome and irritating, their distorted twist to the game is more serious. Shari and Tim raise their hand in a gesture that threatens a smack. I realize it sounds ridiculous that a raised hand is the cause of my intense anxiety. But it is. Why do the Andrewses need to threaten me? I leave socks on the floor, Mom. I'm not an impossible child; I'm human. I coward into submission upon recognizing a hand positioned for a strike; it's a Pavlovian response. Tim is the worst offender. While his hand is lifted above his shoulders and his teeth are clenched, he claims that he would never use physical means to punish, although he admits I push him to the brink. It's his threat that frightens me, more than any smack across the face. I smell the beer on his breath and look into his bloodshot eyes. They don't get it. Their simple gesture of control connects me to the full impact of a violent beating that left me gasping for air. Mom, you left me a legacy. All the beatings, all the times I slid down the wall, all the bruises, and all the welts—you set me up. I wish you could know the hidden scars you left me to bear. I'm different because I know violence and violation. I'm separated from the kids in school not only because I'm a foster child but because of the shame I carry deep inside. That's all my foster parents have to do is raise their hand and I bend to their demands. I do my best not to be head-shy, but it is an ingrained response. Being alert to a physical threat kept me alive all those times you were in a rage. Nadine no doubt divulged our private history to the Andrewses, Mrs. Lareau, and Patrick Muldune. I'm not surprised my older sister crossed that barrier, the one I dare not even approach. You didn't say, but we understood. The beatings were to be kept secret, and there's no reason to tell anyone now. I think telling them was Nadine's way of revenging on you. The Andrewses seem to have capitalized on the information rather than heeded it. They probably appreciate the terror you instilled in me. All they have to do is raise a hand; you did all the work.

This I leave out of my weekly phone conversations with Mrs. Lareau, the shame of being a victim of your quick hand. Mrs. Lareau won't help me. What can she do about a raised hand in the air? How can she know the fear?

Empathy, no one can teach it to another.

*****

Shari was fuming by the time I walked home from soccer practice this afternoon. She met me on the driveway, clenched her teeth then said, "Get into the car, Miss Ariana."

Halfway to the hospital, the floodgates burst open. "Your father is lying in the hospital from an asthma attack, and you have the gall, the absolute selfish gall to go to soccer practice while I'm sitting at home waiting for your pretty little butt. You were at soccer practice. What is wrong with you? Who do you think you are, a princess? And when your father is seriously ill and asking for you?"

Shari took advantage of the red stoplight. She stared through me and waited for my answer. I knew my foster mother was geared for an attack. No matter my response, she was going to pounce on it. I spoke up knowing I had only one other choice: opening the car door and jumping out. It was a tempting alternative to remaining in the car, yet it would have been suicide. Considering Shari's volatile state, she was capable of running me down.

"I didn't realize you were home waiting for—"

"Where do you think I was going to be?" The light changed. She turned her hate from me and directed it toward the traffic ahead. "He's sick. He's very sick. You're at soccer practice, and he's in the hospital."

It angered me that she assumed I would know to skip soccer practice and meet her after school. I also realized that if I came home from school instead of going to soccer practice, she would have found another excuse to spew.

"I didn't realize how—"

"You don't stay in the hospital overnight because you're breathing on your own. He's being monitored and medicated to make sure he stays alive."

"I'm sor—"

"Oh please. I don't want to hear your apologies. You always have some lame excuse why you do things. Let's face it, you're a selfish brat. You don't act like you're a part of this family. You don't act like you give a hoot about Tim or me. You're banned from playing soccer."

"You can't—"

73

"Oh really. Yes, I can. I'm your mother. I'm the one taking you to the orthodontist once a month. I take you shopping, I make you dinner, and I bring home the groceries. You sit around on your pretty little butt and play the daughter. I'm sick of it. The only reason I'm even in this car with you is because Tim was asking for you. He's asking for you. He's very ill, and he's wondering where his daughter is. I'm telling him you were at soccer practice."

We arrived at Baptist Hospital. Shari continued yelling at me in the parking lot. A nurse walking toward the entrance turned around and looked at us. I stared straight ahead. My foster mother stopped mid-sentence and headed for the hospital, not looking back to see if I was following. I thought about running. I thought about screaming. I thought about the consequences.

My cleats tip-tapped on the carpet-less floor, I disliked drawing attention to myself. Shari stood by the elevators. She refused to look at me, facing the metallic doors instead.

While the sluggish elevators descended to the first floor, my mind scanned which friends I could live with until I was eighteen. As images of friends passed my mind's eye, I realized that two years was too long. The Catholic Services Bureau would not be able to overlook the legalities. I thought about group counseling. It hadn't resumed after the summer break. I suddenly realized why. There were no teenage foster children left after the summer, except me. Then I thought about the foster children in group counseling and wondered if they ran away or went to a group home like Victoria.

Tim smiled when I rounded the corner. I gave him a kiss and an awkward hug. Tubes leading from his nose and arms connected him to bottles and monitors. Shari stood at the foot of his bed. I swallowed hard. The sight of him reminded me of you.

My visit with Tim was brief. His energy was low, but his eyes sparkled past his pale face. Shari asked to be alone with him. I was happy for the reprieve; the silence between the three of us was noticeable.

While sitting in the lobby, I wondered what Shari would be saying to Tim if I were not around, if I were not their foster child. Who else or what else would receive the brunt of her anger, the impact of her fear?

Not a word was uttered during the drive home. Sometimes silence is worse than the screaming. I went to my room, bypassing the kitchen where Shari parked her purse. I didn't know she was on my heels. As I closed the door behind me, she blasted it open and sat on the bed. Well, more like she threw her body on the bed, landing in a sitting position.

"I want to know why. Why weren't you here? Why didn't you call while you were at school? Why didn't you come home for lunch to check in with me at work? Why?"

I drew in a breath and felt fear. Shari was close to slamming my head against the wall. My next words were critical. I thought about telling her the truth, but I already attempted that on the way to Baptist Hospital. Then I thought to plead with her. My mouth opened and said, "I hate hospitals." I don't know where those words came from. I think I was momentarily possessed.

"You hate hospitals. You hate hospitals. Your father is very ill in a hospital, but you won't go to see him because you hate hospitals. Maybe we should have had him meet you outside in the parking lot to prevent you from the stress of entering the hospital." She drew in a breath and raised her fist. "I'm this close to knocking you silly."

I stood by the closet and stared at her. I was totally defeated. She won. She demanded that I bear her pain, her anger, her frustration, her disappointment, and worst of all, her fear. The weight of her emotions anchored me to the floor. The buzzing sound in my right ear filled my head. I could hear Shari's words, but they were muffled by the drone.

"What? Is it because of your mother? When your mother died in a hospital? Is that what this is all about? Another pity me party?" Shari turned toward the door. "You disgust me."

The image of you dying overcame my vision. Tears trickled down my face, and I could hear Shari singing as she slammed my bedroom door behind her, "Feelings. Nothing more than feelings..."

I don't know how long I stood by the closet, motionless, void of thought, void of reality. I don't know when I pulled out your letter and began writing. I don't know what I've written. It's late now. The kids have not been fed. I wonder if Shari has gone to bed. I'll feed them in the morning. Skipping a meal won't kill them. The blind is open, and I'm looking up to the sky, but all I see is black.

Jordan Russo probably went home after football practice and had dinner with his family. He pulled out his books and read his chemistry chapter before turning off the light. Why can't I live a normal life like Jordan Russo?

My hand is heavy. I don't think I can reach to turn my light off. It will have to stay on. Nothing matters. You're gone. I can't escape enough.

CHAPTER 9

Jordan sits behind me in French class. That's where we pass notes containing our intimate thoughts and feelings on subjects ranging from education to premarital sex. Replying to his question, I wrote that I was a firm believer in virginity until the honeymoon. A few days later, Jordan began dating a cheerleader. I'm having second thoughts about my pristine views on human sexuality. Being Jordan Russo's thou-shall-not-touch friend is not what I had in mind when I signed up for French class.

No matter my current status with Jordan, there is hope. I've officially bloomed, and to boot, I'm five-foot-three. Evidently, a breast reduction won't be necessary in this lifetime. I wasn't counting on it either. It's a relief to know that I'm not physically stunted, though it is clear that I'm damaged emotionally.

Nadine hasn't had a breast reduction, yet. But she has written me and asked how things are with the Andrewses. I'm impressed with her boldness to break from the chains the Andrewses had shackled to her, and I told her so in my reply letter. It was a short letter. My sister knows what I'm facing. The Andrewses' desire for the perfect daughter has not changed since Nadine left. Why bother with the details?

Nadine is living with Samantha in Indiana and waitressing to put gas in her junker car. Not surprising, your second daughter failed out of college in her first semester. She hasn't heard from Nina. I should give Nina's mom a call.

I contemplated the things I would have written Nadine, if I thought she cared. A feeling of hollowness is what stands out the most. Pervasive silence is constantly with me. The house whispers over the buzz in my ear: I hear the clock on my dresser mark the passing seconds with a measured tick, I hear Nikki's breathing when she's lying next to me, and I hear the door slam when Shari comes home.

The house and I have become the focus of Shari's attention. We are expected to be perfect, and when we veer from her heart's desire, I am reprimanded. Mrs. Lareau has imparted some survival techniques. I write a list of the chores that need to be done around the house each day and check off the completed ones before I go to bed. My counselor also suggested that I say "I love you" more often. Those three simple words are hard to say when being asked to say them.

The daily check list is working; there's less friction with Shari due to my neglect. At her request, I sent Mrs. Lareau the lists from last week. She called on Wednesday and said she appreciated my humor. When I reassured her it was not a prank, Mrs. Lareau mentioned her next phone call was to my foster mother. My counselor was going to suggest that Shari get a maid instead of a foster child. For fear of reprisals, I begged her not to discuss my household duties with Shari. Mrs. Lareau dropped the matter, reluctantly.

Saying "I love you" more often engendered an unexpected comment. Shari accused me of being sweet in anticipation of a lucrative Christmas. It's amazing how my foster mother's mind works. I've decided not to communicate Shari's accusation to Mrs. Lareau; she'll think I'm making this stuff up.

I asked Tim if he was planning any big Christmas items this year for Shari, hinting that I would be willing to chip in babysitting money. He indicated that the burdens of being foster parents have left their bank account trim. Tim said my savings account has a larger balance than theirs. I got the picture; it will be a light Christmas this year.

The girls soccer season ended. I barely had any game time mainly because I lack the ability to throw straight when the ball goes off sides. I have long legs and skillfully run the ball up the field, but throwing a soccer ball was beyond my range. Besides, our opponents knew about my handicap: running out of my cleats. I was their favorite target to trip from behind. We have a dreadful win-loss ratio; I won't bother writing it down. At our awards banquet, Coach stated how proud she is of a ragtag group of girls who became a team. I appreciate her perspective.

Jordan attended some of our games. He always patted me on the back and said "nice game" even though I played substitute for winded players. I felt embarrassed whenever I saw him in the stands. Jordan is kind and supportive, and it makes me cringe. He's captain of the football team, how would he know what it feels like to be second choice?

I know joining the girls soccer team was a whim, but I'd like to find something that allows me to shine. Even academically, there's always someone smarter, a higher achiever. In chemistry, there's a student whose father is a college physics professor. Compared to him, our class is on the level of kindergarten.

I joined the Soccerrettes, the boys soccer team's version of cheerleaders. We don't cheer, at least not in formation and with short skirts. Instead, we proudly wear our matching T-shirts at the games and fill in the stands. I demeaned myself by becoming a Soccerrette so I can inconspicuously flirt with Jordan after the games. He and I talk about death, college, love, and sex, thus placing me further in the category of friend. I've noticed he says nothing about his family. I suspect it's to avoid rubbing in my foster child status.

Being friends with Jordan has afforded me some notoriety, although it's not the kind I want. I was on my way to English class when I overheard a conversation two freshmen were having in front of me. Among other things, they said I'm saving myself for Jordan Russo, waiting for him to finish dating the cheerleading squad. I purposely cut in front of them, hoping to embarrass them. Neither one had a clue I was the owner of my name. What is it about me that makes me so invisible?

My less than flattering reputation hasn't blinded Daniella. Perhaps that's because her focus is on sports instead of the gossip grapevine. Soccer is where Daniella and I met and became friends. Not unlike the rest of the tenth graders, Daniella is a couple of years older than me. Some of Jordan's friends tell me that Daniella is gay. Guys can be so cruel. Daniella wears her hair short, is on the girls volleyball team, and she's pigeon toed—none of which define her sexuality. But try telling that to a seventeen-year-old boy.

Melissa is an official druggie. She's barely living at home and occasionally drops by school for a class or two. I hope it wasn't Shari's book I lent her that prompted her most recent blunder. Melissa is dating a local rock band member; I think he's twenty-two. Anyway, she tells me sex is almost as good as drugs. I wonder if she knows how bad she looks with scraggly hair and dark circles under her eyes. Melissa asked about Carrie, and I sorrowfully admitted that I too had lost touch with our bus stop buddy. I wonder if Carrie still smokes. I should call her.

My student counselor has been hounding me to apply to college. He said that when I graduate next year, I'll be eligible for financial aid. In addition to potential scholarships, I'll have Social Security death benefits and the college Pell Grant. In other words, my chances of paying for college increased when I declined adoption, especially considering the Andrewses' depleted savings account. I am, however, paying the emotional price for that decision. Shari has a long memory.

Mary Pat Brennan wrote me a few weeks ago. She's considering going to the University of South Florida in Tampa and wants me to apply there as well. I promised her I would consider it. I didn't bother to tell her that college is a dream at this stage of my life. Right now I'm concentrating on waking up each day and turning away from the thought "I want to run."

*****

Christmas came and went. The highlight was a surprise phone call from Tasha and Cammy. They had a white Christmas and went snow tubing near the meadow before opening gifts. Hearing their voices reminded me of memories that had seeped from me with the passage of time. For a while anyway, I remembered that I have a family.

Tasha seemed to want to say something but didn't. I had a feeling someone besides Cammy was around. Maybe Uncle James was monitoring their conversation. Mom, I hope your two youngest daughters are as happy as they claimed. I can accept Nadine and Samantha being, well, being who they are and how they are, but Tasha and Cammy deserve to have the world in their palm.

Though she doesn't celebrate Christmas, Daniella insisted that we exchange gifts on Christmas Eve. When she pulled up to the Andrewses' house driving her Hanukkah gift, I realized why all the fuss. Daniella's parents are divorced. That wasn't the gift. For months they had argued about who would drive Daniella to and from school events. I know because she would end up at my house waiting for one of her parents to pick her up. Now Daniella's parents have the perfect solution, and she has the perfect gift. Daniella is the proud owner of a new VW Rabbit. Not bad for a sixteen-year-old with a brand-new driver's license. To say I am jealous would miss exposing the delight I feel. If I don't have a car, at least Daniella does.

Tim is escorting me next week to my driver's license test. I hope I pass. I'm nervous about it. Not the written portion; it's the examiner climbing into the car and directing me to parallel park that terrifies me. Though I passed this maneuver in driver education, I passed by the skin of my chinny-chin-chin.

During the last week of Christmas break, the Andrewses and I went camping. Considering all that transpired, I wish they had gone by themselves. The more I'm away from the Andrewses, the less trouble I'm in.

A few days after we arrived at our Key Largo campsite, a troop of boy scouts set up camp three sites behind ours. The Andrewses were immediate friends with Steve, the boy scout leader. I decided I didn't like him the moment we shook hands. Steve is a psychologist when he's not playing in the boy scouts. Tim and Shari must have thought they hit the jackpot having a professional so accessible. They huddled with him and sipped on wine coolers at the nightly campfires on the beach. As usual, I became the topic of conversation. I'm no longer embarrassed by the Andrewses when they solicit opinions about me. It's more like an irritant, bug spray in the eyes. I've learned to walk away instead of attempting to disrupt the menacing cloud. So I walked away when the boy scout leader was around. Within twenty-four hours of meeting him, Steve appointed himself my personal psychologist and set out to fix me. I'm afraid of people who want to fix the world before they understand it. I wonder if he's a card-carrying member of Ego Maniacs Anonymous. In retrospect, it was probably a mistake to reject Steve's efforts to mold me into the perfect daughter. Instead, I fed fuel to the Andrewses' fire and bruised Steve's fragile ego to boot.

America Outdoors has a small game room where Jeremy spent his life savings. He's one of the boy scouts and almost my age. I'm inspired by how worldly ninth graders are these days. Jeremy taught me how to play pinball and French kiss. I didn't know what I was missing all these years while in the honors classes. Shari ended my practice sessions with Jeremy; thankfully, it was on our last day of camping. I knew the instant I glimpsed her image that adoption would have been less painless than what I was about to face. In front of Jeremy, Shari pulled me out of the game room by my ponytail. Before my feet landed on the sandy path, she opened her dragon mouth and spewed fire. I didn't have the guts to look back to see if Jeremy was watching as I was dragged to the campsite. I knew he could hear.

"What do you think he has between his legs? Do you know? I doubt you do. It's called a penis. Is that what you're looking for? You want to screw some boy you just met? What do you think you've been doing? What's wrong with you?"

These were not questions. They were accusations that I had learned were best left unanswered. She released her grip on my hair but had her arm around my shoulders and shook me with each sentence she screamed into my good ear.

"You've insulted and embarrassed your father and me. We came on this camping trip to be with you, and you've spent ninety percent of your time with some boy who's trying to bed you. Why are you acting like a common whore? Why? In front of little boys to watch you. You disgust me."

She meant it, Mom. She was as disgusted with me as Aunt Erika was with Nadine. For fear of reprisals, I spent the afternoon at our campsite. The Andrewses wandered off. I was too disgusting to be around. The Atlantic Ocean was too cold to drown myself in, so I crawled into the hammock and stared into the cloudless blue sky. I considered running yet felt weary from Shari's attack. She has a way with words.

Evening approached. It was time to pack the camper for our drive home. I lacked the energy to move and remained in the hammock, fully knowing it would earn me another disparagement. Jeremy snuck over to say goodbye.

He whispered as he crouched down next to me, "Shari and Tim are in child psychology discussions with Steve. You still upset?"

"Yeah."

"I brought you a token from the pinball machine. You left it behind. Hold onto it until you meet another penis then throw it away, along with what she said."

He gave me a warm hug then a passionate kiss before he headed down the path. I'm not sure if it was his words or his kiss that brought life into my listless body. While Shari and Tim filled their mental notebooks with Steve's fix-it advice, I quickly packed the camper and Jeep, leaving me time for a walk to the water. Nikki insisted on joining me, and I succumbed to her request when she tilted her head to the side. After throwing the leash over her pointy ears, we walked toward the boats.

A man in his twenties was standing in Nikki's spot. He was looking out toward the Atlantic Ocean as if it were far away. I noticed his left leg was cut off at the knee. My normal inclination would be to find another spot, but something inside said to stand next to him. For a while we said nothing, not needing to acknowledge each other's presence. I found solace standing on the edge of the sea wall, feeling the dolphins. I imagined they were close and could hear my thoughts.

He leaned on his crutches for support then twisted his body toward me. "My name's Robert."

"Ariana," I replied as I extended my hand to shake his.

"Your mom has a set of lungs."

"You heard."

Robert smiled. "They heard her in Miami."

I breathed in salty mist and humid air. "She's not my mom. She's my foster mother."

"Oh. That explains it," Robert said then turned back to the Atlantic Ocean.

"Explains what?"

"Her jealousy of the penis you were spending ninety percent of your time—"

"Jeremy."

"Jeremy's lucky."

"Jeremy is a good kisser."

Robert smiled and gave me a side glance. "Ariana. Beautiful name. Does it have a meaning?"

"Very holy. But as you may have gathered, that description of me is quite disputable today." I paused and said to him, "Actually, I'm borrowing it from my father's grandmother. She's not using it anymore."

Robert nodded.

I examined his face from the side. "Are you looking for something when you look out like that?"

Robert maintained his gaze toward the ocean. An uncomfortable minute passed. He must have been searching for an answer that contained the same amount of honesty I put into my question.

At last he said, "The other half of my leg." Robert's words carried a twinge of a smile to soften the punch of his candor.

"I look for dolphins. When things get bad with the Andrewses, I think about standing here and imagine dolphins come to me. They tell me to let go. Ya know…the words, the hurt. They take it all and cut through the waves stopping only when they reach the edge of the world. They release sadness so far away that it can't come back." Tears blurred my vision. I looked down and pet Nikki. She stared into the rolling water as if she were listening to the dolphins. The waves splashed against the sea wall, dowsing us. Its assault reminded me of Shari. "I'm not a whore, Robert. I wanted to know what it's like to French kiss and… I like it."

"I've never seen a dolphin. I haven't seen a lot of things."

"Have you French kissed?" I asked.

"Yeah. I've French kissed. I like it too," he said, nodding agreement. "I wish dolphins could swim cancer to the end of the earth and banish it forever."

"Have you asked them to?"

Shari's voice interrupted the waves, the sea spray, the peace. It was time to leave. I turned around and pulled on Nikki's leash, yet she held her ground.

"Nik, I'm not in the mood to get yelled at again." I gave another tug, and she looked up at Robert instead. He turned to face me. Exasperated, I slapped my hands at my side and felt the game token in my jacket pocket. I tossed it to him, saying, "Nikki can hear the dolphins. They are nearby. Tell the dolphins to take this with your cancer, Robert. Throw it as far as you can 'cause dolphins don't like coming too close to shore."

Robert said nothing, yet he smiled. I noticed his eyes had strength shining in them. He turned his head away from me, balanced on the crutches, and drew back his arm, readying for a strong throw.

*****

There goes my perfect average. It was bound to end some day; I'm just embarrassed that it happened in my favorite subject. Mrs. Roth gave me a stinking B on my midterm English exam. She answered my objection with a simple statement, "You have more ability than you're expressing."

Jordan reminds me that I have a semester to make up for the undeserving grade. He says I'll end the year with all A's. Jordan Russo is kind, thoughtful, encouraging, smart, has a truck, and is good-looking. Mom, he's too perfect. There has to be a flaw somewhere. And I hope I don't find it.

I told Jordan about Jeremy, leaving out Shari's tantrum. I was hoping he would ask me to demonstrate my kissing technique, but we're just friends. That's what I get for telling Jordan what's in my heart. It takes away the mystery and suspense, placing me in a category of trusted friend.

Being the youngest in my class creates an awkwardness for me. I was surrounded by freshman in driver education. I know it sounds petty or ridiculous, but driving is a status symbol. Juniors have had their driver license for more than a year, and a lot of them have their own car. Though I have a driver's license, a couple of years later than my classmates, I don't have a car. And after experiencing the woes of ownership through Daniella, I'm not eager to acquire one either. Driving is fun. Paying for gas and insurance is not. Daniella is faced with a dilemma: quit sports and get a job, or park her prized possession until the summer. Originally the car was to alleviate transportation problems Daniella's sports caused. Things are not so simple, are they?

This semester I'm taking the other half of driver education: firearms. It's strange how the Dade County school system lumps the two into one course. Lucky for me they are. It was my desire for a driver's license that led me to this hidden talent—I'm a natural marksman. I was discovered while at the shooting range. The instructors were impressed with my eye-hand coordination and introduced me to skeet shooting. Skeet shooting is my forte, not that target shooting is difficult; it's boring. I wanted something that would allow me to shine, but this is not what I had in mind. Tim seems delighted with my new hobby. What else can be expected of a man who goes to the local country diner every Sunday morning for two eggs, cheese grits, and bacon? My foster father is a redneck. He has a bumper sticker that embarrasses me as much as he feels pride in it. It reads, "Will the last American out of Miami please bring the flag."

Shari and Tim told me to make plans to work for the summer. Though I had my heart set on going to Indiana, I dared not argue. Besides, they're right. It's time to earn my keep. Mrs. Lareau had suggested I apply at the YMCA. I sent in an application and was accepted without having to bother with an interview. Apparently, my counselor can pull strings when she wants to.

I'll be a junior camp counselor at the YMCA summer camp in Sebring, Florida. This summer I'll earn money, get away from the Andrewses, and be surrounded by a billion screaming kids. I can't wait.

CHAPTER 10

It's been a few months. Obviously Shari is keeping them. I should've known she would. I know better than to trust my foster mother to pick up my developed film. I'm trying to remember if there are any embarrassing shots. Most likely the roll was loaded with them. That's probably why she has confiscated my pictures. It's frustrating that Shari won't confront me with them. I guess she doesn't want to hear that it was clean, innocent fun.

There we were, two teenage girls home alone on a Saturday with a camera. We drank enough Cokes to drown then an attack of the giggles ensued. Daniella and I had borrowed her mom's lingerie. We modeled when we weren't pretending to be a fashion photographer. I know Shari looks at those pictures and sees immoral hussies. To her, the photographs are undeniable evidence. I won't bother asking for them back; they aren't as important to me as they are to her.

I bet my last babysitting job that when Tim looked at the pictures he said to Shari, "She's got nice legs." He said that the last time we were at the Polanskis' house. As soon as the words came out of his mouth, Shari's eyes bulged. Poor Tim, he didn't notice. I did. I thought Shari was going to decapitate me for whoring myself again. She controlled her temper, though I saw invisible steam erupt from her ears.

Tim's not a bright man, yet he has a good heart. Behind his inappropriate comments, I hear a man conveying his fatherly pride. My foster mother misses Tim's sincerity. Instead, she hears something entirely different than what Tim says. Shari is not only deaf, she's blind as well. She refuses to see how she's destroying her dreams.

My foster mother has been coming home late and sometimes drunk. Home-cooked dinners are a thing of the past. I eat canned soup until there isn't any. Toward the end of the week, Tim picks up pizza on his way home from work. When she spots pizza boxes in the garbage, Shari yells at me for not preparing dinner. She forgets that I don't know how. I'm capable of cleaning a house from top to bottom, but cooking is out of my league. Salads and sandwiches I can manage, yet Tim complains. He says he feels like a rabbit after eating my version of a supper. Potato chips and beer, that's Tim's dinner at least twice a week. I've suggested vegetables instead of the chips, even resorting to serving cheese, celery, and carrots on a platter. My foster father laughs and bites into a hunk of cheese out of courtesy. I end up eating the carrots and celery.

In our quest for nourishment, Tim and I have become pals. He includes me in his Sunday morning ritual while Shari sleeps in. As soon as the kids are fed, we hop in the Jeep and take the back roads to the country diner. Cheese grits aren't as bad as I thought.

Tim and I don't talk about what's going on at home. Things are rather obvious; words would be a waste of effort. For instance, our family camping trips have ended. Shari never said so, but we know. I'm not a girl anymore, and the camper is too small. Sleeping a few feet from one another is too cozy for Shari.

Tim has done nothing or said anything that compromises the father-daughter rapport we've established. I feel safer with him than with Shari. I think Tim is afraid of her as well. Months ago, he stopped waking me up in the mornings. I miss him yanking my foot and saying, "I have to work, you have to go to school, and the kids, well, they're lucky. They get to stay home." I now have an alarm clock to wake me.

Shari wonders why I don't bring my friends around. I shrug to her question. She doesn't remember the day Jordan dropped me off after a soccer game. And I can't forget. My foster mother seeks fuel for her raging fire. To her, my friends are fuel.

After that soccer match with Killian, Jordan drove me home in his mom's car. I stood on the curb and leaned inside the passenger window to hear his description of how Fuad's injury lost them the game. As she drove up the driveway, I caught Shari's facial expression then hastily ended my chat with Jordan to avoid introducing him.

Shari was gearing up for her whore accusations. Jordan drove away as Shari opened her car door.

"Who was that?"

"Jordan Russo. He was dropping me off from the soccer game. They lost."

"Did he get a good view of your lovely breasts? You could've broken his window leaning in like that."

"It's his mom's car. His truck is in the shop. And my jacket is zipped up as you can see, so no, I don't think he got what he was hoping he'd get."

"Did you go to the game like that? Your butt is hanging out. You look like a common whore. Why wear shorts when it's cold enough for a jacket, Ariana? You just have to have your butt hanging out; don't you?"

"Yeah," I said, turning to go into the house.

"Get your pretty little legs back here, young lady. I have groceries in the car."

Things escalated in the kitchen and ended with me walking to my bedroom while Shari called me an uncaring and ungrateful brat. She picks fights, and I walk away. I'm tired of the ugly words, the screaming, of having to walk away.

I don't understand what I'm doing wrong or what's wrong with me in Shari's eyes. She should have a week with one of my friends. They do things they'll probably regret all their lives, if they live past their teens.

Melissa's mom is going to be a grandmother. I don't think she's ready for another mouth to feed. The father-to-be skipped town; he joined another band. And Melissa is attending night school to earn a GED.

Things twist and turn. Words, faces, smiles, bodies, and lives twist in turn.

*****

Tim was in a serious car accident. While on his way home from a client meeting, he fell asleep at the wheel and slammed the Jeep into a concrete light pole. I didn't know anything had happened when I got up the next morning and readied for school.

Shari wandered into the kitchen where I was feeding the kids. Displaying no emotion, she told me about Tim's ordeal. I braced for her attack. I mean, my foster mother had all night to convince herself that I knew Tim was in serious trouble, yet I, the selfish daughter, decided my sleep was more important than him. I figure she had the whole scenario worked out in her warped mind. The princess slept through the night while the queen agonized over her husband's near demise. The queen realized I, the princess, was the villain who caused the king's accident.

I was amazed. Shari didn't attack. She asked if I wanted to see him. I knew better than to refuse even though she told me his face had been intimate with the steering wheel. I stood behind the Andrewses' bedroom door and peeked in. Tim looked up at me from worn eyes. He seemed embarrassed. I felt bad for him knowing his pain was probably worse than his appearance. The Jeep was totaled, and so was my foster father's face. In the weeks that followed, Tim's face transmuted many strange and unusual colors before reverting to his original skin tone. Now he has eight new front teeth and a bill from the Florida Department of Motor Vehicles to replace their light pole.

Tim's accident scared Shari. It also changed her focus. Tim went through total neglect and misery to get his wife's attention. But he got it. He hasn't had to scavenge for dinner ever since.

Shari is talking about selling the camper and her beloved piano. Those toys are yesterday's thrills. Besides, my foster mother wants to redecorate. With the house in her sights, maybe now she can satisfy her quest for perfection. By now, she has probably realized that I'm further away from being perfect than the house is.

So far, my foster mother has acquired two round sofas. They look more like catcher mitts. I have yet to climb out gracefully once I'm in their grasp. I usually resort to crawling. The cats have already sanctioned them. The males have a tendency to anoint anything new or left on the floor. There's no experience on this planet that can compare to going through a semester with a calculus book that smells like cat pee.

I've almost completed the eleventh grade, that or it's almost completed me. Mrs. Roth is determined to give me a B. I'll be glad to be free of her class, and oddly enough, I'll miss my firearms class. I've become somewhat of a legend.

Tasha and Cammy wrote. Apparently, Indiana's weather is unsure if it will succumb to the urge to manifest summer or hang onto the turbulence of spring. Is there an unwritten law that says letters must contain an update on the weather? Anyway, my sisters are disappointed that I won't be visiting this year. Part of me wants to go to Indiana. Most of me wants to go to camp.

Granddad still writes. I'm surprised that he has yet to run out of his antique baseball stationery. Your father complains that I don't communicate much when I write. What do you write to a man who says the rosary every day? I mean, I don't think he can relate to Melissa's predicament or Daniella's gay reputation. It's a challenge to the creative writer inside me to be informative yet leave out details that would give Granddad another stroke.

Mrs. Lareau is going to Canada for two weeks at the end of the summer. I asked her to bring back snow. She laughed, although I wouldn't be shocked if she mailed a bottle of water labeled snow. She tends to find humor in the small, sometimes overlooked quirks life presents. It helps that Mrs. Lareau is quick to find the lighter side of things. During our weekly conversations, we laugh more than talk. I like her way of counseling.

Jordan is planning on securing a summer job. He's been dating the same girl for three months and tells me it may become serious when I'm gone. I'm not stupid. I realize he's young, horny, and has a truck. Who could resist carnal temptations when you have all that going for you?

*****

School mercifully ended yesterday, Friday. I was counting down the days I had to endure Mrs. Roth's face. Thankfully, she doesn't teach twelfth grade honors English.

Coffee in the morning to get him going and beer at night to calm him down, thus is my foster father's biorhythm. While Tim cleared the fog from his head this morning, I fed the kids and packed last-minute items. Before the sun had a chance to burn off dew, Tim and I had loaded his father's army trunk into Shari's car. Tim named her old Cadillac the Houseboat. I swear that monster weighs more than me, I'm referring to the army trunk, not the Houseboat. We heaved it in the back seat after realizing it would be too heavy to pull out from the Cadillac's trunk if we dropped it in there.

Having completed our chores, Tim invited me to breakfast. I accepted and dutifully pointed out that today is Saturday. He acknowledged the deviation from our Sunday morning ritual saying he would go again tomorrow, without me but in honor of me. I actually crave cheese grits, thanks to our weekly breakfasts at the country diner. When I expressed concern about grits withdrawal symptoms, Tim reassured me that every self-respecting camp serves grits.

At noon, we arrived in the middle of Florida and were warmly greeted by mosquitoes and Paul, the camp director. From a distance, I noticed he was a tall, blond man. Up close, I forgot about his height and was lost in his three-dimensional blue eyes. He invited the Andrewses and me to join the tour he was giving counselors and their families. Shari and I walked Nikki while Tim maneuvered the Houseboat under a shady tree. My foster father was worried the ice cooling his beer would melt too quickly if he parked in the direct summer sun. Finally, we caught up with Paul and his entourage then explored my new home for the next two months.

The YMCA camp is tucked among white sand dunes, Florida scrub brush, and one-hundred-year-old oak trees protecting a lake. Sandy paths leading from tiny cabins connect to a dirt road that ends at the main building which is a large dining hall with a kitchen attached to the back. Nikki met Sammy, the camp cook; they became instant friends. Sammy handed her a ham bone when I had my back turned. The Andrewses managed to walk next to Paul. I said a quick mental prayer swearing my firstborn son to the priesthood if God would prevent my foster parents from soliciting the camp director's professional opinion on maladjusted foster children. Paul seemed to have been forewarned by Mrs. Lareau. He gracefully avoided being labeled a foster child expert.

The tour was quick and sweet. Watching Nikki leave was not. I bit my bottom lip when she stuck her head out the back window and whined. Tim waved then blew a kiss. Shari smiled and pointed her finger saying, "Don't come home pregnant." As they traversed the dirt road leading back to the highway, a cloud of dust followed behind.

Not all the counselors have arrived. One guy is coming all the way from Athens, Georgia. He'll be arriving tomorrow. During supper, Paul gave us an overview of what we'll be offering campers and identified the counselors associated with each area of instruction. He suggested that we water-ski before the campers arrive next Saturday. Chances of skiing would be slim after that since those classes are usually filled each session.

I brought your letter this time believing it is more secure with me than at home, vulnerable to Shari's snooping eyes. My first night in the quiet of camp isn't so quiet. Crickets are sending out their mating call, and the older counselors are running around out back faking wolf howls. It's a poor rendition. I'm alone in the dining hall with your letter. The buzzing sound in my ear is more pronounced probably because my awareness of sounds is heightened. I can hear some of the counselors talking in the girls' cabin. We'll move into our assigned cabins when the campers arrive. In the meantime, we sleep with our same gender. This is the first summer that girls will be attending this camp. I seem to be building a legacy of being among the first to crash all male traditions. Enrollment was down this year putting a crunch on the YMCA camp budget, opening the doors to girls opens the door to more money.

I learned that a junior counselor is second in command, behind a senior counselor. The senior counselors attend college. They'll have cabins to themselves. I'll be sharing cabin duties with another junior counselor, Tammy. She has a Southern accent straight from Louisiana and a beautiful smile to match her drawl. Tammy and I will get along beautifully especially because we won't be working in the same areas. She's on the swimming staff. I'm the target shooting instructor, the first female in-charge of riflery. I wonder if breaking traditions is my destiny.

Shari bought a pile of postcards and asked me to send one a week with at least two sentences written on each card. She even pre-stamped them. I should have done the same for her; the Andrewses aren't letter writers. I worry about Nikki's addiction to fence jumping. My foster parents haven't had the honor of chasing her down the street, and I'm afraid once they do, they'll rid themselves of Nikki. In their eyes, she's no different from a piano.

I have no idea if it's late, but I'm feeling tired enough to crawl in bed. I forgot my flashlight and hope I find my way to the cabin. I can always ask one of the wolves to show me the way.

CHAPTER 11

Counselor bonding week officially came to a close this evening when Paul gave us our cabin assignments; Tammy and I have the ten-year-olds. We're meeting them at the bus tomorrow and can't wait. I'm hoping a few girls from our cabin will sign up for riflery. Paul told me to expect only boys with a penchant for squirrel shooting.

I had the guns out yesterday, cleaning them. Today I was sighting them. Mark, the guy from Georgia, is impressed with my unusual hobby. He volunteered to help me sight our twenty-two caliber, single action rifle guns. I quickly discovered that even with a perfectly sighted gun, he's a hopeless shot. Mark is as good at water-skiing as I am with guns. And unfortunately, I'm as hopeless in two skis as he is with targets.

The ski instructors had me in the lake on Sunday, behind the boat. My body was lost inside the floating lifejacket all Mark could see were my hands clutching the ski rope handle. He hit the throttle, and within seconds my head popped up through the ski jacket, and I was hoisted to the top of the water's surface. Despite my courageous struggle, the skis spread apart, and I got my first enema. I was too embarrassed to inform the boat crew of my unexpected purging and insisted on swimming to shore, feigning a desire for exercise. Today they had me on one ski, a slalom. That's more my style. I went the full length of the lake before losing it on the first turn, going over the boat's wake. Mark said I looked like a natural. I said the same thing to him when he was loading bullets in backward.

A representative from the Red Cross spent an afternoon with us in the dining hall. She brought visual aids and spoke to us about masturbation, sexual behavior, female menstruation, social diseases, and activities children commonly do when in a group. We were coached on how to approach campers that may be engaged in a game of doctor or exploration and what to say if we were questioned about sex and sexual feelings. I thought about Shari and her reaction to my sexual curiosity. I almost asked the woman from the Red Cross to stop by Shari's office and give her the same lecture. You know, to debunk Shari's misconceptions.

Thanks to the Red Cross, I'm now certified in CPR and lifesaving. I didn't realize that no matter their area of instruction, all YMCA counselors are required to be strong swimmers. I like the idea of feeling capable of rescuing a distressed swimmer, although I probably won't see many being at the target range. It's on the other side of camp, surrounded by sand dunes and scrub brush.

Paul introduced us to the camp's scout fraternity. Starting this summer girls will be welcomed into the revered brotherhood. That is, when those girls demonstrate the qualities that earn them an invitation. Paul revealed some of its secrets since none of the female counselors are members. The brotherhood is headed by the master of ceremony, Paul, and meetings are held once during each two-week session. Their meeting is at night, in the woods, and during it, campers are initiated into the brotherhood. New members are given a bandanna to wear, signifying their honor. It sounds exciting. I have a feeling the campers will take it quite seriously.

To celebrate the conclusion of counselor bonding week, Paul treated us to a pizza bash this evening. Sammy is a great cook, but he's no competition to Pizza Hut when it comes to pizza. Three pickup trucks loaded with bonded counselors descended on the small-town restaurant. I didn't realize how isolated we've been for the past week until we sat down and ordered. It's an odd experience to be waited on after a week of total self-service.

In between bites of pizza and glasses of Coke, someone started a game of questions. The first question brought me back to Key Largo. "What one thing would you put in a time capsule to be sent off in space to let another civilization know who we are?" I considered placing a sculpture of a dolphin with the words, "This is the best we've to offer, and yet we kill this, our brother, without a second thought. Don't come to earth just yet. Wait until we kill ourselves off." I didn't share this. Instead, I yielded to the consensus which decided the Bible would best reveal who we are.

In just one week, Paul has taught us the dozen or so games we are to teach and encourage campers to participate in. Nothing like games to crack a smile on a shy camper's face. We were shown how to start campfires and how to put them out and learned the words to several traditional camp songs. Paul plays the guitar and sings off tune. It's wonderful, Mom. This past week has been heaven.

The trunk Tim lent me has turned out to be quite versatile and perfect for camp life. Not only is it an impregnable locker, I use it for a table when I'm writing, and when I'm not, it's a nightstand for my clock and picture of Nikki.

Tammy is a year younger than me yet is more experienced or at least more prepared. She had been a camper for years. Tammy gave me two bags of hard candy and one bag of bubble gum telling me these are essential items to have when it comes to counselor and camper relations. We have one day off a week. Tammy plans on sailing during the day and going to town for a movie at night. My co-counselor has this camp thing down to a science.

*****

I received a long letter from Tasha describing their disaster in the garden. The cherry tomato fight we had last summer had calamitous, far-reaching results. Tomato plants are growing everywhere. Uncle James had to plow the area between the barn and the driveway, but it hasn't halted the invasion nor discouraged the cherry tomato's natural impulse to propagate.

Tasha is tall enough to work in the cornfields this summer "de-tasseling," as she described it. She didn't say, yet I have a feeling she's taller than me, by a few inches. Such a fate I have to be short in a family of tall women, to have a younger sister taller than me. Nadine's words repeat in my mind, "bad karma." I don't know what karma is exactly. I suspect it means I am getting what I asked for. I have to be more careful with my wishes. I remember in fifth grade how much I liked being called cute.

Tasha's letter filled me in on Samantha and Nadine. They have had their differences. Okay, they had outright cat fights. Nadine moved out and is now living with her boyfriend. Samantha is working double shifts to compensate for the stuff Nadine stole from her. These things I hope you cannot see. These things I am ashamed of us for doing. We should be carrying your memory with more honor and dignity.

I haven't heard from the Andrewses, and it's been three weeks. Sammy says I'm depressed. I've never been depressed that I know of, so I don't know if he's just saying that because I'm not eating his meat-invested food. The visiting nurse suggested I exercise less and eat more. I'll cherish hearing those words one day, I'm sure. Paul sat me down for a one-on-one. He said it was normal to miss the Andrewses and that if I looked deep enough, I would find that I love and miss them.

As requested, I send a postcard once a week to Shari and Tim. I do miss them, Nikki especially. When I turn off the light and snuggle into bed, I send a kiss to her, a hug to the Andrewses, and I place my heart in God's hand saying good night to you. I wonder if you already know this.

I'm sitting next to the trunk, alone in the dark night while ten campers sleep a few feet away from me. Tammy is on her day off and will be crawling into bed probably after midnight. I have a night light plugged into the wall next to my bed; it substitutes for a reading lamp. Your letter seems mysterious in this muffled light as if it is here one minute and lost in the cosmos in another. Maybe that's what dying is like. I almost had my life snuffed the other day. If it weren't for Mark's determination, my spine would have been crushed.

That afternoon was bright and particularly hot. Ominous clouds suddenly appeared. Within minutes the sky transformed then intensified. I ended my class abruptly. Purple and gray clouds laden with an electrical charge hung in the air as I led future sharpshooters to the cabin area. I saw Mark by the dock helping stragglers out of the water and ran to the lake to assist, sending my class ahead to their cabins.

Lightning struck the lake as we ran up the hill, desperate to reach shelter. Then I saw light flash in front and on the sides. It was difficult to determine where the strikes were landing. Thunder was as immediate as the lightning. The frightened campers were screaming as they darted for Mark's cabin; it was the closest structure in sight. Mark and I followed behind.

He grabbed my hand and pulled me along; I had slowed my run to cover my eyes from the flashes of light. Our hair stood on end, and my skin crawled just before a bolt hit a tree branch arching over our heads. The soundwave pushed me to the ground, and Mark pulled on my arm screaming, "Run, run!" My legs were moving before I realized the tree had been struck.

Electricity engulfed us. I felt light zap the atmosphere as we ran into his cabin. The storm was furious, and as fast as it gathered momentum, it discharged its power. Sunlight was drying the moistened ground in less than an hour, yet we remained in Mark's cabin and played games until supper. I was shaking inside and doing my best not to show it to the campers. Later inspection revealed a large tree branch had broken off, landing on the ground where I had fallen. There were singe marks at the end of the broken limb. I don't know who was more frightened though, me or Mark.

On our day off, Mark let me drive his car. He invited me to join him for an afternoon movie in town. Mark is a James Bond fan. I was inspired by the action adventure and asked to drive back to camp. Operating a manual transmission is more complicated than it looks. I stalled everywhere—at lights, turns, and finally on the dirt road leading into camp. Mark convinced me to give up before we reached camp. He reminded me of the price I would pay if any of the counselors witnessed my ineptness. I like that Mark is two years older than me. He's experienced most of what's new to me and explains it all with a sweet Southern accent.

Mark is an outstanding kisser. Lucky for us his braces were removed before he was fifteen. I doubt we could survive the incessant teasing if we locked braces. I'm over the embarrassment of having metal in my mouth. Braces have done more than straighten my teeth; they've taught me that things are not so permanent. I had no idea my teeth were movable. If teeth can shift because of a thin wire, anything can change. What I once thought was solid, is not.

His talents go beyond kissing; Mark is quick on his feet. I learned that fact while being his opponent captain during war. War is a game Paul taught us. Four teams with an identifying color spent the day in the shrubs, woods, and by the lakeshore vying for the game's prize, a white flag. It was tied to the dock.

The rules of war are simple. The goal is simple. Doing it, now that takes skill, cunning, and quick feet. My team, True Blue, had the best strategy. We lured the other team's fastest runners away from the flag to capture it ourselves. This tactic was a good one since I happen to be among the fastest runners in camp. I used to think I was the fastest; however, Mark takes that prize as well as the title of captain of the winning team when he outran me and grabbed the coveted white flag. It turns out that the white flag was Paul's old T-shirt, and he wanted it back after supper. It's funny what people will do for a smelly, old T-shirt when they're told it's a prize.

My cabin campers have asked me, with tact I might add, to read to them instead of sing when I tuck them in bed. Though I inherited your desire to sing, I didn't acquire your angelic voice. I'm tone-deaf. Tammy says I'm fine when there are other voices to drown me out. I'm concerned that everyone in camp knows I am less than a songbird.

Speaking of birds, my darling campers who signed up for target shooting nearly killed me. I was changing targets when a bird landed on the wire. Somewhere deep in the psyche of a little boy is an irresistible urge to aim and shoot at anything that moves. With the first crack of a rifle firing, the bird flew away, and I ran for safety, shouting, "Guns down! Guns down!" My shoe took a bullet in the bottom of it. I checked my body twice for bullet holes. Lucky for them I wasn't leaking anywhere. Paul suggested that in the future, I have the eager hunters change their own targets.

The target range is remote and has unique problems because of that. Besides bringing out a young boy's urge to hunt, the range has a slight infestation of scorpions. One crawled on my leg while I was leaning back in my chair. The boys volunteered to shoot it off me. I thanked them for their offer and declined. Mercifully, I didn't have to do anything; the venomous visitor continued walking onto the table and down to the concrete ledge. Killing is too easy.

*****

We are into our third session, and finally the Andrewses write. They tell me Nikki has developed a nasty habit of jumping the fence. Oh well, I knew it would happen. Shari says she's been busy with the redecorating. I'm concerned considering her initial choices—the round sofas. They're planning to take a week vacation, staying home to fix up things. I'm glad I'm not there. Shari asked that I send the pictures I took of Mark. I hope she doesn't pin them up in the post office under the Most Wanted posters.

Mark and I spend our days off in town. He takes me to a movie then to dinner. I give him my standard reply, "Pizza," when he asks, "Where do you want to go for dinner?" In an obscure way, Pizza Hut reminds me of Key Largo. I miss the ocean.

Although Mark and I talk about it, we don't engage in more affectionate displays than kissing mainly because I hear Shari's voice in my head repeating, "Don't come back pregnant."

One of my cabin campers tucked a letter under my pillow. I didn't find it until after the bus left with her on it. Mom, it touched me and brought me to tears when I read it. She said that I was her hero—being a foster child, being a camp counselor, and "best of all having a cute boyfriend." I had forgotten how it feels to be ten years old. Things are simple, and they are clear. At ten, you see to the heart of someone and look to that instead of the details surrounding them, defining them in other people's eyes. It humbled me to know she saw me as a hero. Me. It gives the next thing I have to share more impact, more realness. It's painful to attach words to the experience. I will never forget Caroline, not ever.

Jon and I sat under a tree, waiting in the oppressive heat. We fought off mosquitoes the size of a small house plant. The second session bus was running an hour late. When it finally arrived, we hurriedly unloaded campers and their belongings. Amidst the rush, she stepped off the bus dragging a large blue suitcase. Jon grabbed it out of her hand and lifted it onto the cart. It was the only suitcase among trunks bought especially for camp. She smiled to him; he didn't notice. Her blond hair was scraggly, dirty. Her blue eyes were made transparent by her pale skin. I stared at her hoping she wasn't assigned to my cabin. She didn't belong.

Caroline is small for her age, and she most definitely was assigned to my cabin. She stuttered the few times she spoke. I didn't put my arm around her as I did the others. I was aloof and observed her from a distance. Tammy is less affectionate than me and more playful, but even she ignored Caroline when we engaged the cabin in card games.

Mom, I'm ashamed to write more, yet I need to confess.

I was preoccupied with being accepted by the other counselors, the other campers. I ignored sweet Caroline. I didn't want anyone to know I was like her. I let her be shunned. No one reached out to her. I know better than anyone the empty, lonely feeling inside when being ignored.

Two weeks go by fast. For the campers that don't stay for extra sessions, in time their faces become a part of the blur. But I can see Caroline clearly. Her imprint is in my heart. She sat on her bunk in a worn, paper-thin nightgown while the girls played cards on the floor each night before taps. She was careful with everything she did, methodically folding her ragged clothes and placing them inside her blue suitcase. Oh, Mommy, I think Caroline has been on the receiving end of a heavy hand. I think she's been beaten. And I did nothing. I stood and watched her, knowing. I know the signs. I recognized the look in her eyes. I've seen it in the mirror. I'm so ashamed. I did nothing to comfort her, to give her a smile or a warm hug. She, above all the others, needed these things.

I remember her tender, fragile smile and her embarrassed, longing stare. And I remember what Paul said to me as I loaded her suitcase on the departing bus, "Caroline is one of the homeless children. A few get to go to camp." He said nothing more. He didn't have to. He could see it all over my face. I, more than anyone, should have looked past her appearance and braved a look inside her. I was afraid I would find myself.

*****

I'm stuck—removed and separated. I'm left behind to lie in this bed, in this dark room. I stare out the window looking to where all the sunshine lives. I have the flu, the cruel and insidious flu.

This is the last session of the summer, and my body has decided to contract the flu one of my campers brought with her. Three days ago, she was promptly sent home. She's probably in bed right now with her mom tending to her. I have the visiting nurse and an occasional flower Sammy leaves on the plate of food he brings to the infirmary. For companionship, I have your letter and a book Mark lent me to read, *Nineteen Eighty-Four* by George Orwell. It's a depressing book. Mark apologized for not having the foresight to bring more appropriate books to camp knowing I would need them when the flu invaded my body. I accepted his apology and agreed with his self-reproach.

Tammy is counselor in-charge during my absence. My campers wave to me through the window. I'm a hostage to this little building. Paul is the temporary target shooting instructor while I recoup from the virus that broke through my body's defenses and depleted me of my energy, my health. I pray that he knows how to load a gun properly and aim it at least in the vicinity of the target range.

For two days I've endured a one hundred and three temperature, yet I refuse to take the aspirin and medication the nurse left me. I flush it down the toilet. I'm not opposed to getting back on my feet; I'm afraid because of the dreams I had two nights ago when she first tended to me. The nurse had given me a dark red liquid to drink, tucked me in bed, and placed a blanket and pitcher of ice water within my reach. I fell asleep in the isolation of the infirmary. No, I take that back. I passed out, finally giving in to my body's dwindling life force. That night my delirious dreams crossed, melded, and transmuted. They were fragmented pieces of reality slipping into sheets of dimensionless nonreality. Although I can feel some of the dreams' images, in my mind's eye, they become ingredients of a disjointed soupy mixture bubbling up to the surface. One dream stands out in my mind. Unlike the other psychotic dreams, this one was cohesive, whole. And it sends shivers down my spine even now as I begin to recount it.

It was night, yet it wasn't. I felt as though time ceased. An eerie stillness hovered over camp as I walked on the dock toward the center of the lake. The camp was shaded in the darkness of night, and the sky was illumined with twilight. The frogs were hushed; the crickets weren't mating. Quiet pervasively hung over the smooth lake. I stopped at the very edge where worn wood meets black, motionless water. I waited for something, and I knew. I had a knowingness of this something that was to come. I looked to the tree line and waited not with anticipation but apprehension and a deep foreboding fear. I listened. No children's voices, nothing penetrated the silence.

An orange and blue light pierced the night sky shooting toward earth with a cloud of white following behind. Then blinding white seared my eyes. The light filled every crevice on earth. I hid my face in my hands, and that's when I heard the screams. Millions of voices screamed in terror. The sound was deafening, yet the voices did not mix into one. I could hear individual screams and knew it was the last breath, the last sound that person would make before being absorbed by the exploding light. Wave after wave, I felt the power of light ripple in the atmosphere of earth, contorting her. Light enveloped the darkness that encrusted over earth until there was white. The released energy burned hate. I woke to the sound of my own scream.

I haven't told anyone this dream. I wonder, is that what it's like to experience a nuclear bomb? Or is it a metaphor? So real, Mom, the dream was so real. It's changed how I look out the window. It could all be gone in a flash.

CHAPTER 12

On the last night of camp, I was initiated into the scout brotherhood. It was all I had imagined it would be, and more.

Paul, the master of ceremony, and high-ranking members fetched me in the middle of the night. Guided by the light of a full moon, we meandered our way through scrub brush until we reached a clearing. I recognized the area immediately. We were on the other side of the target range. I had suspected this was the brotherhood's meeting place. There were mornings when I noticed suspicious footprints on the sandy path leading toward the target range, more footprints than my classes accounted for.

We sat in a circle surrounding a small campfire and listened to Paul's stories. He narrated a parable for each of the values held most dear to this, my brotherhood: integrity, honor, loyalty, friendship, and love. I felt his warm pride when the master of ceremony recounted how I had demonstrated those virtues. I didn't realize anyone noticed me or my deeds. Paul placed a first level bandanna on my shoulder, and the brotherhood piled their hands on top, welcoming me. I'm the first female to be initiated into our brotherhood. The master of ceremony concluded the meeting for the night and adjourned for the year.

I felt like an honored guest wearing my bandanna the next morning at breakfast. Because it was the last day of camp, campers set aside fluffy pancakes and sticky syrup to hand out awards they created in arts and crafts. Sammy was the recipient of "Cook of the Year" award; he acted surprised, although he is probably given one every summer. Paul was sanctioned the "Best Director," and Mark was bestowed an "Oscar" for his talented performances on skit nights. I was given two awards: "Best Looking Target Shooting Instructor" and "Award of Luck to the Only Counselor to Survive Lightning Strikes and Shotgun Free-for-Alls in the Same Summer." My second award required two sheets of construction paper.

After the campers said their teary goodbyes and waved from the bus, the counselors met Paul on the dock. Our beloved camp director handed a red rose petal to each of us and said it was a symbol of the bond we share. He then instructed us to toss our petal onto the lake, releasing this summer and opening our hearts for the next summer. Unlike the other counselors, I didn't watch the drifting petals. Why wait for the inevitable?

As I hugged Paul goodbye, he said, "The Muses are with you, Ariana." I nodded to him as if I understood his meaning. I do not.

Although it was ready to be hoisted into Mark's car, I quickly unloaded the contents of the Andrewses' trunk in search of my trusty dictionary. Mark patiently waited while I read. "Muses are nine goddesses presiding over the arts and sciences." I laughed then said, "I still don't get it."

Mark answered, "Oh, he meant that you've been given nine lives. You used two this summer."

Mark lacks insight, but he's all heart.

After I hastily repacked, Jon and Mark heaved the trunk into the car. The extra weight caused his Datsun to sink lower to the ground. Shari and Tim had accepted Mark's offer to drive me home in exchange for a stay overnight before his long trek back to Georgia. I was surprised by the Andrewses' change of heart toward their competition. I suspected treachery. I revealed nothing to Mark about the ways of my foster parents. Warning him would not prepare him for what awaited us in Miami. Mark's innocence protects him.

Before pulling out, Mark and I stole one last look at the empty cabins. Sammy stood in front of the dining hall and waved to us as we joined the caravan of departing counselors driving down the dirt road, leading us from camp.

We arrived at the Andrewses' house before the sun set. Shari and Tim offered kisses and hugs as we walked through the front door. I stopped short in the living room. Shari waited for my response, yet I had none to give; I was numb. The Andrewses had transformed the house. "Redecorated" is what they call it. At first glance I thought it was another prank and this was someone else's home.

During their vacation, my industrious foster parents had torn down a wall, thus combining the living room with the dining room. Proudly displayed in the middle of the house are two round sofas. Mirrors and wood slats are glued to the walls, even to the kitchen counter. There are no words to describe the Andrewses' home. Well, two just came to mind: tacky and distasteful. If this is going to be the style of the eighties, I want to go back to the sixties.

We were halfway through dinner when I connected with Shari's aloofness. She was terribly disappointed that I had not commented about her interior decorating endeavors. I apologized saying that I was still absorbing its impact and admiring the details. I doubt she wanted to hear that I was embarrassed.

It had been two months, yet the pressure to wash dishes immediately following dinner outweighed my urge to shield Mark from the Andrewses' prodding questions. Shari and Tim sat on the patio with after dinner drinks in hand while Mark stood on the firing line, unannounced to him. Nikki lay next to him. She's not shy about demonstrating her protective side.

Nikki has grown into her body with grace. Those oversized puppy paws are perfect under her sturdy, adult legs. I intermittently snuck a peek out the window to see her. She didn't lift her head but wagged her tail each time I looked.

The nervousness I felt before I went to camp waited for me to return so it could assimilate back into my system. It's a familiar feeling, one that I was happy to leave behind for the summer.

Nadine's old room was crowded with Shari's crafts, yet there was enough room to make the bed. Mark and I sat on top of the covers and talked about school and camp. We promised to write every day and call once a week. I knew I was going back to Jordan, and he knew he was going back to college. We chose to ignore the obvious and continue with our happy fantasy. Tim came into the room to say good night, and I accepted the cloaked yet tactful hint to find my way to my own bed.

I waited until Mark left the next morning to thank Shari for her permission to have him drive me home and stay overnight. She said we had plenty of opportunity over the summer to copulate, why should one night be any different. My foster mother has a way with words. What she says delivers her spite and haughty intent with precision.

Nikki is attached to me as if we have an umbilical cord connecting us. She lounged in my room while I readied it for another school year, my last year in high school. I draped my brotherhood bandanna over Nikki's picture and adorned the bulletin board with my camp awards. I thought about Jose of all people and wondered if this was his last year at Harvard. As a senior at Archbishop Curly, Jose seemed more mature than I am now.

Without the slightest inclination to hide her affection, Nikki insisted that some part of her body touch mine as we lay next to one another on the kitchen floor. I pet her nose, her ears, then her paws as I spoke with Mrs. Lareau on the phone.

Evidently, the Andrewses had given my counselor a list of complaints, the least of which was my sexual promiscuity. I informed my counselor that I have maintained my virginity. Mrs. Lareau didn't seem to care.

"Shari's concerns are with your attraction to Tim."

The mere utterance of those words triggered a repulsive shudder. I exclaimed into the phone not masking my disbelief, "He's my foster father."

"I know. She's insecure and needs to hear it from you. Patrick and I have done all the talking we can do. Shari is afraid."

"Afraid. Afraid of me? What's there—"

"She's afraid of a seventeen—"

"I'm still sixteen but getting closer to that coveted seventeen."

"A sixteen-year-old girl who's growing into her sexuality. She's afraid of you seducing her husband. She's a frightened, insecure woman who needs your reassurance to feel safe in her home, living with a young, beautiful girl who's becoming a woman with each day that passes."

"What can I say to her? You know whatever I say is twisted and bent into some contorted perception she has of me. I can't break through this woman's insecurity. I'm tired of trying."

"Don't give up. You've been there too long to give up. I know you love them—"

"Yes. And the fact that I'm growing into a woman's body, a natural thing that happens to the female gender, is not the issue. The problem is Shari. Can't you counsel—"

"She refuses. She says you're the one with the problem."

"Is she correct?" Up to this point, I had avoided putting Mrs. Lareau on the spot. I had to know where things were going.

"No. You're perfectly normal. A little too smart for your own good, but you're perfectly—"

"Normal. With an abnormal home life, an abnormal relationship with my foster parents. One who thinks I'm seducing the other."

"You have a point," Mrs. Lareau said in her thick French accent. "There are not any foster homes to place you in, Ariana. I've looked into it. You have to salvage this."

"What's my alternative?"

"You don't have one."

"What is it?" I demanded.

"A group home for girls. They're rough, tough, mean, and you don't belong there."

"No kidding." I drew in a breath and tilted my head looking at Nikki. "What does Tim say about all this?"

"He's heartbroken. He loves you very much, but Shari wears the pants."

"Yes, she wears the pants. Maybe she's lesbian and attracted to—"

"This is nothing to joke about. This is serious. Try to spend more time with them. They complain you stay in your room—"

"I do it to get away from her nasty mouth. You know that."

"I know that, Ariana. Shutting yourself off and getting away from her closes down communications. It further separates you two and causes more problems than it avoids."

"Fine. I wasn't going to play soccer again this year."

"You have to do more. You've got to spend time with them after dinner. Talk with Shari. Find out what she does at work. Meet her for lunch tomorrow. Surprise her. School starts next week?"

"Yeah."

"Go to the movies this weekend. Spend a little of your camp money and treat the family to a movie."

Mom, you would have been proud. Today I dressed up, rode the city bus, and surprised Shari at work asking her to lunch. She could not have been happier, and I hated every minute of it. It feels as though she wins something from me when she has her way. I resent it. Enduring her gloating leaves a bad taste in my mouth. Shari gloated while she grazed on a salad then sucked on her cigarette.

I commented on the healthy plants in her office and asked who cared for them. Shari gave me a side glance. I admitted that I figured out she had replaced my ivy plant. After delivering a fake embarrassed laugh, my foster mother said it died before she remembered to water it. I thanked her for being thoughtful enough to replace it, yet inside I was burning. I see it as another insult, another thing she has ruined. She could've at least attempted to buy the same variety of ivy.

Tonight, we're going to the movies. I can imagine the discussion we'll have on the way. The solution is simple. If Tim and I don't agree with Shari's choice, there will be a hefty price to be paid later on.

So here are my choices as I begin the twelfth grade:

1. I can give up on Shari and go to a home better suited for delinquent juveniles who in all likelihood would slit my throat the first hour of my arrival.

2. I can succumb to Shari's whims until I either burn up inside or make it through school. Once I graduate, I'll be closer to turning eighteen. "Close enough," as Nadine would say.

I can't believe I'm writing this let alone feel it. The fact that you died has made my life unbearable, Mom.

*****

Being a senior is no different from being a junior. I had hoped for a feeling of excitement. That sensation is absent. Almost everything is the same as it was when I left school last year. The classes are no different nor the faces, the teachers, the building. Jordan is different. He and Tanya did it. The first day back to school I saw them in the hallway by the lockers kissing as though they did it. I pretended to be happy for him, but I wasn't. Our hurried conversation during lunch ended with the question he had been burning to ask me since we sat down to eat.

"Did you?" he asked about Mark and I.

I lied and said we did. What can I say? In the face of total melt down, I lack the integrity, the courage to stand my ground and support my principles. I have no principles. I have a quick wit and low self-esteem. I readily admit it. Being virgin I'm reluctant to admit. I'm a senior in high school. I should have lots of life experiences to reflect on. Instead, I avoid conversations about parents, family, and sex. That leaves disco, school, and college plans. I feel limited and isolated. Jordan, he's on cloud nine. His enthusiasm for our last year in high school is overflowing. He's on top and going to enjoy the next nine months of his reign.

I have nine months of going to the movies and looking at Shari's smug smile while I sit on the patio after dinner wishing for a hurricane to hit. I'm tired, Mom. I'm tired of being afraid of opening my mouth and have words slip out that earn me a reprimand. I'm tired of having to secure Shari's approval for everything I do, including how I think. I've learned that if I don't, invariably Shari stings me. Tim doesn't step in, although I know he sees what's going on. He takes a swig from his beer and lets out a giddy laugh. Nine months of being their instant daughter who is perfect in every way, that's what I have in front of me.

Mrs. Lareau is my foster child counselor, not my friend. I realize her mission is to provide me with a foster home. In her eyes, the Andrewses are better than a group home. She asks what I'm doing to open myself to the Andrewses and snuffs any remarks that reflect my honest resentment and resistance. Shari has won. I don't know exactly what she has won though.

If there was another foster home available, I'd be in it. But there isn't, and it's not worth wishing for one. Besides, I couldn't leave Nikki. As it is, she's yelled at daily for pawing at the kitchen window, usually smearing it with mud and sand. Cleaning the window has become one of my afternoon chores. I do it so that Nikki only receives a raised voice instead of a scolding then being chained to a palm tree. Tim let it slip that is what Shari did over the summer while I was away, chained up Nikki.

I'm thankful for Mark. He's faithful to his promise and writes every day. My Georgia college friend has a way of converting Shari's behavior into a comedy routine. He actually draws cartoons and adds captions. I stare at his letters before I go to sleep. Mark's words bring a smile to my face especially when I superimpose his Southern accent on them. He tells me what life at college is like, at least for him. Although I don't look that great in red, I wear the Georgia Bull Dog T-shirt Mark sent me.

I was hoping Jordan would be jealous of Mark, but he's not. He says he's impressed. Dating a college student is considered a coup.

Daniella spent the summer with her grandparents somewhere in the Midwest. She rode horses, fed piglets, and came back with a flawless pig call. We go to the lake after school; that's where she teaches me pig calls. Mostly we talk and stare at the water. I can't figure her out. For hours we'll talk about Mark and Jordan, and when I ask Daniella who she has an eye for, she gives me the same reply, "I prefer not to mess my life up with a relationship."

I think she has a mature approach to our strange compulsion to bond with a mate. We forget that the honeymoon eventually ends. Daniella has a lot of experience in relationships that don't work. She's the referee for her parents.

I often wonder who is the child, the parent or the offspring?

*****

Flashback. Similar to a drug-induced psychotic experience, Patrick Muldune and Mrs. Lareau were at the house today. This time I wasn't asked to leave with Tim's pager and come back when it beeped. The discussion topic was me, not Nadine. I had the pleasure of staying for the full ten rounds for this bout. Shari jabbed, I ducked, and Patrick Muldune played referee. He sent us to our separate corners when he blew the whistle for water breaks.

The stakes were high on this Saturday afternoon. Depending on my conditioning, I could rid myself of an impossible home life and land myself in a group home or stay and continue playing daughter to a woman I despise. Shari's rewards were equally enticing. If she was quicker than me and more ruthless, she would have the choice to either rid herself of a daughter who cannot get the role right or accept the daughter she has, as is.

I'm unsure which ignited this final bout, if it was my outrage or Shari's. In the week leading up to the main event, Shari made comments about things she could not have known unless she was reading my letters to Mark. I had no evidence yet suspected, going with the feeling in my gut. By Friday she had slipped. Or better termed, my foster mother flipped.

Shari came home early yesterday evening before I had a chance to complete my afternoon chores. She burst into my room complaining of my neglect. How could I be studying instead of preparing the castle for the queen? I shook my head and stared out the window, my silent reply to her protest. My gesture was enough for her to know what I was thinking, and she said it. Word for word Shari repeated my recent letter's description of my beloved foster mother. "Witch in the strongest sense of the word holding back none of the tools of the trade—a wicked tongue, a piercing stare, a threat with her hand in the air, and a heart forever frozen with hate."

She had proudly confirmed my suspicions and flaunted her horrible deed in my face. It was the last slap I would allow her to deliver. This time I didn't turn my other cheek. I no longer feared being dismissed from my position as a daughter to a childless couple. Rage engulfed my body.

Stealing my letters to Mark, Shari crossed a sacred line. This violation she perpetrated was beyond an irritating attack designed to establish her reign. Shari had virtually pulled out a gun and loaded it with her insecurity, fear, and disappointment. As my foster mother, she holds the power. This is her home, and I am allowed to live here as long as she deems me worthy. The price I am asked to pay for the privilege is to bow to her, to give up privacy. She was used to getting away with pistol-whipping me. No one was willing to stop her. Friday, I took my fate in my own hands.

Shari failed to see that I was no longer a scared child; I was done being bullied. My foster mother had declared war. I grabbed her weapon from her. I unloaded her bullets and loaded it with my own unspoken resentment, revenge, and resistance to her endless barrages. Pointing the gun at her, I knew it meant my days with the Andrewses were over. I understood it meant I failed at being their foster daughter. I did not hesitate. I shot my hurtful words into her face. She withered from my explosion. Standing before me, she winced as each word impacted her fragile ego. It is a bad idea to pull out a gun and aim it without the intention to shoot, her mistake. When I reached for the gun, I knew the instant I put my hand on it that I would unload all the words I felt, all the words I had squelched. When I aim, I shoot to kill.

Shari had no retaliation. She attempted one more insult by saying that she had been reading my letters all along. I was angry at myself for being so foolish, placing them in our mailbox. Mark received my letters only after Shari carefully opened, read, then resealed them. There was nothing further to say after the gun was emptied. We were at a stalemate.

As she sat on the opposite round sofa this evening, Shari looked at Patrick Muldune and said, "I can handle it if she were pregnant. If she were on drugs. If she were flunking out of school"—she pointed to me and finished the debate—"but I cannot handle that."

Mom, I honestly don't comprehend what Shari cannot handle. I would think my being pregnant, drug dependent, or unable to stay in school would be major problems. What is it about me that this woman cannot handle? She invades my privacy and reads my innermost thoughts then punishes me for having them. She violates with a capital V. How does she believe a thinking, feeling human being would respond? With love, respect, honor, and my other cheek? Dutifully, I sat with Patrick Muldune, Mrs. Lareau, Tim, and Shari, knowing this was a required procedure and necessary to document it for my file before the final words were written. "Ariana is no longer welcomed in the Andrews home."

Words, words, words—symbols that carry our emotions, reveal our intent, cloak our lies, and seal our fate.

Acting upon Shari's final decree, I retreated from the queen's audience. The boxing match had ended. I threw in the towel as was expected of me. I knew my next obligation without being told. I gathered up and loaded my belongings into Mrs. Lareau's trunk. Somehow Patrick Muldune had maneuvered a last-minute reprieve while I was absent from the living room. Two weeks. I was given two weeks. The Andrewses had agreed to a time out, to reconsider. I suspect it gives Patrick Muldune and Mrs. Lareau precious time to find me an emergency foster home.

My fate is obvious, I have no illusions. Shari cannot accept the words I had thrown back at her. She has delivered too many in the course of two and a half years. My emancipation was concentrated, and each word carried my heartfelt resentment. There is no going back. I have attacked the queen. Thus was the ending to my stay with the Andrewses.

Casualties of war, Nikki and I must separate. I hate being a foster child. I am homeless. My parent is the state. I own what now rests in Mrs. Lareau's trunk less the contents of a liquor box we quickly packed when Patrick Muldune walked out to the driveway with news of the postponement. I haven't taken anything out of the liquor box except your letter. It's the one thing I value above all else. I feel safe knowing Shari has not desecrated it with her eyes.

Nothing. I have nothing in this world except me. Before I let go of my words on Friday afternoon, I did not even have me. My bedroom is a room connected to someone's house and offered to me at a deep, personal expense. The Andrewses' rent for my bedroom grew too steep when I was asked to give up myself. For a while I was willing to release even that. This fact scares me, Mom. If I sell myself in exchange for a home, what do I have left?

I sit here on a Saturday night by the window. I have your letter propped on a book and I wonder. Have I failed you? Have I failed myself? My fate is precarious, Mom. I saw the worried look in Patrick's eyes. I heard the strain in Mrs. Lareau's voice when we packed the liquor box. She said things could be worked out. Why do people use words to mask how they feel?

What will I do without my Nikki? I'm familiar with everything in this house as if it were my own. It is not. I've cleaned every centimeter and cared for every plant surrounding the exterior, and yet none of it was ever mine. None of it mattered. I'll be gone. Jordan will forget my name. Mark will continue sending letters to Shari's house, and she'll hoard each one.

CHAPTER 13

Friday afternoon Mrs. Lareau drove to the Andrewses' house, alone. Patrick Muldune's services were no longer needed. There was nothing further for him to do. Negotiations had concluded. The war was over. Shari had fulfilled her agreement to wait fourteen long, awkward days then delivered her final word at the end, "Out." As hoped, the two-week deferment gave Mrs. Lareau enough time to find me another foster home. By some miracle, I was spared the group home alternative. I am grateful, Mom, if you were one of the angels working on my behalf. Divine intervention had to be in play. Foster homes are scarce, and foster children, well, we seem to be increasing in numbers exponentially.

I waited in the front yard for Mrs. Lareau's car to pull up the driveway. Nikki whined. She knew that more than the fence was separating us. I comforted her, gently clutching her and the liquor box. We had said our goodbyes, yet letting go of Nikki, walking away from the fence, and ignoring her whines when Mrs. Lareau opened the car door ripped off a piece of my heart and left it behind the fence.

As we backed out of the driveway, my eyes glanced over to the Boston ferns growing along the walkway. I wondered how I would explain things to Granddad. Indiana is light-years from the Andrewses' home. An urge to rip up the ferns and take them with me flooded my veins. Then an intense light flashed inside my head. Suddenly, I was living the dream I had at camp. My head dropped into my hands, and I heard the screams again. This time I understood. It was not a nuclear explosion. This was my life melting into nothingness. The screams were mine. All of the unheard cries remained trapped inside my mind as the light seared my brain cells and burned through my memories. The dream had been a warning of what was to come. I reflected on my situation as Mrs. Lareau drove me from reality. I had sustained many blows during my war with Shari; I am not only deaf but am now blind. In a flash, my world died.

Mrs. Lareau was bubbly during the drive to Coral Gables. I should have detected that something was up, but my mind was on the crushing ache I felt in my heart and the blinding light in my head. Mrs. Lareau told me about my new foster mother, preparing me for my new foster home. I had been through this routine before. Knowing what was ahead of me didn't ease the terror burning inside.

My fate and my life hung balanced on two-week increments. Jessica Lareau, using her French accent ever so eloquently, neglected to tell me that my new foster home was temporary, very temporary. Luanne's home was meant to be a depot. My counselor needed more time to find me a permanent foster home. During her debriefing, I'm glad Mrs. Lareau forgot to mention Luanne agreed to be my foster mother, for two weeks.

Luanne had recently earned a master's degree in psychology at the University of Miami and was volunteering at the Catholic Services Bureau, until I came along. My new foster mother is a sexagenarian and widowed nearly ten years now. I was disappointed to learn I was moving in with a woman who was alone. No children, her five had grown. No cat or dog, but she has a garden. A luscious vegetable garden in the backyard, that's how I met Luanne. She was wearing muddied clothes and a warm smile.

Luanne stood by the front door and apologized for the dirt on her arms and shoes as she gave me a hug and welcomed me to her home. Ignoring the inside of her house, I was immediately presented to Luanne's backyard. It is a miniature paradise in the middle of Coral Gables. Like a centurion, a huge ficus tree stands with branches out spread, touching every corner of her sanctuary. In the back near the fence are pineapples, ginger plants, and banana trees. On the sides are lemon trees readying to bloom fragrant, tiny white flowers. Scattered in between are exotic plants like the fig vine that crawls up the trellis near my bedroom window.

Luanne's garden reflects her personality. Neat rows of carrots, lettuce, and tomatoes are protected by a perimeter row of delicate herbs. My mouth waters when I breathe in the aroma of crisp basil. An avocado tree stands over the garden providing would-be thieves an alternative meal. It didn't take me long to figure out that I must watch where I place my feet when near the garden. Half-eaten avocados wait for an unsuspecting foot. The squirrels often pluck, nibble, then leave exposed avocados for less agile scavengers. The first time my foot found one, it reminded me of stepping in dog poop, but it was of course an awful green oozing between my toes instead.

After being introduced to the most important feature of her home, Luanne ushered Mrs. Lareau and me inside. My foster mother cheerfully opened the door to my room. She stood in the doorway as I timidly walked in, feeling amazement at its size. The closet was bare, the dresser empty. I glanced at the queen size bed with a handmade quilt draped on its end and knew I was home. It had been waiting for me. Luanne was careful not to walk beyond the doorway. I looked back to her and smiled. Her weathered face and wrinkled grin sparkled with delight.

Mrs. Lareau was happy to unload her car saying she felt as though a body was in the trunk. As she gave me a goodbye hug, my counselor said, "The Andrewses will never be given the custody of a child again. You are the closest they'll get to having a daughter. If you can find it in your heart, stay in touch, include them in your life even in the smallest way. It would make two very lonely people happy."

I gave her a kiss on the cheek then nodded to her knowing it would be a while before I called the Andrewses, if ever.

Mom, why do I have to turn the other cheek? Why can't I wallow in my rejection? Why can't I turn them into a lifelong resentment? Why do I have to be the parent?

The contents of Mrs. Lareau's trunk lay on the bed, waiting for me to do something with them. I reacquainted myself with my possessions then organized them. After carefully placing my precious mementos in boxes Mrs. Lareau had collected for me, I stashed them along with the emptied clothes boxes in the closet. My clothes filled two drawers leaving the rest of the dresser empty. I tucked your letter in the top drawer knowing Luanne respects me and my privacy. Luanne's eyes will not glance at this letter without my permission.

My room is barren, yet loneliness is absent.

Looking through white wooden blinds, I noticed Luanne was in her garden plucking weeds and delicately touching the new growth of her loving efforts. The enticing sunlight caressing my bed was too much to resist; I lay my body down telling myself, "Just a short nap before I go out to the garden."

There was a knock at my door, and I opened my eyes to Luanne's image standing in the hallway wiping her wet hands with a kitchen towel. The sun was setting, and its gentle light filled my room and illuminated Luanne's face.

"Are you ready to make a salad?"

"I must have fallen asleep," I replied, feeling embarrassed.

"Naps can be regenerative for the emotionally exhausted." She turned and walked toward the kitchen.

I followed behind. "What do you want in your salad?"

"Whatever you put in it," she said.

"Oh. Well, do you like—"

"There is no right or wrong, Ariana. Make your own choices. I'm sure a vegetarian knows how to make a salad." Luanne smiled to me, opened the garage door, then shut it behind her.

I stood before an open refrigerator and scanned for choices. Luanne came back into the kitchen with a load of clothes in her hands.

"I hope you like onions," I said.

Luanne stopped in her tracks and turned to me, saying, "Ariana, put each ingredient in because you want to, not because you want to please me. I'll pick out what I don't like. There is very little grown from the earth that I don't like."

She meant what she said. With gentleness, she picked out the onions then ate the salad, not hiding her delight. My first dinner with Luanne set the tone for our relationship—polite and peaceful. I'm free to express, and she listens, considers, responds. She has had a lot of practice with teenagers; she has been trained by her own five. I suppose that is why she recently earned a master's in psychology. I'm guessing she has a lot of insights to offer the world.

That night, we discussed school, and Luanne encouraged me to make my first decision about my future. I chose to continue going to Miami Sunset. It's only September, yet the thought of attending another school is, well, it's inconceivable. This commitment I've made, in order to have some continuity, has a price tag. I'm up at five in the morning and on the street corner by five thirty, waiting for the city bus. The ride to school demands an hour and fifteen minutes, but it doesn't seem that long. My nose is inside my books until I step off the bus.

We were in Naples when I learned the truth about Luanne's intended brief role as my foster parent. Exactly a week after I had arrived, Luanne made sandwiches and packed her old, powder blue Lincoln while I rode the city bus home from school. Within minutes of walking through the front door, I found myself in the passenger seat with the seatbelt fastened. The sun was setting as Luanne drove west across the one lane highway cutting through the Everglades. My sixty-year-old foster mother put pedal to metal, passing trucks and slow motorists. Her adventurous nature transformed the long, straight highway into a blur. We were in the oncoming traffic lane more often than not. I found comfort looking at the landscape instead of ahead. Low, puffy clouds hung in the horizon and reflected the sun's light. Yellow and pink refracted off shallow standing water and danced on cypress tree trunks. The Everglades is a magnificent, shallow river oozing with life. I discovered Florida's backyard and fell in love with cypress trees while Luanne sped down State Road 84.

Annie, Luanne's daughter, was astonished by our "making such good time." Evidently for some years, she hasn't been a passenger in her mother's car. With a grin stretched across her face, Annie pried my white knuckles from the car door handle. I staggered into her two-bedroom villa, saying a silent prayer of thanks for our safe arrival.

No one seemed to notice I was not a part of the original plans. Annie has lived in Naples for less than eight months. New job, new friends, new area for Luanne's oldest daughter, she had invited her mother for the weekend on the west coast of Florida to see her new life. Annie seemed delighted to share it with me as well. She treated me as if I were a member of the family. We went boating, swimming, shopping, and out to dinner with her new friends. With her camera in hand, Luanne's daughter documented our entire weekend. I like Annie and not because we share a passion for photography. She spoke to me as if we had been friends for a lifetime. Annie noticed the parallels in our lives, her recent divorce from a possessive husband, my recent divorce from…well, do I have to write it?

Before I braved the trip back to Miami across the Everglades with Luanne at the wheel, Annie pulled me aside. She said, "Mom needs you. You need my mom. That means she has to change her two-week status as temporary foster mom to permanent foster mom. It wasn't hard to convince her. She says you two are a lot alike. I can see her in you. Aren't your birthdays a week a part?"

I nodded.

"If she becomes too much of a pain in the butt, you come live with me. Okay?"

I nodded again, holding back the tears. For being twenty-six, Annie has an uncanny ability to remember what it feels to be sixteen.

*****

Mark called this past weekend. He said he labored for weeks making a billion phone calls to track me down. I had almost forgotten about him, but I didn't say so. Instead, I explained that his letters have yet to catch up to me at my new foster home. Apparently, Shari is a slow reader. Mark wants me to move to Georgia and stay at his mom's to finish high school. I declined. He's a great kisser, but my heart is in Florida. Mark was disappointed I hadn't called or written despite my recent move. He doesn't understand. It takes time to adjust, to remember where the silverware is, where the dishes go, and if it's okay to say pseudo cuss words like poop or dang. Jordan doesn't get it either, although he would never admit it.

Jordan had no clue that I moved, and I was reluctant to tell him, yet I had to. I had to explain my remiss in my duties as president of the Soccerrettes. Because of the city bus schedules, attending the

Soccerrettes meetings means I don't arrive home until seven thirty, when it's dark. I don't mind taking the city bus in the early morning; the bus driver knows me and expects to see me standing there at his first stop of the day. The evening bus passengers intimidate me. It's unsafe riding the city bus after dusk.

I made Jordan swear he wouldn't breathe a word about my situation. I know he won't. He's solid that way. His girlfriend, Tanya, is in the Soccerrettes, and she's the one doing most of the talking. She complains about my recent absence. She's right, although much of her venom is directed toward me for personal reasons. I had approached Coach Friedman ready to give up my post, yet he rejected my resignation. Coach knows about my transportation problem, and why I have one. In exchange for being sensitive to my circumstances, I've tied his hands. I've asked him not to say anything to the disgruntled Soccerrettes in my defense because I would rather have the girls think that I'm a lazy club president than a pathetic foster child.

Coach Friedman is my psychology teacher as well as the boys soccer team coach. He's eccentric on and off the field. To illustrate the chapter on probabilities and guessing, Coach Friedman implemented a contest using football scores forecasting. So far, I've won the extra credit points every week. He decided my lucky predictions are extraordinary and asked that I take a psychology test. After weeks of his relentless insistence, I took the test. The results were surprising to me, but not to him. According to his insignificant psych test, when it comes to extrasensory perception, I'm at the mastery level. For a while I thought I was a victim of one of his famous psych experiments, yet my classmates insisted that wasn't the case. To convince me that the test results are valid, Coach Friedman brought a memory computer game to class. As he hoped, the game demonstrated my unusual talent in front of witnesses. Though I try, it's hard to deny what I did. Coach Freidman's goal was not to measure my memory capacity. He theorized I could accurately predict the computer's future selections. I did, without error. He exclaimed to the class, "She can see into the future."

He wants me to take more psychology tests, and I've refused. I have enough that separates me from the normal. Coach Friedman thinks I've "developed a hypersensitivity in response to a sense of lack of control." Whatever. He's a psychology teacher. I chose Coach Friedman's psychology class because it's the last one of the day. I figured sixth period psychology would be a good way to end the long days at school, sitting around analyzing the abnormalities of human behavior. God knows I've spent years doing that contemplating the Andrewses.

Coach drove me home yesterday after the Soccerrettes meeting. I think he wanted to see where I live to be sure I actually have a home. In the driveway, Luanne and Coach Friedman chatted about psychology and Freud. I was afraid the subject would digress into a discussion about me, yet it didn't. I must break this conditioning the Andrewses inflicted on me. I don't want to go through life feeling fearful that people's conversations will eventually lead to a psychological analysis of me.

I just experienced an insight. Perhaps that's what Coach Friedman was referring to. I was thinking about how pervasive fear has been in my life. Fear triggers my feeling of being out of control. The most intense, fearful time in my life was about a year before you died. I knew cancer was going to take your life and reluctantly, but eventually, I had accepted your fate. Oddly, I was terrified a car accident would steal you from us sooner than the cancer. I was overcome by the fear that the precious few months we had a mother would be stolen by something out of our control. Fear is a powerful force; it's capable of bending the mind. Coach Friedman is right. I see how my life has been out of control, creating my need to compensate. Is that why I can predict the future? To prepare for it, to brace for life's hiccups?

Another cognition just entered my mind. When I think about what will happen to me in the future, my mind is blank. There's a darkness in front of me. I can imagine Daniella's life still to unfold; I can see Luanne's and the Andrewses'. I have no sense of myself in the future. I wonder, why?

*****

I pulled out the vacuum a few weeks ago and thought Luanne was going to faint. She was wondering when one of us would find it. It appears my tolerance for dirt is lower than Luanne's; she can ignore it longer than me. I've established a weekly cleaning routine, neglecting Luanne's room and laundry, thus honoring her request. She says I'm not a maid. I'm glad she noticed.

Luanne and I are planning to celebrate our birthdays on her son's boat. Samuel has promised to anchor by the mangrove flats so we can snorkel. I understand it's a great place to find horseshoe crabs and nurse sharks. I'm looking forward to being in the water again.

Samuel lives in Coral Gables with his wife, Monica, and their two-year-old daughter, Emmy. They've asked for my babysitting services, and I've avoided committing. I don't want anything to cut into my standing social appointment with Daniella. We go to Coconut Grove and listen to local bands Friday and Saturday nights. Unfortunately, we're not allowed in the bars, so we sit outside and engage in some serious people watching. Luanne's house is Daniella's personal weekend retreat. I think she loves the backyard jungle more than I do. We lie in the sun and listen to the guy next door. His jazz band, five music students from the University of Miami, religiously practice every Saturday afternoon.

Luanne has been hinting for me to get a job. I loathe the idea. I'll have the rest of my life to work, why push the inevitable? She tells me that after having five teenagers, she can see the signs. She says, "Financial independence is a socially acceptable expression of self-identity." Luanne's psychology-speak loses something in the translation.

My sexagenarian friend has few rules for me to follow. She heavily relies on life to teach me. There is no curfew, no punishment for saying what is on my mind, and Luanne doesn't put me on restriction for leaving my clothes in the dryer. She puts my clothes aside and does her laundry around mine. There is one rule Luanne has asked that I never break and that is to tell the truth, always.

Luanne says we create our life by the choices we make. I have choices instead of being forced to live by the laws of another. I don't have to respond to someone's words, someone's voice, someone's intent. No one has control over another. This is an amazing revelation. I am my own person. I wish I had figured this out while I was in Mrs. Roth's class. I would have declined her invitation to read out loud. I had a choice. Mrs. Roth, she would have failed me if I declined. But I had a choice to fail or read in front of the class. I didn't realize that.

Mrs. Lareau said Luanne and I are either having an unusually long honeymoon or are extremely compatible housemates. Luanne explained to me what has been occurring. Teenagers naturally separate from their parents. I'm in an awkward position because of my situation. I'm being asked to bond at the same time that I feel a compulsion to separate. I'm determined to correct the mistakes I made with the Andrewses. I'd rather avoid separation altogether. Almost two months have passed since I first walked through Luanne's front door, and I've finally made a choice. I've decided Luanne is not my foster mother—she's much more. She's my friend.

CHAPTER 14

Initially, Mrs. Lareau called weekly to check on my progress. Lately, however, her phone calls have dwindled to once in a while. I have a feeling she's realized that I've a personal counselor right here at home.

This afternoon Luanne and I were in the backyard pruning banana trees, pulling weeds, and raking avocado leaves. We were knee-deep in trees, weeds, and leaves when she decided this would be her last year of vegetable gardening. It bothered me she would eliminate the garden from her backyard sanctuary, and I said so. Luanne knows how to hear beyond words. She promised that she would stick around until at least the year two thousand because "Life is still interesting. Gardening, however, is hard on my back. So I'm gonna let that one go." I believe her, that she'll be around at the turn of the century. I know I can count on her.

Luanne talks for hours about her five "darling" children. I know everything there is to know about them, yet I know next to nothing about their mom. I ask questions about her life, and she tells me about her husband. He was a surgeon. They met when he was finishing medical school. After their small wedding ceremony, Luanne and her young doctor shipped off to Panama where he was commissioned in the army's war effort. It sounded romantic, almost like a fairy tale. Unlike fairy tales though, there was an ending. Twenty some odd years later, her husband suffered a heart attack and died, leaving Luanne to an empty house that now echoes with the voices of grandchildren during the holidays.

As we bagged up yard debris, my mature friend asked me why I had no boyfriend, and I told her about Jordan. She smiled at the end of my sad, very sad story.

"So you're gonna be an old maid?"

"Probably. I'm a senior in high school. No car, no boyfriend, no life."

"Since there's no one in your life right now, why don't you spend your time being the best you can be to attract the best him available?"

I tilted my head to the side.

"I didn't marry until I was almost twenty-five," she continued. "When I was your age, I knew I was destined to have a husband and children, but I wasn't sure when it would come. My wise mother suggested I go to college since there was no man in my life when I graduated high school. So I went. There still was no man in my life when I got out of college, so my mother said I should get a job while I was waiting. So I did."

"How did you meet your husband?"

"My sister was graduating from medical school. They were lab partners. I went to her graduation, and the rest is history."

"What are you going to do now?" I asked her.

"Find another hobby when this garden is done producing and be the best foster mother I can."

I smile thinking about Luanne's words as they repeat in my head, and I write them down for you. I thank God that I found her and her garden. Sometimes when the lights are out and the house is quiet, I slip out of my bed and open the blinds. I stare at the garden and wonder if you can hear my thoughts. I wonder if you know that I feel a deep anger when I think about your quick hand that delivered more blows to my face and young body than I can count. I wonder if you know I love you, and I wonder if you regret beating the only things that mattered in the end, your five daughters.

This letter has to end. Soon, I will no longer be a foster child or a child for that matter. I will be an adult, legal age. I bet I'll get carded even then—I look like I'm twelve. I'm five feet four inches with dimples. I define the standard set for being cute. People at school mistake me for a freshman.

Mom, I have no idea what I'm going to do with my life. So far, I've spent it struggling to stay alive. That's all I know. What do I do when I graduate in the spring? What do I do when I turn eighteen? I can't work in a bakery all my life. They don't pay that well, and eventually I want my own house. Did I write about my job? I was hired because I promised to learn the Spanish names for all the pastries.

On the corner of Bird Road and Red Road is a family-owned bakery. It's within walking distance. I work four afternoons a week and proudly report that I now have a decent grasp of Spanish, speaking it with an almost perfect accent. And I've gained a few pounds eating croissants and flan. Flan has eggs in it, but I can't resist.

The bread baker teaches me popular Cuban cuss words and phrases. I practice them on the cake maker who gets red in the face and yells at his brother for teaching me such things. When they raise their voices, I find an excuse to head for cover. They've been known to throw handfuls of flour and dough to make their point.

I missed the city bus last week, so Daniella drove me to work, causing her to be late for her job in Dadeland Mall. We're working women now. Gas money isn't a problem for us anymore; it's her reputation. The grapevine has labeled her a lesbian. I wonder what they think of me. It doesn't stop me from being her friend. Daniella is part of my new family.

Luanne's son, Samuel, says Daniella is a tomboy, not a lesbian. She has been on Samuel's boat for several mangrove snorkeling trips. It was she who discovered the ship door and nearly pulled it out of the water before Samuel had a chance to maneuver the boat closer to the sandbar. The wooden galley door is completely intact. It's stored in Samuel's garage. He has plans to convert it into a cocktail table.

Of all our adventures on Samuel's boat, so far our birthday celebration was the best. Luanne and I toasted to a combined seventy-eight years of living. Daniella, Samuel, Monica, and Emmy lit candles they hastily pushed into a lopsided homemade cake. They had hidden it in the cooler. Holding hands and taking in a deep breath, Luanne and I blew out our candles together. There weren't seventy-eight candles. Samuel explained that safety outweighs tradition. We ate cake before lunch because Luanne and I like to devour dessert first. We unloaded sandwiches and drinks on shore—best lunch ever.

In between sandwich bites, Luanne revealed her wish to me. "I wished for another sixty-one years and told God that if there's not that many years left, then let however many there are to be as happy and fulfilled as the ones I've had." I didn't tell her my wish. I simply hoped for all the years ahead of me to be as happy as this day, unlike the years I had lived before.

I tested Luanne's curfew, and sure enough, there isn't one. Last Friday, Daniella and I stayed out all night. We started with swimming in her neighbor's pool, then drove to Coconut Grove, and ended up at the beach yelling pig calls before the police pulled up and sent us home. The next morning, after two hours of sleep, I woke to the sound of Luanne's voice. She said Samuel had called and was on his way to pick us up for our boating excursion.

When I declined, she reminded me, "This is one of those moments that life is going to teach you consequences. You agreed to go boating with us before you went out last night. You made a commitment."

"Yeah, but I have a headache from pig calling."

"You have no curfew except your own common sense, and if you didn't use it, that's not Samuel's fault, or mine. Get up, get your suit on, and make sandwiches. Remember no onions on mine."

Luanne has not raised her voice to me. She's done worse. She makes sense and is logical. Luanne treats me as an adult, leaving me no room to fall back on the role of a child.

That morning, I rolled out of bed and eventually onto Samuel's boat. The waves were two to four feet, and I felt every boat bounce in my head. I no longer have an urge to stay out all night, let alone scream until my head hurts.

Speaking of no more hurt, my braces were removed. My tongue constantly passes over my teeth; it's wondering where the sharp edges have gone. It's amazing how slippery enamel is. Thankfully, I have a job; I had to fork over seventy dollars for a retainer. The orthodontist said he has to reimburse the lab. In other words, my retainer isn't a tax write-off. I'm supposed to wear it until I'm thirty years old. What a strange thought, me being thirty. The orthodontist told me that if my wisdom teeth grow in, they have to be removed surgically to prevent my teeth from shifting. Surgery sounds radical. Why do we have wisdom teeth? Does it indicate that time in our lives when our bodies are completed with the process of growing thus marking a time of maturity? I wonder if I'll grow wisdom teeth.

This weekend I called Shari and Tim. They sounded excited to hear from me. The only reason I called was because I felt badly for them. The orthodontist mentioned the Andrewses had separated for several weeks after I moved out. I never thought that Shari and Tim would contemplate divorce. My leaving had more impact on them than I previously believed.

Nikki is doing well. She gave me a hello bark over the phone. Shari and Tim invited me over their house for Christmas Eve, and I accepted. I hope Daniella doesn't have plans because I'm not going to the Andrewses without her. Besides, I don't have a car, and I prefer that Shari and Tim not know where I live.

Since the holidays are fast approaching, Daniella and I made plans to go shopping together. I have a long Christmas list. In addition to Daniella, there is Tasha and Cammy, the Andrewses, Mrs. Lareau, and Luanne and her family to buy for this year. Did I mention how thankful I am that I have a job?

I have a Jordan update, and it hurts me to write these words (not really). He broke up with Tanya. Yes! I don't have time after school to visit him as I did, but we have our lunches together now that Tanya is out of the picture.

This week, one of the counselors from the YMCA camp, Jon, transferred to Miami Sunset. He ran into me at lunch, literally. While I brushed spaghetti off my jeans, Jon asked about Mark then admitted how jealous he was of my Georgia college man. Jon said he was still in love with me if I could ever see past Mark. I thought Jordan would keel over backward and drop dead hearing those words. It was perfect. Jon reached out to give me a hug, and I made sure it was an extra-long one, for Jordan's sake.

My dear Jordan remains a friend, yet I know he feels deeper for me than our lunches at school indicate. I don't know why he hasn't asked me out. The closest he's come to dating me is escorting me to my class following lunch. I really wish he wouldn't respect me so much.

Luanne tells me that dating is a social ritual beset with codes, signals, mores, insecurities, and mysteries. Why can't it be simple? "I like you, would you like to go out?" Why can't he say those words to me? Why do I have to know the intricacies of his college plans and his views on premarital sex, but not have a clue what the inside of his truck looks like?

I asked Jordan if he thought I was lesbian. He nearly swallowed his tongue as soon as the words left my lips. Jordan knows I'm not. I should have said, "So then what's the problem? Why don't you ask me out?"

I'm a foster child. Perhaps that's the reason for his hesitation.

*****

I'm writing to you on Christmas night. Luanne's children have collected their kids and gone home. Quiet is descending upon the house, yet I can hear their voices in my head and see camera flashes capturing smiles and goofy poses.

We shared an elaborate holiday dinner this evening; I had the honor of contributing bread and pastries to our feast. They were freshly baked yesterday morning at Red Road Bakery. My employers surprised me with a large container of flan when I stopped in to pick up my order last night. I work for the best bakers in town.

Throughout Christmas morning and afternoon, various family members meandered into the kitchen to assist me and Luanne with meal preparations. Luanne's family asked about school and my plans for college. They wanted to know how many years of higher education I plan to pursue before beginning my writing career. I appreciate their assumptions.

Annie wandered into my room and noticed the boxes stacked in my closet. She met up with me in the kitchen and asked why I was storing empty boxes in my closet.

I answered, "I may need them."

"For what?"

I shrugged my shoulders, but we both knew why.

The next thing I knew my closet was emptied, the boxes were flattened and dragged out to the curb, and I was no longer holding onto a notion of temporariness.

After dinner, Annie asked to see a picture of Jordan. I whipped out Miami Sunset's first yearbook and proudly presented his many sides. She's the only person besides me who noticed that Jordan's right eye squints more than his left when he smiles.

Luanne's children were touched by my thoughtfulness. She told me it wasn't necessary to give them gifts. I didn't do it because I felt obligated knowing they were coming over on Christmas Day. It was a natural gesture of affection.

In contrast, the Christmas Eve visit with Shari and Tim was strained and mercifully brief. Shari prepared a crustacean seafood buffet leaving seaweed for me to munch on. I haven't been gone enough months for her to forget that I'm vegetarian. The Andrewses, Daniella, and I exchanged gifts and hugs and few words. Daniella said my voice was about three octaves higher than usual. I guess that's what happens when I pretend everything is wonderful when it's not.

Daniella loved her Hanukkah gift; she cried. I gave her a stuffed animal, a life-size foal, with a red ribbon tied around his neck. Taped to the ribbon was a short story I wrote for her titled "Fury's Baptism."

Remember our beloved horse's first bath? Mom, I had been the butt of many family jokes for years because of it. At least now I can laugh about it, and write about it. At the time I was mortified. I naively accepted my responsibility to clean Fury's back legs and rear end and honestly believed that our revered horse lifted his tail to help me. Daniella laughed out loud as she read the part about how my sense of pride gave way to sheer humiliation when Fury expelled gas in my face with so much force that it blew my hair. Too bad all my sisters witnessed my equine baptism. Events like that create family legends.

Daniella said my story helped her understand what it must be like to be a foster parent. With keen insight, my friend hinted that caring for and loving another being is a labor of love. I felt more compassion for Shari and Tim after she said that. So today I called and thanked the Andrewses for the Christmas Eve gathering, the gifts, and their love. Tim cried on the phone. He said my phone call was the best Christmas gift they've ever had.

Granddad's hearing is slipping further into nothingness, and his handwriting is barely readable, yet he managed to write Christmas cards this year and enclose a check. I imagine he's already asleep having stuffed himself with turkey and cranberry sauce. Aunt Ruth is a good cook and a compassionate companion to an aging man. I hope they weren't lonely today.

Tasha and Cammy called this morning to wish me a merry Christmas and tell me they loved the gifts I sent. They have yet to figure out how to play the computer game I sent them. It's similar to the one Coach Friedman used in class. I guess my propensity for ESP isn't genetic. Well, I had to know.

My sisters asked about the weather. They regretted their question when I told them it was eighty. I reluctantly admitted I was wearing a pair of shorts then quickly said I wore a sweater in the morning. It didn't ease their envy. They said Samantha and Nadine had to waitress today and called before they went into work. The guy Nadine is living with is a pig farmer. I never pictured Nadine with a devout meat-eater let alone—I can't write it again. I bet they had ham for dinner.

Tasha is on the swim team and doing quite well. Cammy is being teased by our cousins and kids in school. She received my share of female endowment in addition to her own. I have too little and she too much. Is there a perfect body for a teenage girl?

I chose this night to write you because I want this Christmas to be complete, being with all my families. Ever since you died, Christmas has lost its sparkle. I attended midnight mass last night with Luanne hoping I would find the spirit of Christmas lurking in church. If it was there, I didn't feel it. I don't know if it's because I'm not a child anymore or if it's because you're gone. Christmas is a day set aside for family and friends. Today, that's what I did. I hope someday I'll find the spirit of Christmas in my heart. This is my hope as I write to you on this night.

Luanne tells me that Christmas is an idea we create in our hearts and manifest in our lives. She goes to church every Sunday, and without fail, she invites me to join her. I prefer the backyard. I think church is an idea and not a place.

CHAPTER 15

Shari and Tim called to announce that Nikki has a new home. She'd been jumping the fence and roaming the neighborhood while the Andrewses were at work. They said safety forced them into their decision. I'm heartbroken, yet I know Nikki is probably better off. The Andrewses gave her to a woman who lives alone. That's a good place for Nikki's nurturing to find expression. I hope the woman has strong arms; Nikki is more powerful than she looks.

I'm in the last semester of my last year of high school. It's astounding that I made it this far in life. My heart is not in the books anymore. I'm looking forward to the things that will help me reach graduation day, like senior skip day. Daniella and I are planning to go to the beach. Seniors have been warned that our parents will be called if we skip. Luanne has already given me the okay. She's proud of my honesty and wants to reward me. Her five children have really broken her in.

Senior Grad Night is around the corner. The execution of Grad Night is quite simple. The entire senior class squeezes into four buses parked at Miami Sunset and arrives at Walt Disney World by late afternoon. Then we combine forces with other high schools around Florida to overtake the world-famous theme park for an evening. A night of mayhem and madness, I'm wondering why I'm looking forward to it, yet I am.

Then there's Prom Night in May. I don't have any prospects since Jordan is back with Tanya, not that I had a chance even when they weren't a couple. I'm not into limousine rides anyway. The last limo I was in drove me to your funeral. Daniella said she would go with me to the prom. That's a reputation I can live without. Maybe she and I will treat ourselves to dinner that night.

Luanne has offered to buy my graduation dress. Though graduation is months away, Luanne can see I'm eager for things to go through transition. This must be the longest semester on record; time is mercilessly sluggish. There is one piece of excitement: Luanne bought a new car. A shiny, black Mercedes-Benz majestically rests in our two-car garage. Occasionally, I take her car to school when I know I have to stay late or there's a special event at night.

There's no comparing a Mercedes-Benz to Daniella's VW Rabbit, yet that's my only reference, and it shows in my driving skills. I was sitting at a traffic light in Coral Gables after a rain shower. The light turned green, and I pushed the gas pedal a bit too hard. By the time the tires stopped spinning and grabbed a hold on the road, the Mercedes-Benz and I were a foot from the gas pumps at the corner gasoline station. I don't know whose eyes were wider, mine or the gas station attendant's. Either it's a coincidence or someone witnessed my near mishap because the next day Luanne suggested that I go easy on the gas pedal, as if she has room to give advice about driving with a heavy foot. It was good advice anyway, and timely. I've no intentions of being torched before I graduate. Luanne's children deserve a lot of credit for training their mom so well. If it were my Mercedes-Benz, I'd have a hidden alarm installed to go off the instant my teenager looked at the car.

Luanne and I have been in discussions about college. She gave me a scenario to consider. I'll repeat it for you to give you an idea how she works her influence on a young mind without bending it too far.

"Imagine this," she said, "you're working in Burger King, making four dollars an hour, and one of your buddies from high school walks in, orders a sandwich, and notices you behind the grill stirring up some special sauce."

"Very funny."

"Well, I doubt you'd be doing the grilling being a committed vegetarian."

"Go on, go on."

"Imagine this. You get out of college and go to your first interview, and behind the desk with your résumé in his hand is your future husband."

"Funny. What does he look like?"

Luanne grinned. "That's not the point."

"Oh, I got your point. I wanna know what he looks like."

"Tall, dark, handsome, and college educated."

"Mmmm. What company does he work for?" I questioned.

"A big corporation that employs only vegetarians. There is a nonsmoking policy and exercise breaks every three hours."

"I like it. So I'm gonna have this wonderful life because I go to college and—"

"Ari, go to college so you don't put a ceiling on your potential. That's all. Try a junior college first. Get used to the atmosphere. Take a bunch of classes that you're interested in. Take marine biology and psychology and political science and—"

"There's always Burger King University in Kendall."

"Take a stand-up comedy class. That would be an easy A."

"I don't think I'm smart enough to go to college. My grade point average has been slipping ever since eleventh grade honors English," I honestly replied.

"You're too smart not to. Go this summer and see what it's like. Go before you're eighteen while you have a place to live. Experiment with life while the risks are low. If you like it and do well, I'll let you stay here for what I get from the Catholic Services Bureau. One hundred and eighty dollars per month after you turn eighteen."

"What if I decide to work instead of going to college?"

"Five hundred dollars for rent and you have to buy your own food."

"You drive a hard bargain, Luanne."

"Indeed, I do."

Indeed she does. I think I'll take her up on her offer now that she has given me a fresh perspective and twisted my arm. There's something I have to do before I sign up for college courses, and Tim has volunteered to assist me. My savings account balance is healthy enough so that by the time I graduate high school, I'll be ready. I'm planning to buy a very, very used car. Transportation becomes a necessity once a person is out of high school. Mom, I may be a virgin for the rest of my life, but I won't go anywhere without a car.

The concept of college is running rampant in my life. And now it will be forever recorded in my high school yearbook. I regret having granted him one when the photographer on the yearbook staff asked for an interview. This year, they're profiling seniors who have demonstrated leadership, and unfortunately my picture will be among them. It doesn't belong. I was pulled out of my English class for a photograph and a five-minute interrogation. I said the weirdest thing. I hope it's the last time my mouth talks without my brain being engaged. I don't know if it was my conversation with Luanne that influenced me or Mary Pat Brennan. My lifelong friend had written informing me that she was accepted to the University of South Florida.

The yearbook photographer had a pen in his hand and a note-pad resting on the railing. He stared into my eyes waiting for my reply to his question. He had asked, "What college are you going to, and what do you plan to major in?"

I stood silent and stared at him. My mind was completely blank. Nothing popped up for me to relay. I waited as he waited. Then I asked myself, *Well? What are you gonna tell him?*

My mouth opened out of obligation since it was my turn to speak, and it said, "I'm going to the University of South Florida in Tampa, and I'll be majoring in child psychology."

What was that? my head asked my mouth. *What did you just say? Child psychology? Where did that come from, and why USF? Who in their right mind goes to USF? Why didn't you say the University of Miami? Everybody goes to UM. If you're gonna lie, make it a good one.*

As I stared off in disbelief, the photographer diligently wrote Child Psych at USF.

He continued as I held myself tight around the waist. "Why child psychology?"

Yeah? my head questioned my mouth, *why child psychology?*

My mouth was angry at me, so I was left with this mess to clean up. I replied, "They're our future. Children are the symbols of our beliefs, our hopes, and our dreams. They are the continuation of our society, of our world. Why not children? Why not seek to understand ourselves through them?"

It sounded good, but I didn't know what I was talking about. I don't think he wrote that part down. He asked more questions, yet I can't remember them. I think I left my body and let someone else stand in front of the photographer to answer his questions. It was the same feeling I had when I was beat beyond the threshold of pain.

It didn't happen enough times, when I floated away from situations like excruciating beatings. I remember most of the beatings and their stinging, aching reminders that sometimes took days to fade. But one time you beat me so relentlessly that I remember it as I remember the photographer's face in front of me, looking at me like you finally did.

The wire hangers you held in your hand whipped through the air making a whirling sound. I watched them land on my thighs as your other hand held me by the hair. After the fifth or sixth blow, something happened. My legs stopped hurting, and I watched you in slow motion. I could hear the hangers cut the air, but I couldn't feel them anymore. Someone else was in my body. I was observing you from another space and another time. My mouth stopped screaming, and my eyes stared into yours. You didn't feel them. You looked at nothing except your target, my legs.

Mom, mindlessly you hit my legs not noticing the blood blisters developing just under the skin. You hit and hit. I don't know what made you stop. Perhaps the absence of my screams or was it my stare penetrating your self-absorbed rage that stopped you. You dropped the hangers and let go of my hair. As you rose up from the floor, your knees cracked the silence. Before you walked out of my room, you turned back. Do you remember? You turned back and looked at me. It was the first time you noticed me when you beat me. It was the first sign of recognition, yet I wasn't in that body. I was already gone, somewhere. Did you know I was gone? Did you want me to leave? Is that why you beat me?

*****

139

Nikki found her way back to the Andrewses. She had continued with her habit of chasing birds, and unfortunately for the feathered friends of the woman who took Nikki in, well, those little souls are now in heaven. Anyway, the Andrewses planted tall bushes in front of the fence, thus impeding the obsessive jumper from her natural compulsion to flee the compound when a male dog has been sighted. It's amazing that the Andrewses didn't come up with the idea to plant bushes in the first place. I'm glad to know where Nikki is, although I wouldn't consider it a home if I were her.

Shari and Tim had called to accept my invitation. This is going to be an interesting graduation ceremony. I will have my former foster parents, my friend Luanne, and my foster counselor sitting in the audience. I wonder if they will have anything to say to one another. Luanne has offered to take us to dinner after the ceremony. What a crowd we'll be, celebrating my transition into the real world. I wonder what I'll feel looking into the eyes of people who are unrelated to me. They didn't bring me into this world, yet they guided me to this point in my life. No doubt their faces and the guaranteed moments of awkward conversation will be etched into my mind when I think of my high school graduation.

The semester is finally coming to a close. Goals are important plateaus to reach. I did senior skip day, survived Grad Night in Disney, and studied just enough to place myself in a good position. If I become brain dead from the bite of a rare spider, I can fail every final and still graduate.

For the first time and hopefully the last, Luanne and I went clothes shopping. We found an elegant summer dress that is more like a wedding dress. White lace on white cotton, but my graduation dress fits perfectly and, most importantly, helps me look less childlike. Luanne made the mistake of saying that I look cute when I put it on. I'll wear it under my graduation gown and keep it for my wedding day so all my guests can say how cute I am instead of how lovely.

Daniella dragged me through the mall searching for dresses for our dinner that replaces the prom. For me, we settled on a white dress with red trim. These white dresses make me feel like a bride with no groom. Daniella found a basic black dress. I'm thinking she has more fashion sense.

Graduating in 1980 means saying goodbye to a decade of disco and bell bottoms and saying hello to debt and dinners in fine restaurants. Now that I have a dress to wear on our "who cares about the prom" dinner date, I have to find shoes. "Details are the things that get you noticed." That's what my ninth-grade English teacher, Mrs. Conroy, would tell me. Her observation makes more sense now. I didn't realize how many shades of red there are and how few pairs of shoes match the red trim on my new dinner dress.

Daniella, Michelle, Vicki, and Carlos will lounge in Luanne's car this Saturday night as I drive us to dinner then to the beach for a walk along the shore. Now that our dinner is a few days away, I'd rather stay home. But I'm the transportation vehicle, the entertainment committee, the one who wanted to go to dinner this night of all nights with friends who find the prom ritual as meaningless as I do. None of us have dates.

Carlos has been in my homeroom for two years. It surprises me that he has no one to take to the prom. He usually has a girl under his arm by the lockers. The lockers are where couples swap spit. He must be between girlfriends. Daniella said he's got the hots for me. I think she's wrong; he's never asked me out. Perhaps everyone thinks I'm gay.

Mom, I don't understand why I have no one calling me for a date, let alone the prom. I'm not convinced that my cuteness has repelled the male gender. My teeth are straight, and I shower, sometimes twice a day. What is it about me? Michelle and Vicki have boyfriends who are in college, out of state. They have good excuses for being dateless. Daniella, well, I stopped asking months ago. Maybe she has a guy on the side and won't tell, sparing my feelings. Did you go through this stage?

Luanne said worrying about centimeters is a waste of time. I had asked her if my nose was too long or my eyes too close together. She said to stop guessing why things are the way they are and continue being the best me. I don't know who I am. I don't know why my dates are group dates. What is it about me?

CHAPTER 16

Tim and I settled on a Toyota Celica which was manufactured before the turn of the twentieth century (exaggeration of course, but hints at the advanced age of my new prized possession), and it was the only car in my price range. There's one slight flaw. I'm sure I'll rectify it in no time, I hope. My dear, wonderful, perfect first car is a stick shift. I don't know how to work a manual transmission, yet. Luanne has offered to assist me, yet I feel guilty subjecting her to more practice runs. I want to give her body time to heal the concussion she suffered during our last attempt.

Samuel's wife, Monica, promises to give me instructions. It'll have to happen soon because classes start in less than a week, and Miami-Dade Community College is not within walking distance. Luanne reassures me that I can drive her car until I learn. I appreciate the thought, and although nothing compares to her Mercedes-Benz, I prefer my car. I just wish I could drive it.

I outgrew Red Road Bakery and moved on. I'm working for friends of Luanne; they own a temporary employment agency. I've been assigned to a permanent part-time job working for a brokerage firm in Coral Gables. Monday through Friday I show up for a couple of hours in the morning to accept quip machine messages. A quip machine transmits documents over the telephone line; it spits out information only a stock broker would find interesting. Quipping is mindless work but pays well. Besides, the hours fit perfectly into my college class schedule. Can you believe it? I'll be in college. I can't.

Luanne is going to London in a few weeks. In her absence, I'll be a college student with the responsibility of running a household for three weeks. It'll be an empty house without Luanne. She said Daniella can stay with me. I have yet to find the right words to tell Luanne.

Daniella is gay. And she found someone to return her affections. I know. I know. I'm dense, blind, and slow. I'll miss Daniella. She said we were having separate experiences. I was having a friendship. She was having a relationship. I'm happy for her, finding love. Daniella's mom called me the other day trying to figure things out. I told her that Daniella is no different from any other daughter. She loves her parents, is a good friend, and needs to feel all that in return. Her mom said I'm a natural for child psychology. She must have read the yearbook.

Jordan has moved on to higher education leaving sweet words in my yearbook and a peck on my cheek, that side of my face I have yet to wash. He said to me as he walked away, "I love you, Ariana. Always will." Out of the blur of experiences I had in high school, I will remember Jordan and how he looked at me, spoke to me, and never asked me out but loved me all the way through.

On the day of my graduation, Luanne asked me if I would go to my ten-year reunion. The answer was simple and quick, "No." I struggled to survive life, and high school was a component of that reality. It was something I did every day, but I didn't like it. My graduation celebration was the same. I struggled through the dinner with Shari and Tim, Mrs. Lareau, and Luanne. Mrs. Lareau gave me a pendant that defines all the things I missed. "Live Love Laugh" are inscribed on a silver heart. I store it next to your letter. It's a reminder of what I want instead of a symbol of what I had.

The countdown is on. I'll be legal age sooner than later—no more foster child status. I plan to make choices and decisions. I'm going to plant my own garden and fill it with the things I need to nourish me. Luanne appreciated hearing me say that especially since the time had come for her to relinquish her own vegetable garden. We converted the garden into a compost. The backyard has grown into more than what Luanne can handle, so she hired a lawn maintenance company. They tend to cut everything in sight and nearly downed one of the banana trees. Did I tell you how important the banana trees are? The parrots from Parrot Jungle fly over in the afternoons and feed from the neighborhood banana trees. I love to hear their squawks in the distance. Most afternoons I drop what I'm doing and look out the window to see brilliant blue and red descend on banana stalks. Our neighbors have figured out the attraction and planted banana trees along the fence to reinforce visits from our feathered friends.

Today, I was lying in the sun and gazing up at the ficus tree. A steady, balmy ocean breeze fluttered leaves that mesmerized me. Suddenly, a branch moved, and I realized it was a lizard—three feet long. I screamed. Luanne looked out the kitchen window, holding a kitchen towel in her hand. She gave a laugh when she realized what I was pointing to.

"Cuban lizard," she said. "They're a lovely bright green, wouldn't you say?"

Luanne has a way of looking at the world. It's brighter, full of mystery, and intelligence. This dear woman has turned a weary heart into an explorer. I am indebted to her soul for all the love and honor she has bestowed on me. Luanne lives her life. She impresses no one. She commands nothing. Yet she has completely changed my life. She has never asked me to love her or respect her. Those are the very feelings I experience when I think of my friend, Luanne.

Mom, I have waited for this time in my life. I have hung on with my nails digging into the fabric of experiences. This moment of transition is here; I am in between high school and college. In between being a child and an adult, I find myself wondering what it means to be a woman. I had believed being a woman was defined by a man. But I look at Luanne and know that no one created or defined her. She is herself. I've heard each of her stories at least twice, yet I don't grow tired of them. Her passion for life is an incredible gift. I wonder if she knows she gave it to me at a critical time in my life. I had a choice when I came here, I now realize. I could have chosen the bitterness of my experiences. Thankfully, I looked to Luanne and learned how to find safety in letting go.

Tonight, as I write you these words and feel these thoughts, I see how much I have released. And still there is more deep inside me. My dear mother, I cannot let go of this letter as I had promised myself I would do at this time. I need to write you. This letter will continue. I cannot let go of you. What will I be if you are really gone?

*****

Monica swallowed two aspirins before we left the house; Samuel had warned her about my less than smooth shift from first to second. We began with the basics. Before starting the engine, my stick shift instructor talked me through the mechanics and concept of the clutch. She said to concentrate on the cable tension when releasing my left foot. Once I comprehended the clutch, Monica coached me on foot coordination. Then she had me practice the gear shifts. I even practiced down-shifting before I ever touched the ignition key. Smart woman.

The big moment came when I started my car. From one end of the University of Miami east parking lot to the other, I put into practice all the information Monica imparted. I feel bad that my car has no shoulder straps, only a lap belt. Monica constantly reached for the dash and door handle to brace herself.

In one grueling afternoon, I was transformed into Richard Petty's competition. I braved a spin around the neighborhood, building up enough confidence to drive down US-1. Monica said my last unknown to conquer is an incline, yet there are no hills in South Florida. At this point in my driving career, I have mastered the manual transmission, but only in flat areas of the world.

Thanks to Monica's bravery, I can now drive my car, which is why the following is an ironic twist of fate. Circumstances bumped into each other until, well, I'll give you the circumstances first.

My life as a college student has become a routine. As soon as I wake up, I stretch for a half hour employing the same exercises my dance instructor taught me in tenth grade plus a few modifications. I'm out the door by six forty-five and finish work at nine thirty. Taking backstreets and shortcuts, I arrive at the Miami-Dade South campus in time for my ten o'clock class. After my first class, I find a table in the courtyard to eat the lunch I stuffed in my backpack. Then, depending on the day, I either study or shuffle off to my next class. My last class begins at eight in the evening. Monday through Friday I have no time to spare. That's why I waited until the weekend to clean and wash the cars.

After her long vacation in London, I had it in mind to surprise Luanne at the airport with a sparkling Mercedes-Benz. Two rainy weekends dampened my plan until finally the weather cooperated on the last weekend before she was to come home.

Luanne parks her car in the garage. I prefer to park in the street as I don't have time to manually open and close the garage door on my side of our two-car garage, nor do I have extra money to spend on a second garage door opener. Since her car was already in the garage, I decided my car would wait its turn while I cheerfully vacuumed the Mercedes-Benz. Right after that is where my problems began. I started Luanne's car and put the seat belt on; it's a habit. I turned around to back out of the garage and failed to notice the driver's door was not completely shut, and the blasting radio drowned the sound of the warning beeps. The driver's door was opening as I was backing.

I heard a crunch then a crack. My left foot was searching for the clutch while my right was looking for the brake. Luanne's car has an automatic transmission. The engine revved. I didn't have to find the brake; the concrete pillar separating her side of the garage from mine found the driver's door and stopped the luxury car in its place. Well, it did a bit more than that. It crammed the door into the side of the engine. Lucky me, I found the brake just as my body was thrown slightly forward, a tad too late.

I refused to turn my head around and face reality. For what seemed like eternity, I stared out the rear window looking toward the street. It didn't help. I wrecked my friend's car, and I wasn't even three inches out of the garage. The driver's door had been relocated, about two feet into the hood.

Using both feet to brake, I pulled Luanne's car forward. I'm unsure which required more time, taking the key out of the ignition or sliding out of the passenger's door. I was shaking to the core and ran into the house. My first thought was to call Daniella. Much to my relief, she was home. I told her what I thought just happened and admitted there was room for doubt.

"Maybe I was having a hiccup in time," I explained. "Maybe this is some weird mind warp and it really didn't happen. I mean what a stupid thing to do."

Daniella convinced me to put the phone down and walk into the garage. She had instructed me to examine Luanne's car, then come back to the phone. I did. And it was. She gasped.

"Can you believe this?" I begged.

"No. No, this is for the record books. All that time you had her car going to school, work, out with me. Now that you have your own, you wreck hers. This is a classic. Do you mind if I tell my mom?"

"No. In fact, get a billboard on Bird Road and advertise it to everyone." I sighed into the phone. "Oh god, I've really done a major booboo. Luanne is going to kill me. No. She's going to scream bloody murder at me, throw me out of the house, and then hire someone to kill me."

"I'd like to say here that you're wrong and that you have nothing to worry about. I can't because I think you know as well as I that you're dead meat." Daniella remained silent waiting for my reply. I was unable to squeak air through my vocal cords. She figured it out saying, "You're crying."

"Yeah," I peeped.

"You didn't do anything wrong. Everybody knows you can't drive. No one can blame you for having a problem like that. It's gonna be okay. Really. You can live with my mom. She's been lonely since I met Janet."

"Your mom's insurance company won't permit it."

"You have a point."

"Luanne's insurance is going to go through the roof. I'll have to pay her for the rest of my life. I'll be ninety and still writing a monthly check to her."

"What're ya going to do now?"

It was a good question, Mom. I hung up after another spontaneous cry, went out to the garage, and stared at my horrible mistake. There was nothing else I could do except go to the phone book. I would need to present Luanne with a financial plan on how I would spend the rest of my life indebted to her, and she would require proof in my figures.

I spent the remainder of that sunny Saturday afternoon driving to three different body shops, obtaining written repair quotes from each.

Coming from a desire to teach me how to be self-reliant, Luanne had imparted her golden acquisition rule. Always get three quotes. She had said throwing out the high quote prevents overspending unless the vendor can prove their worth. Dropping the lower quote avoids a potentially undesirable situation where "you get what you pay for." The middle quote is the answer to any purchase decision.

Unfortunately, Luanne was not privy to my body shop quotes when she disclosed this valuable guideline. I think six quotes would have been more prudent considering their range. One shop owner quoted five thousand; another shop manager wrote in tiny letters next to his eight-thousand-dollar quote, "and up depending on availability of parts." What that meant I was afraid to pursue, so I did not. Twelve thousand dollars was the high quote, and my heart nearly jumped out of my chest when I heard it. Three seconds of driving can be expensive these days.

Luanne's car was drivable, yet it looked so wounded and hurt. I dutifully pulled up into her side of the garage for the last time, careful not to damage the washer and dryer. I thought about packing my things and loading them into my car. Then I realized there was nowhere to go. I contemplated blowing up my car. Playing out that scenario in my head did major damage to my car yet didn't help the Mercedes look any better. I decided not to vacuum or clean my car. It would have to remain neglected so long as Luanne's was bearing the scars of my carelessness. All weekend I practiced how I would say, "I wrecked your car." Actually, I came up with every sentence available in the English language except that one. It was too direct. Then I wrote a short goodbye speech, preparing for the ultimate doom to descend once the fateful words had departed from my lips. By Sunday night I had a plan. I would have to inform her of my horrid deed before Luanne discovered it herself. She would accept being picked up at the airport in my ancient Toyota. Knowing my adoration for the small junk heap I call a car, Luanne probably wouldn't ask why I left the Mercedes-Benz at home. Upon walking through the front door, careful not to go through the garage, I would put her suitcase down in the foyer and tell her I need to speak with her in the backyard. Mentioning the backyard would send up flags. Luanne would then know something is up if she hadn't already detected it during the ride home from the airport. I knew when the time came, the ficus tree would be there for me. Anything important to be said had always been done in the backyard under the ficus tree. I pictured us sitting side by side on the old wooden bench positioned under the gentle giant. The bench is secured between huge roots that jut from the surface of the earth and cradle it. I hoped the roots would reach out and cradle me after my throat vibrated the words that would decide my fate. I would tell what I had done, hand her the three quotes, then brace for Luanne's rage.

It was a flawless plan except for one minor point I had not considered. On Wednesday evening we sat down under the ficus tree. I drew in a deep breath then told Luanne how I disfigured her expensive new car. I clung to the bench waiting for the impact. There was none. I turned to the side to look at her. Luanne's eyes were reading the quotes. Believing she had not yet grasped their meaning, I waited for my words to reach Luanne's consciousness. She remained silent.

After glancing at the last one, the highest quote, she asked, "You did this on Saturday?"

"Yes. I drove it to three local shops as you can see, and I'm deeply—"

"You got three quotes."

"You said three is good for any decision, but I think that six may have been better in this case. On a Saturday, I doubt there are six body—"

"I'm so proud of you."

"What?"

"You got three quotes."

"Yeah."

"Ariana, you have grown into a young woman. I'm so proud of you." Her eyes filled with tears. She even sniffled.

I was prepared for her screams, threats, rage, even foul language, yet I had not considered her tender tears, especially not her pride. I was dumbfounded. I sat looking at her not knowing what to think. The words "thank you" came to mind, and I barely uttered them. I was convinced something was terribly wrong.

"I've wrecked your car, Luanne."

"I know."

"Why aren't you screaming at me?"

"A car is a car and can be replaced, repaired, junked. But you have demonstrated a maturity, a sense of responsibility, and a nobleness that moves me to tears. I'm sorry the only thing I can say to describe it is that I'm so very, very proud of you, Ariana. I'm proud of you."

As I write these words now, I realize that Luanne is a saint. At that time, all that ran through my head was disbelief. I had assumed that I was a failure and a disappointment. Without trying, without making any attempt, I became a noble person. On Wednesday night, I stopped being the sneak you labeled me as being. I was no longer the liar, the whore, nor the cheat Shari decided I was. In Luanne's eyes, I was someone worthy, and I was nothing less than a blue-blooded noble sitting under a ficus tree.

We hugged and again she cried when she saw her car. It wasn't exactly tears of pride; that time she felt the hurt I inflicted on her Mercedes-Benz. My proud foster mother called her son, Samuel, to let him know she had arrived home safely. With a tinge of excitement and joy in her voice, she told him how proud she was of me. Fifteen minutes later, Samuel was knocking at the front door. He wanted to see what I had done to deserve his mother's admiration.

Before I came into my room this evening to write you, I went outside and hugged the ficus tree and thanked him for his love. I have no doubt that our backyard centurion hugged Luanne and I that night as we sat under him, opening our hearts.

Ironically, one of the body shops I visited currently warehouses Luanne's car. Her insurance company uses that body shop for repairs. The quote he gave me was more than three times the amount his shop is charging the insurance company. I have to pay Luanne's deductible. Considering all things, five hundred dollars is more than worth it to find out that I am a noble person. I've always wanted you to be proud of me, Mom. You didn't live long enough to see me as a woman. Can you see me now? Do I look different?

*****

I've made it through the summer semester at Miami-Dade Community College and can happily report to you that I have a perfect four-point-o average. College is much easier than I had imagined. Luanne's daughter, Annie, told me during her visit last week that junior colleges are easier than a university. I didn't take it as an insult. She doesn't deliver clandestine ridicule like Shari.

Annie is moving to Tallahassee for a career advancement and spent her remaining vacation days in Coral Gables, playing tourist. She came at a perfect time. I was between semesters, and Samuel was itching to use vacation time before the summer ran out. We did more snorkeling, boating, swimming, walking, and laughing than is rationed for one lifetime. Luanne was pushing herself to keep up with us. I knew she wanted to be with her oldest daughter as much as possible. She would never admit it, but I think Luanne is upset that her Annie will be eight hours away instead of two.

It's an incredible experience to be in nature with a botanist. Annie described the history, origins, and the families of plants I have seen all my life. I felt blessed to see Florida through her trained eyes. Palm trees are from the grass family. A banana tree is actually an herb. I'm amazed at how quickly the indigenous Florida vegetation is being squeezed out of existence by plants imported from South America that were originally intended to be landscaping for homes. Every time Annie is around, I look at Florida with more appreciation in my heart.

The night before she drove home, Annie sipped on Luanne's homemade potato soup and helped me select my fall class schedule. I'm loading up this semester, taking the maximum number of classes permitted. President Regan has cut back social security death benefits and promises to continue the trend, eventually eliminating my benefits. I do a financial juggle between the Pell Grant, death benefits, and earning an income. I pray my savings is enough to fill in the widening gap long enough for me to earn my four-year degree. At the rate things are going, the faster I can go through college, the more I will be able to afford it.

Luanne took advantage of Annie being around. She enticed her daughter to gang up on me. Luanne's nephew, Joey, has a Fiat he wants to trade in for a BMW. It has twelve thousand five hundred miles on it, and he's willing to sell it to me for the same amount of the trade-in. "It's a steal."

I'm hesitant to commit to the depletion of my savings, although Luanne is convinced my dependable car isn't so dependable. I tell her rust is no indication of a car's health. Luanne has a way of wrinkling her face. It means many things depending on the situation. In this one, it meant that the rust is significant. Annie remained relatively neutral admitting to her mom that she had a Fiat Spider and learned Fiat stands for, and I quote Annie, "Fix It Again, Tony."

Luanne managed to drag Annie and me across town to inspect Joey's car. It's a blue-gray, five-speed, two-door sedan. Two years ago, Joey drove it out the dealership lot when the leather seats were still soft and supple. I have time to ponder my decision since his special edition BMW won't be arriving for some weeks. Joey threw in the floor mats he ordered for the Fiat, making the deal sweeter. I don't like putting my hard-earned money in a car. Luanne said it's really an investment in myself. I think she's stretching things with that comment. I'm beginning to see through her inspiration speeches. My gentle foster mother is equally cunning.

There are four criteria Luanne uses as a guideline when making a decision. Luanne puts all four into a question, "Is it educational, inspirational, useful, or entertaining?" Luanne's husband used this system before he passed on. I've adopted it as Luanne's family has adopted me. I concluded that a Fiat meets none of the decision criteria until Annie reminded me that the Fiat is bigger than my Toyota, classifying it as useful. I gave her a look.

Annie grinned and said, "You've lived with my mom long enough to flawlessly mimic her facial expressions."

Luanne put her two cents in saying, "Ariana had a repertoire of facial expressions before she came to live with me, Annie. All I did was refine them."

CHAPTER 17

His mom asked all the questions. She was the early bird who called at seven thirty on a Sunday morning inquiring about the car for sale. Having barely enough time to brush my teeth before the doorbell rang, I didn't bother checking my ad in the *Miami Herald* because obviously the phone number was printed correctly.

She was loaded with questions. His mom wanted to know why I was selling, how long I had the Celica, the names and addresses of the previous owners (I'm kidding, of course), and if it had been in any accidents.

I stared into her eyes and said, "The engine is rebuilt. I haven't wrecked it. My friend, Tim, and I bought it from a Jamaican gentleman. I doubt he was the original owner. I'm selling it for less than I bought it because I already have a car." I pointed to the Fiat parked on the street. "My insurance company will cover both cars for thirty days. It's priced to sell. It's my first car, and I happen to think it's wonderful. It safely got me back and forth to Miami-Dade."

"Is that where you're going to school?" She sounded shocked. "You don't look like you're in college. You look like you're barely out of junior high."

"I had my eighteenth birthday last week. Tim made sure the title read 'or' so I could legally sign it over without his having to cosign."

She nodded then said, "My son's car died on him during summer break."

"What school are you going to?" I asked the shy boy standing behind his mom.

"Florida State in Tallahassee."

"Does the AC work?" his mother asked.

"Try it out," I said, fully knowing the condenser was blown centuries ago. The sky had doused the neighborhood with a rain shower minutes before my buyers arrived. She turned on the air conditioner and was pleased to feel cool air blowing on her face. The fan works perfectly, and on a rain chilled Sunday morning, it simulates an air conditioner.

We shook hands, and with that, my precious first car was sold to another college student. I met them the next day and exchanged the title for a cashier's check. It was a simple transaction. The hardest part was watching him drive off in my car. In my mind, I wished them both good luck, my car and him with the overbearing mom.

Luanne was proud of me; all by my lil' ol' self I had sold my car. I hadn't recognized my accomplishment until she said something. I've always been self-reliant, yet no one noticed before, not even me. Luanne's efforts to encourage my self-awareness are paying off, although I don't always view myself in a positive light.

For a while, I worried that the male gender attending Miami-Dade perceived me as a child prodigy, really not belonging to the student body. I was offered smiles and hellos but no dates. That changed when Claudio spoke up for his friend. Every day I sit at the same courtyard table to eat my lunch. And for more than a semester, I failed to notice Alonso's struggle. I tend to bury my head in my books when I'm eating. He faithfully sat near me yet was too shy to drum up conversation. Fearing his grasp of the English language would fail him, Alonso had his friend vie for my attention. Claudio's Colombian accent is thick and difficult to understand. Thankfully, Alonso's timid nature gave way to his attraction, rescuing me from Claudio's bungling seduction.

By the time he introduced himself, Alonso had been speaking English for eight months, although it sounded more like only two weeks. Shyness coupled with a Venezuelan accent challenged my right ear while deep hazel eyes pleaded to be understood.

Since that fateful lunch, our communication skills have improved dramatically. We've settled on teaching one another our native languages. I converse in Spanish and Alonso in English. For months I've been watching Alonso's lips contort and form words resembling the ones I use to communicate without a second thought. Language, I've learned, is no barrier to physical attraction. Furthermore, I barely notice Alonso's struggle with English. My attention is lost on his long dark brown hair which emphasizes his thick lips and penetrating eyes. Luanne has been hinting that she wants to meet Alonso, and I've been hedging. I want him to have a better grasp of proper English before they meet. He tends to use the cuss words Claudio taught him.

Alonso's dream is to be an electrical engineer. And true to his nature, he has his education precisely planned. After graduating from Miami-Dade, he'll attend the University of Florida in Gainesville and earn a degree in engineering at the end of two years of hard studying. I know he'll do it. Hopefully by the time he graduates from UF, he'll be able to say engineering without sounding like a drunk.

I'm inspired by Alonso's determination and have decided on a career track. Business administration appears to be the most logical path for me to take especially considering my natural prowess in sales. This semester I'm taking an introduction to marketing. When it comes to stimulating my curiosity in human behavior, marketing stands above my philosophy, art appreciation, music history, biology, and political science classes. Although, I must admit, marketing is shoulder to shoulder with my psychology class. Alonso warns that most psychologists don't earn an income worthy of their education.

Beyond his contagious zeal for an education, Alonso Martino has exposed me to his world. I'm developing an appreciation for Latin music, food, and dancing. Most of Alonso's friends are from South America and have a healthy attitude toward school. They feel studying should be properly balanced with partying. I've been the token American to more than one of their gatherings.

Among my new friends is Margarita Consuela Maria Alvarez-Fernandez. She's from Bogota, Colombia, and has the accent to prove it. The moment we met we were instant friends. She loves to say my name and repeats it at least fifty times during a conversation, "Ariana, how do you say..."

True to her name, Margarita is an elixir. She has an unquenchable excitement for life and transforms its hiccups into opportunities. I've introduced her to Coconut Grove, and she's been ecstatic about it ever since. Margarita attracts people like a slice of watermelon attracts flies on a hot Florida day. Somehow she convinced me to sail with a group of high school students she met while she was wandering around Coconut Grove's boat docks. They were preparing for a Saturday afternoon sailing trip and invited us to join them. Normally, I would refuse, but Margarita has an infectious way of being totally enamored with living. While lost in a crowd of ten high school students, I fell in love with sailing. I wanted to sail around the world and was disappointed our adventure ended before dusk. It didn't matter to me that there was no more wind. I wanted to be on the ocean.

*****

Sex. Alonso has suggested it more than a few times, and I think about it more than anything else. I'm eighteen, and I'm a virgin. I'm probably not the oldest virgin, but close. Well, not counting nuns and Mother Teresa. I know I was taught to wait until the honeymoon. I, however, don't go to mass anymore, so I don't think I'm bound by the pope's moral dictate on this matter. I'm kidding, of course.

Mom, I really don't know what to do. Should I wait until I'm married? What if I don't get married? I mean, it has taken me a long time just to be asked out on a date. Alonso said he lost his virginity at the age of twelve to the maid. You would think that bothers me, yet it doesn't. Actually, I wonder about the maid, not Alonso. I'm glad he's more experienced. He said he matured early. I guess so.

The voices of advice roll through my mind late at night. Love, devotion, feelings, emotion, compassion, passion—I hear it all. Luanne tells me to follow my own way, my own heart. I'm afraid to let go of my innocence. What if I have intercourse with Alonso and find out that I'm a repressed nymphomaniac? Sometimes I think virginity has kept me from jumping into the sack with every guy I see who makes my heart skip a beat. That's a lot of guys.

Margarita's sister visited for a week and gave us sisterly advice on life in the eighties. My ears perked up when the subject of sex rolled around. She said it was better to get it over with while we're still young, thus giving us the eerie warning that if we wait, we may never do it. That may appear to be bad advice, yet I have to say it makes some sense. I tend to dip my toe in the water to test it out. In the arena of lovemaking, one either jumps in or doesn't. I'm afraid if I wait too long, I'll lose my chance of becoming a sexual human being. Thus, losing any hope of swimming in the waters of primordial urges.

I understand the mechanics of sex; I don't quite grasp the stuff that surrounds it. When I consider it from a logical point of view, sex is no big deal. But sex is not logical. It's not a mindless act people engage in for extracurricular activity. Well, not all the time. If it were, then we could go to some place to have sex like we go to the theater to see a movie. Sex is intermeshed with compelling emotions such as love and desire. It's used to gain power, control, even to dominate. There's so much more to sex than the mere act. My curiosity is not about the act other than maybe discovering how it feels. I want to comprehend sexuality. I want to know. I feel as though I don't know something. It's as if someone told a joke and everyone laughs except me. I don't get the punch line because I lack the experience to appreciate the humor. I miss innuendoes because I simply don't have a reference. Mom, I wish you were here so you could explain. I wish you could tell me what it was like for you, what you'd change, what you would do again. I feel lost in all the advice. I wonder if I'll look back on my final decision and feel regret. What will I be committing myself to if I have sex with Alonso? Shari's infamous words roll around my head: "What do you think he has between his legs?" Is that all Alonso is after? If I say no, will he go away? Will I regret his leaving, or will I wish I took a leap past my logic, past my fear, and land in his arms saying, "*Te quiero, Te quiero.*" I doubt a translation is necessary. The words, "I want you," sound the same in any language.

Margarita is on the hunt for her first experience. Her approach to sex is quite simple: "Why not?" She prefers American guys, and they prefer her. I'm sure she'll announce it over the phone one day soon, exclaiming, "I did it!" I hope she uses the protection we bought at the drugstore.

I thought taking the time to write all this down would help things become clearer. It's not. I'm back to do I or don't I.

*****

I had forgotten she has a lead foot; it proved to be beneficial as we raced through Miami's traffic on a busy Friday afternoon. Luanne wasn't rushing; she was flying. Margarita and I had asked her to hurry, worrying we would be left behind. Everyone was to meet at Claudio's apartment at three in the afternoon, and it was four o'clock by the time we left the house, thirty minutes away.

We arrived just when Claudio and the others were loading the van. Margarita and I were actually on time. You'd think by now my mind could grasp the difference between Latin time and Miami time. Margarita tells me they're at least sixty minutes apart. After pulling out our sleeping bags and duffel, we each gave Luanne a kiss and a hug before she peeled out of the parking lot.

Alonso had declined the invitation to go camping. He wanted to study for finals. His English is improving, yet he tends to overkill. Alonso was shocked that I chose to go without him. My classes are easier than his for one reason, and the other is I would never turn down an opportunity to go camping. It had been too long since my last stint in Key Largo.

I shared the driving with two other front seat passengers while the rest of our group sat in the back of the van with the camping equipment. Constant complaints were directed our way regarding our infrequent stops, but we had to reach the KOA before it closed. From Miami, traveling to the middle of Florida is like driving through two states. I gave up my front-seat privileges three-quarters of the way to High Springs. Claudio got gas, and I don't mean the kind at the gas station. He said rice and beans usually don't affect him. It was affecting me; I could barely see straight.

Setting up camp was an impossible feat. Eight college students should have enough know-how to erect two tents in the dark. We didn't. What was left of Friday night I spent outside under a pine tree, zipped up in my sleeping bag.

Discomfort was washed away by the Ichetucknee River the next morning. We rented floats, tied them together, and drifted for hours in seventy-degree water. Cypress trees reached out to us, sometimes leaving stumps in our path. Clear, cold water bathed our souls while light gray clouds hung above us and guided us down river. Margarita peered at the shore looking for native wildlife. I borrowed snorkeling gear and spent most of the slow drift with my head underwater. Occasionally, Margarita would nudge me and point to a bird or to river otters playing on shore.

By Saturday evening, our tents were pitched on top of soft sand near the edge of the riverbank. Over our campfire songs, we could hear the trickle of river water. I sung fairly well in Spanish once they taught me the words. Latin music is similar to American folk songs, with a splash of a longing to dance.

Juan Carlos. That's the name of the guy who snored all night. He positioned his sleeping bag next to mine. I didn't think anything of it until he fell asleep, thus keeping the rest of his tent mates awake. Margarita had a brilliant idea that did nothing to hush our noise maker. She placed a partially melted marshmallow in Juan Carlos's hand and tickled his face. On the way home Sunday morning, we had to listen to Juan Carlos's screams as he combed his hair. I wanted to shoot him, but he's a photography student. I have a soft spot for anyone that has a passion to capture moments, vistas, and emotions on film. In the tent while he was snoring the rest of us into madness, I took a picture of his short black hair covered in white marshmallow. I doubt he will appreciate my angle when he sees the developed film.

Alonso was at Claudio's apartment when we arrived. I think he was relieved to see I wasn't arm in arm with any of his buddies. We unloaded the van, sprayed Juan Carlos off with the hose, and raided Claudio's refrigerator before leaving. Alonso drove me to Luanne's house and sipped hot broccoli soup while I described my adventures. Luanne appreciated Margarita's marshmallow prank saying her "darling" five children were known to have similar sparks of creative revenge. I'm too old for my age; I worry about the details in life. My creative flashes rarely lead to pranks.

I miss camping. I want to go every weekend. I know it's not practical, neither is studying until my eyes are bloodshot and black letters on a white textbook page begin waving. This time I'm not letting final exams run my life. I'll study, take my tests, then go Christmas shopping. Checking the mailbox twice a day for my grade report is ridiculous. I'm over this obsessive-compulsive behavior. It's time I enjoy being a college student and—

Oh, forget it, Mom. This isn't working. I can't settle for anything less than a four-point-o. As soon as I put your letter away, I'll pull out one of my class notebooks. I'll spend hours reading and highlighting until my hands are yellow then call Alonso before I drift off to sleep. It's my life. I'm committed until I have a degree. After that well, I have no idea what I'll do. Whatever I do, I'll have a degree in business administration to do it with.

Before I tuck your letter back into the drawer, I want to write down what I feel. I love you. I used to miss you, but I've grown accustomed to your absence. I was looking at myself in the mirror today and wondered if I look like you. I don't have any pictures of you; they're somewhere in Uncle James's house. I remember your striking blue eyes and brown hair. How did I end up with gray eyes? I thought when I turned eighteen, I would somehow look like you. I thought I would look like an adult, yet I don't. "*Que lindo.*" That's what my friends say. It means how cute.

CHAPTER 18

Shari and Tim invited us to what is becoming a traditional Christmas Eve gathering. Alonso drooled when he saw Shari's seafood buffet spread out on the dining room table. My former foster parents adore my Venezuelan boyfriend. He's all the things I am not. He loves seafood, wine, and found the Andrewses quite charming. I said nothing to sway his opinion. Shari and Tim are charming when they want to be. So am I. I greeted them and their friends as if I had never moved out, as if I had always been in the Andrewses' lives and in their photo albums.

I was smart this year. I anticipated Shari would conveniently forget I'm vegetarian, thus subtly exclude me from the Christmas Eve celebration. Luanne and I sat down to a small dinner, vegetable soup and a tomato sandwich, before I drove to Alonso's house. The Martinos live ten minutes from the Andrewses.

I practice most of my Spanish on Alonso's parents. His father is from Spain, and he speaks proper Spanish. Mr. Martino finds my Venezuelan accent appalling. I find his pronunciations nearly impossible to comprehend. Mrs. Martino loves feeding me when I stop by their house; she thinks I'm too thin. I've learned to accept and eat whatever she serves; otherwise, it becomes a horrible family squabble. On Christmas Eve, she handed me a tray of homemade cookies and a glass of milk. Alonso quickly drank the milk while his mom left the room to find a gift under their Christmas tree. Moments later Mrs. Martino handed me a wrapped giftbox and told me to open it. Tucked inside red tissue paper was a handwritten note. Alonso's mother wrote me a Christmas letter, in English. She had been taking an English class without anyone knowing. It reads,

My dear Ariana,

This Christmas I want for you to feel happiness in your heart and you feel the love of my family. I want you to know you bring this for me and my son.

With my love, Rosanna Martino.

I was moved to tears and hugged her tight. Alonso was shocked to learn his mother was taking a class behind his back. He was not surprised, however, by her words reflecting her love. He told me on the way to the Andrewses that she wants me to be her daughter-in-law. He said nothing more, and I dared not reply. I'm still thinking about having sex. Marriage is another subject for another time.

On Christmas Day, Luanne and I visited her children's homes. At each stop we gorged on Christmas cookies and exchanged gifts. Quickly, I discovered a family conspiracy and realized Luanne was behind it. The gifts so generously bestowed on me had a theme: car safety. I received a first aid kit, jumper cables, a blanket, flares, flat tire kits—you name what has been invented to make driving a safer and more pleasurable experience and I got it for Christmas. Additionally, I was the recipient of more driving jokes than anyone should have to endure in one lifetime let alone one Christmas. Luanne eased the stings, saying, "Did you hear the smiles in their words?"

We decided we prefer driving to Christmas celebrations. It was easier than having one at home. "Next year," Luanne said, "I think we'll offer a Christmas breakfast. It's easy to do eggs and muffins. Then we'll get invited to everyone's house for lunch and dinner, thus saving ourselves from filling up on cookies."

We think alike, my cunning former foster mother and I.

Tonight I'm working on my New Year resolutions. For number ten I wrote, "To have sex before I get old." I think that's a good resolution; it doesn't force me to do it in a year. Number one was to write Granddad more often. He sent a Christmas card and tucked a check inside. This year he included a clipping from the town newspaper. Every Sunday they feature a section called "From a Child's Perspective." In October, Granddad had submitted the short story I sent him when I was in high school. I had no idea he'd do that. Mom, I'm published. My first byline stares at me, though I can't believe my name is in print. This flimsy newspaper clipping I will cherish for the rest of my life. I've included it with your letter because it belongs nowhere else.

"Sitting on Hearts"
Ariana Oman
(Gustav VanHusen's granddaughter)

I was four years old when I finally met him. Mom told me to be on my best behavior as she tied the bow attached to the front of my new dress. He came all the way from Indiana to meet us. I wanted him to like me, so I quietly waited for him to finish his rounds. First, he had to see my two younger sisters. No one could resist their dribbles except me, of course. Then there were my two older sisters hanging on the poor man as he walked into the family room where I stood petrified. This was the moment of truth; he stood before me. He asked for a kiss. Gently he pulled a thumb out of my mouth then wiped a tear trickling down my cheek. He was so big, and his cigar smelled so badly, but he sure could hug. Only grandfathers give hugs like that.

Soon, I was in his lap screaming with laughter as he nibbled at my ears. I can still feel the weight of his head as he leaned into me and tickled my belly. It was then that he decided my name was to be changed. Ever since, I've answered to

"Monkey." Feeling perfectly safe, I forgot my screams would lure Mom back to the family room. She came to his rescue and reminded me of his age.

Mom led her father to another room, away from rambunctious children. I watched him ease into the living room chair. He sat next to the window and lit his cigar. Granddad's features were blurred by Florida's bright sunlight piercing the room. From the family room, I stared at his silhouette and thought to myself, "So this is Granddad. I like him. I like him a lot."

The next time we met I was thirteen. I knew he had not forgotten me when I walked up the porch stairs. The screen door swung open, and he yelled out, "Monkey!" My heart skipped a beat. He looked the same, only tired. Although we were visiting because Mom was dying, it didn't take away the joy of seeing my granddad.

Summer days crawled. Granddad passed the time as he always did, sitting on the porch chair listening to baseball games on the radio. My sisters and I grew restless and bored until Granddad decided it was time to impart the sacred secrets of his favorite game.

Five eager granddaughters sat in his dimly lit kitchen while Aunt Ruth poured us lemonade and Granddad passed out the cards saying, "This is not for girls, but you might as well know. I taught your mother how to play poker."

The game is called Hearts. He beat us every time until we learned how to cheat. Sitting on the right cards would insure our chances for the next game. When our trick was discovered, he admired our determination, although he felt compelled to point out the lack of virtue in cheating.

That summer Mom succumbed to cancer, and it was then that I realized he too was suffering a loss. He sat in a dark corner of his big old house with rosary beads dangling from his fingertips. My sisters comforted one another in a room upstairs. I sat on the porch swing, alone. Through the window I watched Granddad's silhouette pray. His pale blue eyes caught mine, and the next thing I knew his shaky hands were pulling me into his lap. For the second time in my life, I felt safety in my granddad's arms.

I could feel it swelling in me. I thought my heart was breaking. I blurted out, "Oh, Granddad, it hurts. It hurts a lot."

What do you say to a girl who's lost her mother? Granddad simply spoke from his heart, "I love you. Monkey, I love you a lot."

Death separated five sisters, yet different homes and different lives did not keep us apart. Granddad writes a letter to each of us once a month. His handwritten letters on baseball stationery remain my connection to that small kitchen when I tried to hold on to a game I was losing. Sitting on hearts is no insurance in the game of life.

I am in my second foster home here in Florida and still I have not forgotten the tender love of my granddad. I cling to his monthly letters that bond us and keep me safe.

What do you write your granddad when you know you may not see him again? Because his gentle strength is behind me, my letters to him begin with, "Granddad, I miss you. Monkey misses you a lot."

*****

I handed her my rent check, and she asked me about the garden hose. There I stood in front of Luanne, contemplating if I should lie or say nothing. I now know there is no difference.

The malicious act happened on Saturday night while she was sound asleep. The neighborhood gas stations were closed. Alonso had enough gas to drive me home from the party, but not enough to reach his house. I offered to him the family room sofa to sleep on. He knew his mother would object to such a poor excuse for staying over. Running out of gas just isn't used anymore even if it is the truth. Then a brilliant idea flashed in his head. He ran over to the bushes in the front yard and pulled out the lawn hose. Before I could say, "Don't you dare—" Alonso cut it in half. The deed was done.

He sucked on the hose connected to the Fiat's gas tank until fluid spurted onto his lips then into the bucket I use for weeding. We poured gasoline into his Mustang's tank, and he was on his way after a five-minute departure kiss. I rinsed out the bucket and put it back in the garage then went into to the house completely forgetting about the hose. The plight of her garden hose didn't enter into my consciousness until I was face-to-face with Luanne.

The look on my face must have been blank because she answered her own question, saying, "I know what happened."

"You do?"

"The lawn maintenance company. They hack everything in sight. Now they got my hose. I didn't need one that long anyway."

"You didn't?"

"Obviously not."

Mom, I know someone with good moral character would have spoken up. I did not. I kept my mouth closed. Now, my lack of honesty is engraved in my mind. Without her knowing it, I learned a valuable insight from Luanne that day I paid rent. Lying is not only an act of giving false information, it includes leaving out details that may shed light on a situation. The hose is not a big deal. That I was willing to blame Alonso's desperate act on the lawn maintenance company is. A sense of honor has drained from me. I have lied to Luanne.

I've decided that lying is a habit. Once lying starts, it becomes addictive, not that I'm a habitual liar—at least not yet. It's comparable to my virginity. The moment I cross that line, what will keep me from becoming a sex-crazed maniac? Margarita lost her virginity over the Christmas break, and she hasn't stopped long enough to look back. I've counted four guys I've seen her with at parties. Thankfully, they were not all at the same time. At least I hope not. She tells me sex is better than she thought. Obviously. Margarita insists I go for it with Alonso. I'm hesitant. I've noticed my tendency to take things to their extreme. That's one trait Nadine and I share. She sent a wedding invitation. She's not satisfied with living with a pig farmer; she wants to marry him. And she wants me to stand up in her wedding alongside Tasha and Cammy.

The wedding date lands just after this semester ends. I was hoping for better timing, like in the middle of the summer semester. That way I wouldn't have to come up with a lame excuse for not going. Luanne tells me I would regret not attending my sister's wedding. She's never met Nadine.

Tasha and Cammy are excited about the prospects of my visiting. Luanne called Eastern Airlines for flight information. I have a feeling I'm going to Indiana for a wedding. At least it won't cut into my plans with Mary Pat Brennan. Alonso will be driving us to Satellite Beach for the Fourth of July weekend. I'm excited about visiting with Mary Pat and nervous at the same time. We're great pen pals, but it's been a long time since I've seen her and a lifetime since I've seen him. Hold onto your pantyhose, Mom. I have Dad's address. Samantha gave it to me. In her last letter, she informed me our father is living on the Space Coast and still working for Harris Corporation. Apparently, he and his family never moved from the area. Samantha made a few phone calls over the holidays and secured his phone number and address. She was planning on calling him but wimped out. I, however, am braver than my oldest sister. That or am more demented. I wrote Dad a letter telling him I would be in the area this summer and asked if he would like to meet. We'll see if he responds.

Once in a while I notice a man who's in his midforties and wonder if he's my dad. I was four years old the last time I saw him, and I was probably eleven the last time I saw his picture. Samantha tells me that for ten years he beat you. I knew that, yet I didn't know he drank his way to the bottom of bottles and seduced babysitters. I had forgotten that you lost five babies before they were born because Dad's violent blows to your body killed them. Samantha also reminded me during our last telephone conversation that our father has never talked to us in all these years, even though you died. I somehow avoided ever thinking about it. I believed he wanted to leave the past in the past. He started over with a new wife and children. Now that I think about it, sending him a letter was probably a bad idea. I don't know what I was thinking. I guess I was hoping to meet my dad. I want him to see how I've grown into a woman. I want to see what he looks like. I want to look into his eyes and know if he is my father or just some man.

Speaking of men, I'm the only female in my judo class this semester. Alonso talked me into signing up for judo saying it was a good idea to learn self-discipline. I need more than discipline to survive this class. I need football padding. Weighing barely one hundred pounds has put me at a disadvantage. When I make a mistake, I pay dearly. The instructor has nicknamed me "Helicopter" mainly because at least once during class, I end up flying to the other side of the gym, with the help of my opponent. We're required to take an oral test at the end of the semester, and I asked Samuel to help with the judo terms. Luanne's son studied martial arts during most of his college years. Samuel cracks up laughing when he hears me say Japanese words using a Spanish accent. I've tried to explain that my instructor is Cuban and that's how he pronounces the judo terms, but Samuel doesn't seem to get it. He sits across the table grinning at me. It's the same grin he gave me when he saw the Mercedes-Benz, after I had the mishap in the garage.

CHAPTER 19

As soon as I finished the final, I flew out of my last calculus class, ran to the other side of campus to my awaiting Fiat, and sped home. I hope I at least yielded at all the stop signs. I don't remember if I did or not. Anyway, I opened the front door expecting to see Luanne standing in front of me with car keys in her hand. Sylvia was there instead. She's a friend of the family and stopped by to visit Luanne.

"Hi," I said. "Where's—"

"She's on the phone. How ya doin', Ariana?"

"Good. How about you, Sylvia?"

"I came by to give Luanne some herbs for her knees then talked her into letting me read her palms."

"Really. You don't do astrology anymo—"

"Oh, sure. I do palms too." Sylvia smiled like a cat.

"That's nice. I'm on my way out—"

"It just takes a minute. I'd love to read your palms."

I knew I was stuck. Sylvia stubbornly ignores my reluctance to dabble in that stuff. I scanned the living room. No excuse was going to rescue me. I decided it was better to get it over with than to argue with Sylvia. So I acquiesced giving her my palms after dropping my backpack and keys next to the front door.

"Are you planning a trip?" Sylvia asked.

"Luanne told you."

"Told me what?"

I sighed. "She's taking me to the airport when she gets off the phone. I'm going to my sister's wedding."

"Where?"

"Sylvia, doesn't my palm tell you?"

"Funny. It says you're going to old memories. You'll be dealing with unfinished business—"

"Indiana."

"You're an old soul, Ariana."

"I feel old."

"No, look at your hands. See the lines? You've lived many lifetimes and learned many lessons. You came back to give the world your—"

"I don't believe in reincarnation. The soul leaves the body and that's it. It doesn't want to come back. It wants to stay in heaven. Like my mom. Why come back to this earth to live another life again?"

Sylvia was undaunted. She continued with her usual intensity, saying, "You have. Many times. Your destiny will take you into the public eye. See this line? That indicates you're able to move beyond intelligence receiving knowledge from innate wisdom. And this is your head line. Smart. Very smart. Do you work with numbers? You're capable of comprehending complex concepts through symbols and numbers. Oh, look, your heart line is very active. You'll have relationships that change your life."

"How many relationships?" I asked, worried this meant that Alonso may not be the only one.

"They'll be meaningful and lasting. How many depends on the men in your life. If they can allow you the freedom to express your strong, creative—"

"Not just one?"

"Probably not."

"Any children?"

"Lots of children, but they won't be yours."

"Great. I'll marry some guy who has—"

"Children will be your destiny."

I pulled back my hands. "No offense, Sylvia, but this is fake. You can't look at someone's hands and know their life. It's dangerous to tell people things that you can't know."

"How did I know you were going on a trip?"

"Luanne mentioned it."

"No, she didn't."

"Lucky guess."

Sylvia explained, "I read it on your palm. And I'm sorry if I upset you." She adjusted herself in the chair indicating she accepted my refusal to hear more information. "How's college going?"

"Just finished the semester." I walked over to my backpack. "I plan on getting my AA degree this December."

Luanne walked into the room saying, "Hello, hello...I got caught up on the phone. How was your final, Ari?"

I looked over to Sylvia and smiled, saying, "Calculus is simple once you figure out how the symbols represent complex concepts." Sylvia grinned, accepting my token of acknowledgment. "Can I interrupt your palm reading to catch a ride to the—"

"Alonso said he's gonna take you instead. He wanted to surprise you." Luanne smiled at me.

I quickly sucked in a breath of air, saying, "Uh-oh. Did you tell him the American time or Latin time?"

"Latin. He already called and said he was on his way over. He'll be here soon. Do you need help with your bags?" Luanne offered.

"No, but thanks. What did Sylvia say your palms show?"

Luanne answered me, saying, "That I'll live until I'm an old woman."

"You're already old," I said without thinking.

They both gave me a look, and I excused myself from the room.

Alonso gave me a departure kiss that made the skycap blush. Before his arms released me, Alonso whispered in my good ear. Using his native language, he told me that the next wedding I would be going to would be ours. I didn't reply. I gave him a squeeze and grabbed my backpack. Sylvia's words swam through my mind as I waved goodbye.

Three hours later, Nadine was at the gate waiting for me with her pig farmer husband-to-be. She shook her head when she saw the guy walking next to me ask which way to baggage claim.

"Of course you would walk off the plane with a gorgeous guy at your side." Nadine gave me a big hug and introduced me to Clem.

"You're as pretty as Nadine said you'd be," Clem said, demonstrating his fine Midwestern accent.

"Thank you," is all I could think to say.

Nadine shot me a smile and said, "We have a surprise for you." By the way she was looking at me, for an instant I thought that they brought a pig to the airport. My eyes followed hers then I caught the image of Tasha and Cammy standing next to the restroom. Tears raced down their youthful cheeks when they saw my face light up. Tasha reached out her arms as I ran across the terminal. My little sisters are at least three inches taller than me. They nearly picked me up off the floor in a synchronized hug.

It had been a long time since my eyes scrutinized theirs. They were dressed for the wedding rehearsal dinner. Mom, you would have been proud to see how poised and lovely Tasha and Cammy have become. A quick touch-up to wipe away tears and we were on the road leading to town.

The wedding rehearsal was short and sweet. I was amused with the idea of Nadine being married in a Catholic church. Clem must have worked hard to turn my sister around. I thought for sure Nadine was destined to a life of drugs and devil worship.

We walked four blocks to the rehearsal dinner. A minor, four-car collision occurred at the intersection as we entered the restaurant. Frankly, the accident was more exciting than dinner. I snapped pictures realizing that being a wedding party member would limit my accessibility to a camera during the ceremony. I aimed my trusty lens at everyone including the scrumptious waiter. During a group pose, Tasha leaned next to me and asked if I had seen our bridesmaids' gowns. I shook my head indicating a negative. A laugh erupted from her mouth. Then I placed my fingers over my lips. Tasha nodded and said, "Cheese."

Clem drove us to the VanHusens'. It's amazing how that house shrinks every time I visit. Nadine's almost-husband was due at his bachelor party. Within a few minutes of our arriving, he excused himself from our family reunion. Before leaving, he reached around the chair I was sitting in and gave me a kiss goodbye. It bothered me that it was on the lips. I thought maybe he had confused me with Nadine, but we don't look alike. Nadine followed him outside.

I looked over at Tasha. She shrugged her shoulders then said, "Clem has heard a lot about you." I wondered what he had heard.

Aunt Beth and Uncle James look the same, though they have more gray hair and slouch further in their chairs. My cousins were smiling, investigating me as much as I was curious about them, their lives.

Nadine, after all these years, has not honed the art of tact. She literally pulled me out of the house. This was the eve of her wedding, and we had primping to do. I could see it in Tasha and Cammy's eyes; they didn't want me to leave, yet this was the script, and it was Nadine's show.

Nadine and I piled into her junker car and drove downtown to Granddad's house. I walked up to the front porch expecting to hear him call out, "Monkey!" He did not. Granddad was in the kitchen waiting for me. I raced through the house straight into his arms. His pale blue eyes still have that sparkle, and he shined it on me.

"Monkey. How's my Monkey?"

I raised my voice so he could hear me. "Short. I got most of your genes."

"You're a beautiful young woman," he said, twinkling his eyes at me.

I smiled to him. "I love you lots, Granddad. I've missed you lots too."

"He waited up to see you," said Aunt Ruth in a loud voice when I stood to give her a hug.

"You did?" I asked him.

"Can't miss seeing you. You have a way of lighting up a room."

"Granddad, can you believe Nadine is getting married?"

"Oh, sure. He's not Catholic though."

Aunt Ruth laughed. I saw Nadine roll her eyes. She had walked into the kitchen with her wedding dress draped between her arms. I dutifully complimented her taste and asked her to put it on.

"My Monkey. How is college?"

"College is good. How's cards?"

"Most of my friends are dead now. I'm waiting for my turn."

I looked up at Aunt Ruth. She smiled and whispered in my direction, "Don't worry. He'll outlive us all."

"Granddad, what's this news about strokes? Are you trying to go deaf like me?"

Granddad let out a laugh then he nodded.

Aunt Ruth indicated it was time for him to go to bed. I gave him a kiss and a hug before your father shuffled out of the kitchen, holding onto Aunt Ruth's arm.

Nadine danced into the kitchen twirling her wedding dress as if she were a princess. I smiled to her then landed the burning question.

"Are you pregnant?"

"*No.* I use protection."

Nadine and I spent hours in the upstairs bathroom. We shaved our legs, talked about sex, cried, and eventually the conversation centered on you, Mom. At this point in our lives, it's the same memories. We grow older, and you, you stay the same.

We fell onto an antique, queen size bed having plucked, shaved, bathed, and moisturized all the appropriate areas of our bodies. Nadine lay on her back looking up to the ceiling. I knew she had talking still left in her. Ignoring my exhaustion, I turned onto my back and said, "No one has mentioned Samantha. What's up?"

"She moved."

"To where?" I asked, not masking my astonishment.

"Florida."

"Florida. Florida! Where in Florida?"

"Westcoast."

"Why didn't anyone say anything to me?" I pleaded.

"She needed to get out of Indiana. She needed to start a life on her own without Uncle James or Aunt Beth or Granddad or Mom's memory or me."

"What happened between you two?"

"We argued a lot."

"I guess so. Did you invite her—"

"No."

I got the message. The subject was to be dropped. "Nadine, you're gonna be a married woman tomorrow. You'll have a different last name than us."

"Yeah. I can't believe it myself."

I sighed then said to Nadine, "Before I turn over, I want to know one thing."

"What?" she whispered.

"Do you still scream bloody murder in the middle of the night?"

Nadine laughed then pinched my butt after I turned over.

I drove the bride's car to church while she sat in the back seat, navigating. Nadine opted to have me drive saying she was too nervous. When I parked the car, my sister said getting married could not be as nerve-racking as watching me put our lives in peril. Driving in Indiana doesn't compare to rush hour traffic in Miami. I'm usually not flustered by driving conditions. It's common for me to see people drive on Miami's sidewalks and slug one another at traffic lights. Potholes. Salt and snow are brutal on the roads up north. I'm just not used to potholes.

I saw the bridesmaids' gowns and gasped. Tasha was standing next to the altar, and Cammy was sitting in the front pew. As Nadine and I entered through the church front doors, my eyes went not to my sisters; they were fixed on their dresses. I must tell you, Nadine selected rose-colored pajamas. I thought Tasha was going to fall over backward when I donned the wretched dress. She laughed hard enough to blow an eardrum. Cammy was too caught up in the wedding atmosphere to notice our fashion predicament. Besides, she filled her dress out. And I mean out. Tasha and I decided the dress style suits well-endowed women. We are not and, from the looks of things, nor will we be well-endowed. Tasha is sixteen, and I'm eighteen, by now old enough to know that we have Granddad's side of the family's endowment.

Nadine and Clem took the plunge. We threw rice on them after three hours of drinking, dancing, and toasting. My rice bag didn't open all the way, and it plunked Clem on the head. Cammy thinks I did it on purpose. Probably, but it was an unconscious, malicious act.

I couldn't wait to disrobe; I plopped the gown in the church donations box on our way out. You never know what some crafty church lady can do with it; perhaps it will be sewn into a kitchen window curtain. Tasha asked if I wanted to go to your grave as I drove to the VanHusens'. I thanked her and said it was bad luck to visit a graveyard after attending a wedding. She agreed, yet I think Cammy had her hopes up. I couldn't go. You're not there anyway. It's just a tombstone surrounded by grass. Cammy doesn't understand, and I didn't attempt to explain. I remember how I saw the world when I was fourteen. It was black and white; gray was not a color.

Your three youngest daughters spent Nadine's wedding night together. Tasha and Cammy gave up the coziness of their bed and joined me on the floor. Snuggled between blankets and their comforter, we talked until the early morning hours of the next day. That night I was transformed. Tasha and Cammy revealed to me the world beneath my illusions, my assumptions. They told me what it means to live with the VanHusens.

All this time I thought they were better off. They are not. They're being shunned, ridiculed, criticized, and purposely neglected. Aunt Beth makes it clear she resents the responsibility of two more children in her already full household. She no more wanted two nieces to care for, to raise, than she wanted a horrible disease. That's how she treats them, as if they're a disease.

It took some prying, but Tasha finally opened her heart and divulged the secrets my two sisters carry, the pain they hide. I learned how Aunt Beth brings her only daughter to the mall every Friday night for mother-daughter bonding. Josie's closet is filled with fashionable clothes, a testament of her mother's love. My sisters are given yard sale clothes to wear to school, marking them as refugees.

My younger sisters have learned their place is behind the VanHusens. They showed me the family album. Tasha and Cammy were photographed separately. And the few times there was a family Kodak moment, my sisters are an arm's length way from the VanHusens. Throughout the years, I was sent copies of these pictures tucked inside letters that described the weather and football games. I never realized, I never noticed how separate they stood from our cousins. I have the VanHusen pictures on my bed staring at me as I write you, and it is so obvious. Mom, how could I have missed it? How could I not see?

I asked why they had not confided in Uncle James. Tasha and Cammy explained how Aunt Beth rules the nest, not your brother. Every day they wake to reminders that they are not wanted. Tasha told me how the chores are divided, the weight being carried by the intruders.

My sisters don't have a Mrs. Lareau to call. They have each other. The stories went on until they could tell me no more. Suffice it to say your youngest daughters are suffering without a voice. Tasha and Cammy have quietly lived like foster children without having a counselor, without having the title, without having the chance of living with a hero like Luanne.

They drifted off to sleep while I lay awake feeling their anguish. For one night I carried it for them. I felt their shame, their worn spirits. My sisters deserve a loving home. I thought they had one, and my heart aches to learn it was an illusion. No wonder they miss you more than Nadine, Samantha, or me. They needed you more. They need love from their mother.

Tasha and Cammy are growing into women. What happens to girls who've grown up with the opposite of love? What is going to become of their adult lives? I have Luanne who caught me in time, who turned my heart from cold to warm. Who will my sisters be as women? How will they learn to love themselves if no one shows them?

The next morning we joined the traditional VanHusen Sunday brunch. The kitchen was the same. The dishes, pots and pans, even the VanHusens were the same. I was not. From Tasha and Cammy's perspective, I saw through the smiles and cloaked comments. I maintained my assigned role as the naive, unenlightened older sister, yet inside I was burning. I imagined screaming out to the VanHusens, "Where's your love, where's your acceptance, where are your hearts?" I knew they were more deaf than Granddad and me combined. The day Tasha and Cammy walked through their door, the VanHusens decided on my sisters' fate. Your brother's family has been deaf, dumb, and blind to anything else. Two young girls invaded their home and would be punished for their crime.

I want to carry their burden. I want to take away their hurts. I know they are not mine to take. You died, and they are paying the price. I'm sorry, Mom. It's you I blame.

I asked Uncle James to stop by Granddad's house on the way to the airport, and he granted me a short visit. I doubt Granddad knows what goes on right under his nose. Your sweet father said goodbye with tears in his eyes. I have a feeling that is the last time I will see his kind face, the last time I will look into his soul and know unconditional love so completely.

At the airport, we said our goodbyes having given kisses and hugs. I turned to walk down the long corridor to the terminal; that's when Tasha reached out then clutched my arm. She wouldn't let go. She held me in place, and I closed my eyes for a moment before twisting my body to face her. She and I knew. We knew that when she let go, I would leave. She would be left behind. My sister would ride back in the car with Cammy and Uncle James. They would walk into the VanHusen house, and all the love we shared during my visit would fade into the background. They would be alone when I walked onto the plane. They would be left behind to bear your cross.

I peered into Tasha's eyes and whispered to her, "It's only a body. My spirit is with you. I'm not leaving you behind. I'll be with you. Do you feel my strength?"

Tasha nodded, looking away.

"Do you feel my courage?" I reassured her.

She glanced at me and whispered, "Yes."

I looked at Cammy. Tasha released my arm. It was a few seconds, yet that moment of truth will last me a lifetime. I doubt Uncle James had a clue what was unfolding before him. We see what we want to see. He saw three sisters saying goodbye. I saw two girls silently screaming for a rescue.

CHAPTER 20

I'm tired of having to explain that the bruises on my body are not from my boyfriend. Judo has left its mark. I didn't realize my arms and legs would take so long to recover, it's already two weeks into the summer semester. Purple and green had become symbols of my determination, but now they're an embarrassment. Alonso tells me they're sexy. It's a poorly disguised attempt to appease my vanity. A bruise is a bruise; it's not a sexual stimulant.

On a whim, I signed up for sailing. If what Sylvia says is true, then I'm sure at least one of my lifetimes was spent on the ocean or in it. I'm a natural sailor and can't get enough of the wind, the water, and the taste of salt on my lips. The sailing instructor has assigned me to her crew. She says sailing is an art, a passion, and a way of perceiving life, and those who demonstrate these characteristics share her boat. It is an honor bestowed on a lowly sailor such as me.

The serenity bathes me when I'm sailing. Time warps, my mind expands, and I feel the freedom I have tucked in my heart. I become one with the elements relying on my instincts to anticipate changes in the wind, shifting currents, sails whipping. I hear the sound of God's heart beating with each wave the boat cuts through. I feel Earth's soul when I'm sailing.

I know it sounds strange to say, yet it's true. Sailing brought me to the memory of him. I wonder if you forgot about him, Mom. I did. Time doesn't heal wounds nor does it shield against pain or cover the scars that mold lives. Time distances us from ourselves until we grow strong enough to look inside. The freedom sailing affords me has given me the space to remember, to remember him. I'm praying it gives me the courage to forgive and the power to forget.

I was standing by the living room sofa looking out to the backyard. Luanne asked me if I wanted an orange. What a simple question. It was the same one he asked me nearly twelve years before. It may have been her voice, yet it was his words I heard. The memory of Mr. Wilson flooded my mind. The backyard blurred, and I saw his face. I grabbed the arm of the sofa for support, except I felt nothing there. I was falling through the years, back to Satellite Beach.

He asked me if I wanted an orange. You said it was too late to eat, so he volunteered to tuck me into bed. Why didn't you go into my room when he did? My god, I wish with all my heart you had. Mr. Wilson didn't tell me it was a secret; I already knew. What he did was wrong. What he had me do was wrong. I wish I had an orange in my hands instead.

Luanne was calling my name. She grabbed my arm, pulling me back through time. I know my eyes were directed at her, yet I was seeing through her. All I could perceive was him, Mr. Wilson.

She asked, "What is it?"

"Mr. Wilson. He molested me. My god, he's molesting me."

"You're in the living room, Ariana. Ari, you're with me. It's okay. You're with me."

I looked into eyes staring into mine, and it was her, my friend. She smiled. I attempted to smile, but the signal from my brain wandered and missed my mouth. I was scrambling to disconnect from Mr. Wilson. I wanted him to stop touching me as much as I wanted her to hold me.

"Who is Mr. Wilson?"

"An old man. He painted our house."

"Do you want to sit down?" Luanne asked.

"I don't think I can."

"You're safe, Ariana. I'm right here."

"I know, Luanne."

Mom, I never forgot, yet I never remembered. The memory of Mr. Wilson has been with me, constantly with me. I've always known. He is my nightmares. Mr. Wilson was the reason I refused to sleep alone. He was the reason I crawled into your bed late at night. My god, where were you when he had his hands on me?

Luanne guided me to the sofa. She sat across from me. I told her about how he would tuck me in at night and how he became your friend. It was just facts, information, stuff that had not been lost in time's void. What hit me so hard was my thoughts of you. I didn't ask Luanne how a mother could be so blind, but I wanted to. And I wanted to scream the question out to you loud enough for you to hear me beyond the grave.

I sit late at night alone in my bedroom and write you questions. Never do you answer me. You're not here for me. You weren't then.

Mr. Wilson went away. He found another family with girls. When their father contacted you two years later, I wonder what you had said. Nadine admitted he fondled her. I said nothing. What was there to say? I knew even then that you would not protect me. You did not protect me like a mother should. Why tell you what he did. It was done. And I knew the woman who gave me life also beat the life out of me and handed me over to a perverted man.

I've thought a lot about what a mother is, who she is, why she is. My psychology book has devoted chapters on mothers. The descriptions are simple and, I think, incomplete. When I'm sailing, that's when I understand what it means to be a mother. Mom, you are the being who breathed life into me. You were my guide into this world. Without you, I had nothing to grasp onto, nothing to build from, and no one to identify with. A mother is a child's world. You took what you gave. I'm empty without you.

Luanne has helped me understand why I suddenly remembered Mr. Wilson. She's helped me cope with the shame. I carry within me not the scars and bruises Mr. Wilson inflicted on my soul. I carry the legacy of your neglect and your inability to protect me. This is the essence of my memory.

Why? Why did you hand me over to him?

*****

I searched all over the house and finally found her. She was in her favorite place, the backyard. Luanne stood up from her crouched position and answered, "I'm by the papaya tree."

"I just got off the phone," I said out of breath. "He said it was Dan and that he got my letter. I know he said more than that, but I wasn't listening. I was trying to figure out who Dan is. Then it dawned on me. The voice was my father. He was talking to me on the phone."

"What did he say?"

"He said he didn't think meeting was a good idea and that there should not be any further communication."

"What did you say?" Luanne asked, sending the question to my eyes.

"I said, 'Okay.' I was still recovering from the shock of hearing his voice. I can't believe that I just got off the phone with my father. I can't believe what he said."

"What else did he say?" she asked.

"No, that was it. I said okay and then he said goodbye and hung up the phone."

Luanne's face twisted. "No 'further communication,' what does that mean? He doesn't want you to write or call? Did he thank you for your letter?"

"No. Maybe he did at first. I don't know. I was trying to figure out who was calling me. I mean I didn't know who Dan was, and I forgot that I sent a letter. I guess it's pretty clear. He wants to be left alone."

"How do you feel about that?" Luanne asked, placing dead leaves in the bucket positioned next to her feet.

"Numb. I just got off the phone with my father, and I feel numb. God, he said his name was Dan…not Dad. My father called me."

"And he told you he doesn't want to communicate with you again."

"Yeah."

Luanne asked, "Want some leek soup?"

Soup is Luanne's go-to counseling tool. The aroma, the warmth, and the feeling inside when I have soup in my belly gives the body and soul comfort. Luanne has no idea that we live in Florida and that eight months out of the year are sizzling summer. She makes soup. I think she makes more soup in the summer than in the winter. I accepted her offer. It was in the middle of the afternoon, and we sat at the kitchen table sipping from our spoons. My friend reminded me that I was to pay rent. She commented on the prolific banana trees and pointed out how lovely the avocado tree has grown. She talked about everything except Dad. I was glad she waited until I was ready.

"Why did he call me to tell me he doesn't want further communication?"

"He has his reasons that you and I may never know. I'm proud of you for trying. It took a lot of courage to write him, to reach out to your father. I'm sorry he's not able to do the same."

"Me too." I spread margarine on a slice of bread. "I guess he has a family of his own and we're in the past. I think he wants the five of us to stay there." I stared through the dining room window, my eyes focused on the ficus tree. "I somehow believed that my father wanted to contact me, but he couldn't. I accepted that I had no father in my life, not that he didn't want me. I told myself he loved me but had to live with his other family. The one he started after my mom divorced him. How can a man turn his back on five daughters?"

"I don't know. But he did, and he wants to keep making that choice."

"Yeah. It's a choice, isn't it? It hurt less thinking he had no choice."

"Well, Ari...now you can move on. You're eighteen, and you know where you stand. Your mother is gone, and your father has a life of his own. I know you had no control over your life up to now. You've made it to adulthood and earned the right to create whatever life you want. You don't have any reason to look back now. You can keep your eyes forward and move on."

*****

Illusions drop away from me as I grow into the body of a woman. Inside feels like the child I was when you died. I cling to the things I know, and time twists them into the illusions they are. Sylvia tells me that change is a catalyst life offers so we may reconnect with our soul. Change has given me a microscope. I'm learning that things are not what they seem when examined closely with laser clarity.

I wonder if the soul is complete and utter innocence. I think dying is similar to returning to innocence. Maybe that's where you are. You shed the pain, the struggle with cancer, the illusion of living, and you became the soul you were before you were born. Why live at all? What did you discover? You endured a ten-year marriage to a raging alcoholic and beatings that killed five of your unborn. You left five daughters to a world that did not want them. Did you find your soul in all that misery? Did Dan find his soul when he beat you? My father denies me. He chooses not to acknowledge my existence. What can my soul learn from that?

It's late. I write you at night because the darkness is home to me. I feel safe in my room, safe enough to write you, to face you. Mom, you're deeply embedded in my psyche and associated with fear. I want to hate you for my fate. I want to. Sometimes I do. Something inside is wiser than me. It's a knowingness. It asks me when I blame you, "How can you hate the one you love?" I know you were beaten before you laid a hand on us. I know you felt the blows of Dan's hands before I felt them through yours. I want it to stop. The cycle of hate has to end.

Alonso doesn't understand my decision. Getting married after we graduate from college is not my idea of creating a life for myself. It means staying stuck in the circle. I want to break out. Innocence expects nothing and accepts everything. No marriage I've seen can claim the qualities of innocence.

He says I'll change my mind. Alonso knows about Dad, he knows about you, and he knows about Mr. Wilson. It has changed nothing for him or his feelings for me. I am changed. What I thought was real is not. Alonso knows I write you late at night. He calls me before he goes to sleep and asks if I've written you. It's just words I write on a page. It's not a letter to you. You will never read this. It's been an illusion, another piece of life I've clung to and still I feel no innocence from my words that spill out in the night. I think that's why Alonso calls me before he goes to sleep. He wants me to have the answers I ask you. He wants me to feel loved and understood. With so much love around me, why do I feel so alone?

Last week I dozed off with a text book in my lap. I didn't hear the phone ring, not consciously. I thought the voice on the phone was Alonso asking me what I was wearing. I answered not realizing it was a sexual deviant calling. Luanne says these people use a woman's voice to experience sexual pleasure. I don't like being used even if I am half asleep. I hung up the phone when I realized it was not Alonso's voice on the other end. Strange that I would accept such a question from him and no one else.

Mary Pat asked a lot of questions. We talked most of the first night while Alonso snored happily in the den. He took to the pull-out bed like a fish to water. Mary Pat and I resumed our friendship as if not one second had passed. We are the kind of friends who pick up where we leave off not noticing years have happened in between. Like we did over a decade ago, we shared her bed, and while staring up at the ceiling, we talked until sleep stole us from our bodies. She wanted to know if I thought about you. How do you describe the loss of a mother to someone who can only imagine? I answered, saying, "Be glad you didn't have to experience that loss as a child."

We exchanged our impressions of college and our views on sex. Since I was two years old, I've admired Mary Pat. She has never questioned if life will carry on. She makes plans about her future assuming it will be there. I dip my toe in the water and wonder if it will dry up in the middle of my dive. Her determined, dominate nature has not changed; if anything, it has blossomed. She is forthright and uninhibited in her expressions. I have spent my formative years imitating her, never quite being her, though I've desperately tried. I wonder if she knows how I adore her.

She delighted in the near-fluent Spanish flowing from my lips. It was an oddity for Mary Pat to hear me speak a different language. She said that her idea of me had remained fixed. Until this visit, her mind had taken a picture of me when I was fourteen. It didn't grow as I've grown. I felt honored to receive her praise.

We spent our nation's birthday celebration on the beach, directly across from the fireworks. I didn't realize they can be so loud. I felt like a war veteran experiencing flashback to the battlefield. While I crouched down in the sand with a towel over my head, Alonso and Mary Pat oohed and aahed until the last boom.

Being with the Brennans felt like home. Satellite Beach has remained a small community; I feel proud knowing we once were members. Mary Pat and her family are the same. I guess loving people have no need to change. Mrs. Brennan shared stories about you. She misses you. Friends are friends in life and in death. The Brennans accepted Alonso as if he were their son. Mary Pat has always considered me her sister, not just her friend.

Leaving for Miami was almost as difficult as leaving Tasha and Cammy in Indiana. I cried for about an hour while Alonso drove down I-95. He said nothing, but he smiled. He doesn't know what I feel when I part from my friends and family. He does understand it runs deep inside me.

Yesterday, I picked up the pictures from our Fourth of July holiday and framed one. It sits on my dresser. Alonso's head sticks out of the sand, wearing an expression of triumph. Two svelte female bodies lay on top of my boyfriend even though he was buried under the sand. Mary Pat fills out her bathing suit better than me. The three of us are laughing. I can't help but grin each time I glance toward the dresser. After staring at the picture, Margarita concluded that Mary Pat and I look like sisters. It's not surprising; we've spent our formative years together and copying each other's facial expressions.

Margarita has been coaching me on the finer points of dating. I take what she says, along with a teaspoon of honey. She usually has one eye on her current squeeze and another scanning the field. My friend from Colombia is enjoying her freedom of sexual expression. She eagerly fills me in on the delights of diversity. Our conversations come back to the same thing: Margarita prefers Alonso to them all. I accept her compliment, although it leaves me with a twinge of worry.

The summer semester has flown. College was easy, and life was hard. Sunlight has a way of burning away the darkness and exposing every detail. Wrinkles, bruises, dark circles—sunlight shows it all.

CHAPTER 21

I'm moving up to the big leagues; this is my last semester at a junior college. In December, I will have earned my associates degree, and I anticipate that my current four-point-o average will remain unchanged. At the rate I'm going, I'll be nineteen and have a BS degree.

Luanne and I have been in discussions. She said it's time I go away to college. I want to stay in Miami and use money as an excuse to support my argument. Luanne's contention, however, is more compelling. She reminds me that Alonso will be in Gainesville this January, meeting new people and living in a different town. Luanne feels living in a college town is an experience I'll regret not having. True to her nature, my persistent friend handed me a package containing everything thing there is to know about Florida State University. Luanne earned her four-year degree from FSU. The fact that Annie lives in Tallahassee is not lost on me either. This week, Luanne gave me a road map with the route to Tallahassee highlighted. She's not subtle with her hints or shy about her opinions. I completed FSU's entrance application and sent it off, telling myself it's prudent to keep my options open especially when Luanne is involved. In all probability, I'll be attending FSU to earn my business degree. I'm nervous about going away to school. It will be similar to living in another foster home. I'll be alone. Alonso reminds me that Gainesville is relatively near Tallahassee. He promises that he'll visit on weekends. I know Annie will invite me over to her house. She says I'll become so involved in college life that I'll forget her. I doubt that. After my four-year degree is under my belt, I have no clue what I will do. I guess I'll find a job and a life. I'm hoping that one day I'll learn how to live instead of survive.

I received a disturbing letter from Tasha. She described how three of your five daughters had been arrested. I suppose announcing that Nadine is pregnant is an important detail. For me, it just makes this story more nauseating.

Nadine took Tasha and Cammy to a drugstore for personal items shopping. A seemingly normal occurrence, but this time as they were leaving the store, an observant security guard stopped them. His suspicions were confirmed. Surprisingly, all three of them had tucked stolen items in their jacket. I don't know if it's a relief that they are lousy thieves or that they were caught. Tasha claims that they stole independent of one another's knowledge. I find that hard to believe. Nadine, being plump and pregnant, spent the night in jail. They were arrested on a Friday night, and on the following Monday, Indiana law had officially changed. At the time of their arrest, what they did was not a misdemeanor as it is now. It is a felony. The details are sketchy. I believe Uncle James drove Tasha and Cammy home because they're minors. Nadine had to remain in jail, and I'm unclear exactly why. Perhaps her husband had to scramble for bail money.

Evidently, Nadine is pleading guilty to lesser charges. Tasha and Cammy are grounded until they turn forty. When I first read Tasha's letter, I was ready for the words "just joking" to appear. But this is no joke. Nadine has lost visiting privileges. She's not permitted to be alone with Tasha and Cammy without a chaperon. I think my youngest sisters are the ones who've suffered another loss from this unfortunate situation.

Nadine. What was she thinking? She's pregnant and she's thieving. I wonder what her baby will turn out to be. The news that you are going to be a grandmother is tainted as your grandchild may become a thief. It was inevitable that Nadine would reproduce. I hope she is smarter after she gives birth.

*****

Luanne and I experienced the same nightmare. Yesterday, I was woken in the middle of the night to the sound of a state trooper's voice. At first I thought it was Alonso calling. I answered the phone barely awake and mostly asleep. The voice on the other end asked to speak with Luanne after confirming this was her residence. I asked if it was important, indicating the late hour. He identified himself again and assured me it was worth disturbing Luanne from her peaceful sleep. The tone of his voice pulled me out of my groggy state. An uneasy feeling churned in my stomach. Someone was in trouble. Without giving another thought a chance to formulate, I woke my former foster mother. Luanne reached for the phone while I turned on her bedroom light. She sat up and squinted to keep her eyes focused on me. For some moments she was silent, yet I could see it in her eyes. Finally she asked, "What hospital is she in?"

It's Annie. She had been in an automobile accident. We didn't know anything except that she was in a Gainesville hospital. By the time Luanne hung up, dawn was a few hours away. My dear friend asked me to make flight arrangements while she stuffed clothes in a suitcase and turned on the coffee maker. Before sunlight broke through the horizon, I was driving her down Red Road heading for the airport.

I waited all day with my arms wrapped around my body. Luanne called as I was undressing for my shower. Her usually strong voice was weakened, and her words sent chills down my spine. Annie was driving alone on a Florida backroad. Late in the evening on her way to South Florida, she had replaced a flat with a spare tire. Annie hadn't noticed the forty-five speed limit warning label on the replacement tire. It may have been due to a pothole, or perhaps she was speeding; Annie's car went end over end. Her body was thrown from the car and was caught in a barbwire fence. Someone found her hours after the accident, although we don't know who. The state trooper who is investigating has not completed his report.

"She's alive, Ariana. I thank God she's alive. We don't know the extent of the damage or if she'll walk. I'll call you tomorrow. Go to school. There's no use staying home."

Annie has a broken back and possibly her spinal cord is injured. Beyond that, we have to wait for tests and x-rays to give us answers. I'm shaking inside as I write these words. So quickly life changes. Annie was on her way to surprise us for Thanksgiving. Now we're praying that her spinal cord is intact and the damage minimal. I can only imagine what Annie is going through. I know what Luanne is feeling. She's terrified.

Mom, if you watch over me at all, if you are near me, I ask you this one favor. Please go to Annie. I'm so afraid for her. Please be with her and comfort her. And when you're done, give a kiss to Luanne. She needs the kiss of an angel to help her through this. She's given so much to me. Please reach out to my friend. If all I have is you, I want you to go to them.

EPILOGUE

This letter to you, Mom, ends abruptly and leaves me with a hollow feeling. Often, I have wondered why I stopped writing your letter only knowing that at some point I did. Between classes, tests, and semesters, I promised myself I would resume. Months turned into years distancing me from you, yet I always knew there were words still left unsaid, unwritten. I gave you to my new family, at that time Luanne and Annie needed an angel's love more than I needed a mother. I released you, yet it was only a partial letting go. Though my body grew into adulthood, in my heart I have remained trapped between worlds just like a foster child.

Whispers and echoes, that's what their voices and faces all those years ago are in my mind. They no longer exist as they were. As foster parents, Shari and Tim and Luanne remain metaphors. They are symbols representing complex concepts, and they are my memories. They were strangers who took me into their homes, their lives, and eventually their hearts. I had the privilege of seeing their secrets, being their secrets. Such hiding places our homes can be.

Luanne still lives in Coral Gables but in a different house. She moved while I was attending Florida State University; Annie needed a home with no stairs to impede her wheelchair. Sweet Annie has since married and gave birth to two "darling" children despite her damaged spine. We have remained lifelong friends, Luanne and I. At her house, I was married, and in her backyard, I told her about my divorce. I didn't marry Alonso. I married a capable, ambitious man who loved me less than his career.

Nadine is married for the second time with five children under her wing. She doesn't do anything in moderation. Cammy has two daughters she brought into the world and was recently diagnosed with breast cancer. She's a fighter, Mom. I believe she will win. I tell her she doesn't have your same fate. Tasha is excelling in her marketing career. Samantha and I live near one another yet find phone conversations more convenient than actually meeting in person. When I do see her, it's no longer a struggle to hug Samantha and smile to her from my heart.

The VanHusens have my lectern. I suspect it is in their living room by the front window with a Boston fern gracing the top of it. It never was mine. The idea that I owned our antique lectern was all I really had. Tasha told me how Aunt Beth called her one evening and apologized for failing her. I know it doesn't erase the years of harsh words and deeds, yet it's an opening for the healing to begin.

Shari and Tim moved out of the country and out of my life when I graduated from FSU. I delayed my graduation until I reached the age of twenty, smart enough to earn cum laude but too ignorant to know how to live my life. My roommate in college envied me. "I hate you, ya know," she would say. "I've never seen you have a bad hair day, you have no cellulite, and in between classes, work, club meetings, sailing, and a boyfriend, you find time to work on your tan. The only thing I like about you is that you can't sing."

I didn't have the courage to tell my roommate who I was and what was really beneath my Florida tan. I have done all I can to be perfect, to hide from the world's probing scrutiny. I couldn't afford mistakes to taint the flawless image I had built. In making no mistakes, wisdom seeped from my experiences. Life became shallow. I was enviable, and inside I was empty. The power of a secret can throw lives into oblivion.

What was the secret I dared not tell anyone, not even myself? You. Your beatings. How you abandoned me long before you died. How I felt unworthy. Two words tell my story with sharp clarity—foster child. There's no way around the truth: Rejection creates a foster child. I understood I was rejected. I also believed that meant I was defective. The longing to be "normal" didn't end when I became an adult; I just learned how to squelch it. I lived perfectly—graduating from college, marrying a great guy, pursuing a worthwhile career. And as each of my hard-earned accomplishments have slipped from my grasp, I remain. All these years I have been waiting for something or someone to foster me and accept me for who I am, defects and all. Today I realize I've been waiting for no one but me to accept me, all of me, including the events I could not control.

I did not, could not, let go of this letter. Tucked inside it, between the lines, was a truth I was unwilling to face until now. Life had to deliver a few blows before I was ready to look inside and find something other than a foster child always needing to prove herself, bargaining with the world, exchanging self-worth for some safety. A divorce, my teetering career, a dwindling bank account—they are reflections. I lived my life in your shadow, your memory. After all these years, why today? Why all of a sudden could I see beyond your image? Perhaps it was the pod of dolphins that swam near shore this morning that stirred me to let go. As I dug my heels into the sand and watched them ride the waves, I saw you, Mom, and remembered our last conversation.

Your face is pictured in my mind as I write these words. We had few moments alone, you and I. For a summer, we stayed at your brother's house in Indiana. The VanHusen household bulged to accommodate five more girls. Two weeks out of that summer, your daughters had a mom. And then you were gone. Warm, precious few were the days before you went into the hospital for the last time. I walked you up the stairs to the privacy of a bathroom. Your bandages needed attention. Excited voices floated in from the open window. Nine kids were engaged in a fierce softball game, but this kid chose to be with you in an upstairs bathroom redressing your wound. I can hear the softball game in my mind. I see your smile. I'll never forget the words you said to me. I vowed that afternoon to live my life by them. "Ariana, no matter what happens, no matter where you go, you'll only have one mother. You'll be my daughter even when I'm gone."

You sat precariously on the toilet lid, slightly swaying, and watched me lay white gauze on the counter. So fragile. You were dying. And you were reminding me that beyond death, you would remain my mom. You were afraid of being replaced, yet I needed to be released. My loyalty has not been to you but to your memory and your fear of letting go.

The familiar scent of soup permeates my home and now brings me back to who I am. Here we are in separate worlds, me on this side and you on the other. That hasn't changed. I'm not looking for a way to reach you anymore. Despite her palm readings and astrological charts, Sylvia was right. Change is the catalyst I needed to reach my soul. Once again, I am alone in my life. No job to support me. No mate to love or tell me I am loved. Not even my sisters can save me from reliving my foster child fears. With precision, I have recreated my struggle to live life without a net to fall back onto, without you. I am afraid, but Mom, this time I am letting go. No net—there never was one. I don't need one. I know I am strong and worthy of love. I'm not looking back again because I know everything behind me has brought me to this place. Another chance to say goodbye. Another chance to live a life not in your shadow but truly shine. All I have is me, and God. And I believe that is enough to begin again.

My parents, all of them, are beautifully flawed. Shari longed for motherhood, and when she felt rejected by my loyalty to you, she sought revenge. My first foster mother, I now understand, was unable to see me. Shari put her needs above all else. She failed to recognize the foster child in her care needed not a mother but a safe home so that I may shed the shadow of death and begin living again. Luanne, absent of the need to become a mother, recognized the foster child I was and helped me reach for the adult I was to become. In her home she provided love and safety, not mothering. After raising five of her own, Luanne became the perfect foster parent for me. She was my guardian angel on earth. With her wings to catch me in case I fell, I faced all three of my tests. The first was your beatings, and I have forgiven you with all my heart. The second was Mr. Wilson's sexual abuse; I admitted it happened. Then I released the pain, shame, and embarrassment. And last but perhaps worse of all because it began with Dad and did not end with you, I faced abandonment. I had to overcome the connotations of that word, *abandonment*. It is created from the failings of those who walk away; I was to learn how to reach for God instead of assigning blame. Luanne taught me how to face myself, heal myself, and move on with life. She made mistakes with me, and all are washed away with time. I cannot recall any of them nor reported them to you in your letter. She reached her goal: She was the best foster mother she could be, and I am eternally grateful God gave her to me. One foster mother mastered the art of loving an orphan; one foster mother wanted the orphan to fill her aching heart. You, Mom, faced death and found life in me.

We were all players. No one was right and no one wrong, just roles that needed to be played. I don't carry blame in my heart. It weighs too much.

It's all done now, Mom. The dolphins are waiting for me. They're going to take this note and your letter. They'll deliver these words to the end of earth along with your beatings, Shari's words, and Mr. Wilson's perversion. I don't need them or you anymore to define who I am. I have the rest of my life to fill in the hollowness and become a woman, no longer a foster child yet in all ways your daughter.

POSTSCRIPT

"A pandemic," the newscaster said, "COVID-19." The wicked virus has been given a name. Humanity has no natural immunity to this microscopic invader. Deadly and easy to contract, we wear gloves and masks to protect ourselves. Government officials tell us to heed the warnings. It is a fearful time. Shelves are sparse in food stores. Neighbors, friends, family, we are in shock and keeping our distance. The governor has called for a Safer-at-Home order; only essential businesses are open. No restaurants, no clothing stores, no traffic, church services are suspended, online connections are encouraged instead of human-to-human contact. Our small business is in jeopardy of failing due to the shutdown. Clients are dropping our services until further notice. For the first time in twenty years, there is a stillness in our home.

Using this break from client projects, my husband cleans and organizes the warehouse. I am doing the same for our home. Kitchen cupboards and bedroom closets and even attic boxes are opened and culled. Tucked deep in an obscure wooden box, I discovered this—your letter. I did not recognize it at first sight. It is yellowed, old. I forgot it existed.

Phones have stopped ringing; even pesky spam calls have ceased. A foreign silence infiltrates our world, and time has slowed up. Every project I can think of has been tackled and accomplished except your letter; it was the only item left on my desk patiently waiting for me to build up courage. I brushed my hands over the top page. Then I recalled that day I stared out at the ocean and watched the dolphins swimming nearby. I had clenched your letter and drew back my arm, resolving to throw it as far as I could. At the very last second, an inner voice screamed. Determination and energy drained from me. I relented and walked away, my hand still clutching the pages. In our newly built home, I hid your letter. It was out of sight and mind. Building a business became my goal, then serving client needs became my life. Twenty plus years has sped past that moment when I stood at the edge of the Atlantic Ocean.

Needing a diversion from COVID-19 fear and shutdown worries, I read your letter, Mom. The world has changed greatly these past two decades, so have I. Soon, I will be the same age as Luanne when I first met her. I hold in my hands my forgotten history. Your letter chronicles my young life's unfolding, and quite unexpectedly, I found something relevant to 2020. I'm glad I saved your letter so that I would read it and be reminded of what really matters in life.

Having been a foster child, I am practiced at starting over. Perhaps I am an expert. COVID-19 asks us all to contemplate endings and consider new beginnings. Wrapped in these pages is a message of perseverance, love, and, most precious of all, hope. Though everything feels lost or crumbled, there is an undeniable force that promises life will continue. We will find our way beyond the threat of COVID-19. No doubt it will change us, our world.

My compassion for foster families remained in my life. At times, I did consider becoming a foster parent, yet clients remained my priority. I knew there was no room for children in my world. My insight into a foster child's reality should not be wasted. Instead of throwing your letter away or hiding it for another twenty years, I will take a leap of faith and publish this letter. Maybe it will inspire a good soul to become a foster parent or save a foster child from despair. As it has done for me, may your letter remind all who read it that God has not forsaken us. There is love even in the darkest moments of life.

ABOUT THE AUTHOR

Ariana Oman and her husband live in St. Petersburg, Florida. They own and operate a small business. Together, they volunteer for a local charity that assists at-risk children.

She continues to write and is contemplating publishing three of her completed fiction novels.

CPSIA information can be obtained
at www.ICGtesting.com
Printed in the USA
JSHW041959140722
28075JS00001B/97